DEREK NEALE is an award-winning short story writer. He was born in Birmingham and left school at sixteen. A graduate of UEA's MA in creative writing, he has written several books about writing for The Open University, and recorded popular interviews with playwrights, novelists and biographers about their art and craft. *The Book of Guardians* is his first novel.

the BOOK of GUARDIANS

derek NEALE

SALT

LONDON

PUBLISHED BY SALT PUBLISHING
Acre House, 11–15 William Road, London NW1 3ER United Kingdom

First published by Salt Publishing, 2012

Printed in Great Britain by Clays Ltd, St Ives plc

Typeset in Paperback 9/12

ISBN 978 1 907773 29 7 paperback

1 3 5 7 9 8 6 4 2

for Beth

CONTENTS

PART ONE

CHAPTER 1

In the matter of the Adoption Act, 1976.
Adoption Application on: Holly Greenaway (now known
as Holly Burns), born 13.3.86.
Matter No: AA212 of 1987; to be heard: 17.6.87, S. County
Court, Family Division.

This report is confidential and may only be shown to the
relevant official parties.

It begins with a crumbling, the ground beneath me giving way. And the feeling that something precious has been stolen. Taken. I don't know what it is, can't pin it down. But it's gone, I know something has gone. When did it really begin? My fortieth birthday – yet even that was just a new recognition. It had always begun. Like all forty year olds, I remembered I was going to die. And . . . and I'd just met her.

It was my last case – there's no such thing, Richard would tell me again and again – my last case and it could have been anyone. But it had to be her; it was as if I remembered her from long, long ago, beyond the reach of memory. A dark wish rising

1

from the depths, I was compelled and thrown. She was a possibility, one I had to pursue despite myself, despite everyone and all other possibilities. God knows there was no shortage of them.

Of course, at first I didn't think any of this. I was just doing my job, looking for the father; that's what I did in those days. I hated fathers, they were always a problem. And, being without prejudice, I was none too fond of mothers either. 'Listen to that,' K would mock, 'hear that good old matricidal malice.' That's why it was my last case: I couldn't take anymore. I was sick of searching through the holes in other people's lives while this gap was growing in my own; a space where something, I don't know what, used to be.

The first meeting was inauspicious, the usual formality. K said there would have been note-taking – 'Subliminal observations, always is with you guys'. As if she was any different. 'Gauging tribal affinities, DNA matches, legs, hair, breasts, you know the scan.' But what did K know? She wasn't there. It was just another mother who was having problems – drugs, drink, men. I had to ask the questions, show my usual attentive charm: so, you wish to be rid of your baby daughter? How quaint; what a wonderful sense of responsibility, and what timing, just coming up to the first anniversary of her birth. What's her name? Isn't that the name of a tree? The canopy over her conception, no doubt; Holly . . . if you say so, so be it.

I was very nearly right about the canopy.

1) I was appointed Guardian ad Litem to Holly Burns on 23rd January, 1987. I received the Schedule 2 Report on 1st March 1987 and began my enquiries from that date, initially by meeting with and interviewing the birth mother, Janet Burns (aka Janet Greenaway).

I didn't get hooked until the second interview, in the clinic where she was being diagnosed: take your pick, anything from clinical depression to Korsakov's psychosis. Holly was in foster care, by all accounts thriving away from her mother. The interview was the only one I managed to get taped: my tape machine was playing up and I was loath to pay to get it fixed or replaced. This case was the last time I would be needing it.

I remember her grey-blue eyes staring through the strands of black hair, waves that never quite curled, as if she were hiding and waiting to be found; teeth crowding, almost greedily, seeming to bite on her roll-up cigarette; cheeks sucking into gentle hollows. There was a hope even then, you could see it as she peered between the petals of smoke with her crescent-moon, half-closed eyes; an expectation that didn't have a voice, not yet, but it was unmistakably there. She was a liability in a place like that, with a look like that; a look that said: I'm interested, maybe, I'm interested in everything, but if you so much as disturb the air about me, I'll kill you. It wasn't the look that made me laugh though, or the fact that she'd changed her name. I'd had enough Nelson Mandelas in my time. No, it was something else. The God thing, that's what made me crack up.

— They tell me you're not who you were?

— I'm Janet Burns.

— That's not what I have down here.

— Well, your piece of paper's wrong.

— I see. Well ... Janet ... that much at least has stayed the same.

— Has it?

I rustled through my papers, avoiding her eyes.

— Now, about Holly. I need to contact Holly's father. When was the last time you saw him? Do you know where he lives?

— No.

— Do you know who the father is? Do you have a name? Or possible names?

Cut to the chase; what did I care for subtlety? All I wanted was to get the damn report written, over and done – I'd already booked my flight, told Sarah and the kids when I'd be leaving, given them a date and sorted everything with Richard, I'd arranged a letting agency for the house. I hadn't told my mother yet, but apart from that . . . I was already running. When something precious, something you covet dies, you want to restore it, revive it, to bring back the past. But you also want to just leave and let go gracefully. I couldn't even bear to look, to see what it was that was dying. I just knew I had to get out: and only this one last case was barring the way, this one last mother and child. 'Birth Father Unknown' wouldn't have been too much to ask, I hadn't had one of those for an age.

— You told your case worker there was a garage?

— A shed.

— A shed?

— That's what I said.

— And that's where . . .

— It wasn't like that, I told you.

— You may have told your case worker but . . .

— It wasn't like that. You can tell them all, case workers, social workers, the doctors and nurses, all of them. Tell them. I've seen their faces, it wasn't like that, it wasn't . . .

Some part of me smirked: well, what was it like then, for you I mean? What was it really like? Some other part of me was irritated: why pretend that this particular father might give a damn, why not put 'immaculate conception' down on the form and be done with it. Little did I know. She looked down into her lap and rolled another cigarette as I fired away.

— It's really not my concern. I'm only interested in how you're faring with Holly, and in trying to locate the father. I only want to help. If you wish to pursue the adoption we need to have Holly's father's consent, that's all. He will need to agree.

— Why don't you get him to look after her? He's the . . . he is the . . .

Father. I should have known from the way she said it, but my eagerness betrayed me, I spied a short cut. Of course the papa would have to show willing; he'd have to jump through the usual hoops, but that was quicker than the alternatives. All I had to do was make the recommendation. All I had to do was find the father and, if he wanted Holly, hallelujah, I wouldn't have court appearances and adoption hearings hanging over me. She looked up, her mouth masked in a thick brown cloud of cigarette smoke. I coughed with purpose but without, I thought, undue aggression.

— Well, maybe we should start at the beginning. Where did you meet him?

— At the allotment.

— The 'allotment'?

I thought for a moment it might be the name of a night-club, but no . . .

— I'd planted some seeds. Carrots and sweet peas.

She looked at me appealing, as if to some prior knowledge I should by rights possess: everyone plants carrots and sweet peas, didn't I know?

— I kept the seedlings in trays in the shed, by the window. It's south-facing. I went in there one day and as soon as I saw them I knew. At first I thought somebody had . . . They'd been watered already you see. Why are you laughing?

I wasn't laughing, was I? I coughed again, without meaning to, I couldn't help myself. The smoke was thick and old, brown and tarry, and I felt like I did with my mother and her Peter Stuyvesants, only worse. This was a grotesque kind of inti-macy: our lungs and bronchial passages commingling in the fluorescent gloom, sharing the smog.

— I'm not laughing, it's just . . . I've got something caught in my . . .

I coughed again, this time managing to clear my throat:

— Now, where were we? South-facing . . .

— I didn't see him then, but he was there, he must have been. It was three days later, they'd been watered again and his voice came out of the corner, behind the sawing horse. Forgive me if I intrude, that's what he said. Like a ghost, I jumped out of my skin. It took me a while to hear him, to understand him, like I was translating from a foreign language, like he was

5

saying something really complicated in some sort of code. Forgive me if I intrude, that's all he said. Just a voice, out of the dark, out of nowhere.

— And?

— And what?

— You developed a relationship with . . .?

— He asked for food.

— And you provided him with food?

— Once I saw him, yeah. When he came out of the corner, I wasn't scared of him once I saw him. You know don't you, you can usually tell.

— Indeed.

— He said I'd get my reward in heaven . . .

I bet he did.

— . . .bread and cheese mostly, he ate it all, whatever I brought him

My heart sank. This papa wouldn't be able to clamber anywhere near the hoops. Things weren't looking bright for Holly's daddy – or mummy for that matter. I'd already tagged her: you don't get mother of the year awards by offering your daughter over to total strangers, as she'd done on a couple of occasions, according to the case notes.

— Did he tell you his name?

— No, but I knew who he was.

— And who was he?

— Yeah, he can look after Holly. He's the Father.

There we go with the big F word again, but still I didn't pick up on it. The tape machine started hissing, and the red warning light came on. I ignored it. I was surprised it had held out this long. I felt another tickle growing in my throat as she stubbed out her cigarette. Another irritation.

— Well, I can only help if you help me. Have you seen him recently?

— His hands were soft. When I saw his hands I could tell. Love and hate, hate and love, on each hand, just there . . .

And she reached out and pointed. I resisted the urge to

retract my hands as the tip of her index finger brushed the back of my knuckles.

— . . . just there . . .

Instead I looked up, avoiding sight of the contact, thinking the touch would be fleeting and therefore bearable. And as I did so I saw her face, not as I'd seen it before, not shrouded in the mists of itself, not layered in mascara and kohl as I'd first thought. She didn't wear make-up or at least to my untrained eye, very little. The goth look was there but with no whitening of the cheeks, it wasn't contrived. Now all I saw was a strange sincerity, full on – as her ash-warm eyes gazed on my paltry knuckles and scrubbed fingers. She saw much more than was in front of her.

— They were soft, so soft. Love and hate, just there. When I saw his hands I could tell.

As she spoke she carried on staring, as if beguiled. Though her touch was fleeting, it lingered on my sensations and something was coming to me – *How love burns* – the lines of a poem or song – *How love burns.* But I didn't know what it was; it came to me too quickly to be grasped and was gone just as fast, as she lulled me away with her cracked whisper:

— Soft, like Holly's, like hers, she's got his hands.

And in the stillness, the old smoke momentarily clearing, I saw the agonised dart in her eye, tears welling, the grey-blue glimmering like a mountain stream: first bright, then black. Hope against hope, I'd seen it all before, but that didn't mean anything. She cares, she cares so much, and yet she's giving her own child away, of her own free will. She is choosing. It didn't make sense. It never did.

— His name?

— Who?

— The father.

— I knew when he left he'd stay with me.

— I'm sorry?

— It was May when he left. Soon as I saw the swallows I knew. May's one of those months.

— You say you don't know his name?

7

— Stays with you, you remember, sticks in your mind. I'd brought him some apple juice and a stick of celery . . . to go with his bread and cheese. Only, I opened the shed door and he was gone. Soon as I saw the swallows I knew. Like he left them for me.

I tried to seek out her eyes to gauge what she meant. Was she bitter and resentful, contemptuous of him? Was she still in love and longing for him? Or was all that too grand by far? Then I lost sight of her completely in a cloud of yellow smoke, sulphured from the match, as she re-lit a nub end. I felt my impatience bursting. The tape machine creaked and squeaked; I checked its reels were still turning.

— And . . . and you say you know his name?

There was an inscrutable pause that crackled and hissed forever when I played the tape back the next day. During this lull, in real time, my arm moved towards her of its own volition, just like when I was a boy and we used to press our arms against walls to get them to rise automatically into the air. Only this arm was intent on more than just rising. I stopped it just in time, as the recorder crackled and buzzed, the crescendo before the end.

— Who was he? Can you just . . .

— I went out and watched the swallows, I just sat there, quiet, while they swooped through the air, laughing and dancing.

— I'm sorry?

— The swallows, they were happy, you could tell.

— I see.

— Then I went back into the shed and drank the apple juice myself.

She giggled like a child, fidgeting in her chair:

— And I ate the food, the cheese and bread, and the celery. All of it.

And she told me how she'd lay down in the shed after eating and drinking, and how she'd slept for so long it felt like days and nights had passed, how she'd felt like sleeping beauty and how she'd had to make her way back in the dark.

— But something was . . . something . . . that day made me feel so . . . so . . . so different.

— Really?

I thought of the cheese and celery as I smelt the clinic's dinners being prepared; that institutional brew of cabbage and custard guaranteed to induce biliousness in the strongest of stomachs. It felt like I was back at school: pinned to my seat by some hideously rancid routine.

— I can't explain, I . . . I . . .

But as she stuttered and tried, I could see in her face: she knew and she didn't know, both at the same time. Words weren't going to help her. Eventually she shrugged her shoulders:

— I suppose it's just from knowing him, this feeling, and the fact that he was gone.

I didn't fall for this drop in tempo, I'd had enough:

— Yes, but do you have an address? Who was he?

And then she told me, simple as that, no qualms:

— God.

Of course. I should have known all along. But as she said it, and the tape machine stopped of its own accord, I squandered those precarious seeds of trust. Now I really laughed. I could barely listen when replaying the interview: that guffawing, crow-like ululation. It was frightening. Later I found out from the full social worker's report that it was the whole deal: divine paternity and conception; no intercourse took place; this was Janet's consistent line, she hadn't wavered. As she turned away, her black hair falling over the side of her face so I couldn't see the glint in her eye anymore, I felt like asking: wasn't there a Hayley Mills' film set in a shed, with Alan Bates? But now even my official questions were met with a grunt. The lady was offended, I'd lost her.

CHAPTER 2

5.) Chronology of Main Events Since Child's Birth

13.3.86 – Holly Burns born, CT General Hospital, S. Birth weight 5lb 3oz, induced delivery.
19.3.86 – Mother, Janet Burns (aka Janet Greenaway), and child discharged from hospital to live at a hostel for single parent families with problems. Mother given help in basic parenting skills, which she was observed to lack.
16.9.86 – Mother and child leave hostel to go and stay in a guesthouse on Bramble Avenue, after mother complains of a 'presence' in her room.
7.10.86 – Holly received into voluntary care (S.2. Child Act 1980), mother goes missing (temporarily).
10.10.86 – Mother admitted to the C. Clinic, S. General Hospital and treated, though diagnosis unconfirmed.

⁂

The next afternoon, after that second interview, I was still listening to her while I opened my birthday post – playing the tape through on my home system to make sure none of it had been wiped. There was a card from my mother, signed without love, best wishes, or even a name – just a squiggle that might on a sunny day be construed as a kiss. There was a joint card from the children – it looked like Rachel's writing on the envelope but both she and Simon had written on the inside: 'Happy Birthday Daddy', and filled all available space with kisses in a lurid rainbow mix of blotted felt-tip. It was a mess, I knew I shouldn't say it or think it even, but it was. They were older than that weren't they? It didn't help, and rather than just missing them I hated them. I wanted to put them straight. It was Sarah's fault, they were on too loose a rein; I really wanted to put *her* straight, some part of me knew that.

Sarah, of course, had sent a present; the postman had woken me up trying to get it through the letterbox. It was just too fat. Now it sat in the centre of the table, as Janet Burns' voice buzzed and droned in the background: shiny brown paper, like old leathered skin, wrinkled and strung; I'd left it there all day, unopened. I knew what was in it. Gifts can be weapons, it's well known. I was waiting for it to explode.

Sarah was a possibility, I knew, an obvious cause for it all. If I hadn't left, I knew, if I'd just worked at it. But there had been nothing to work at. The hole was already there, I was running from it then. That was three, nearly four years ago. An age, a lifetime, a moment – but if I'd stayed, if I'd tried then the hole might have gone away, I knew. It might, possibly. I knew that word well enough. Yet I was the one who didn't try, the one who'd never tried, that's what my mother said. 'You've no heart,' she said. My own mater – she of the ill-fitting frock. She was the worst. But I *did* try, I tried like no one else tried. And I avoided clichés: the third party, the other woman. I was honourable.

When I left Sarah I started walking, rain or shine, everyday. I got the urge to seek, though it's hard to say exactly what it was I was seeking: taking solitary perambulations is hardly the best way to meet a new amour or to take your mind off the old one. I walked because I wanted just that. Something in the motion quelled a strife; it was a cure, or as much of one as I could muster. Sometimes I thought about Sarah, yes, about all that had gone wrong, and some of the things that had gone right. But that wasn't the point, that wasn't why I walked. I wasn't flushing the system; I'd think about everyone when I walked – Rachel and Simon, Sarah, my mother, they all came up at one time or another. More often than anyone I'd get to thinking about my father. That was another possibility, a big one. I kept getting sightings of him on street corners as I walked – a balding pate, the singed embers of red-headed youth around the ears, a creased suit and cranky tie, just a flicker in a passing face; sometimes an older apparition, the fragile flurry of grey hair in the park, a walking stick, a man with his grandchildren, all red hair and hot blood gone; sometimes a skeletal face creeping up on me in the mirror. These impossible visions seemed to have some long-sad meaning, one that had all too obviously died and been interred with him.

I thought of him then briefly – eating his poached egg on wholemeal toast in his lodgings, a locum placement with one of his landladies tending to him. I saw the crumbs around the obscured corners of his lips and was struck by an impulse to wipe them off, to restore his dignity, knowing that however well the landlady might have looked after him, however well she may have cooked or cleaned, she would never have done that. This ancient father of my crumb-raddled memory looked more like a geriatric patient than the doctor he was and, while listening to the Janet Burns tape, I realised that he was probably only a decade or so off my present landmark. His years of being a locum had seen the onset of his old age.

The remnants of my own lunch still lay around on the desk – a mug with coffee dregs, a plateful of burnt crusts and the acrid sniff of the toaster still wafting through from the kitchen. I touched the slab-cold window pane with the end of my fingers, as Janet Burns rambled on about hands and knuckles and tattoos of love and hate. It was spring again; it sent a shudder through my forty-year-old, birthday bones. The sycamore buds in the garden looked like prehistoric, reptilian phalluses – ripe, swelling, about to burst. It didn't seem natural somehow: the sort of thing I'd moved back to my home town for, but it felt just too much. And now all this talk of sweet peas and celery and May and swallows. I searched out of the window, past the sycamore, through the trellis fence, and the line came back to me again, *How love burns*, only this time it was all there, complete, as far as I knew, out of nowhere – *How*

love burns . . . How love burns through the putting in the seed.
Obviously, and literally, sparked by what I was listening to,
I hadn't a clue where these words had come from, who the
author was or how I'd come to know them. It was one of those
memories that hits you when you're trying to focus on something else. It had a will of its own and wouldn't go away.

I searched on through the trellis, over into the garden next
door, over at the ground elder creeping round the black patch
of soil where my neighbours, the Lovetts, burned their autumn
leaves. I wondered whether the weed was in possession of
some miraculous intelligence and knew about the history
of flames and smoke, whether something told the rampant
blood-green shoots to keep clear. *How love burns . . . how love
burns . . . how love burns through the putting in the seed.* The
first hail stones hit the window pane as I searched, and the
sunlight that had been up until then flooding my room, illuminating children's hand prints on the bare walls, suddenly
buckled. Mrs Lovett rushed out to retrieve her washing from
the clothesline, Mr Lovett cast a final shot of blood and bone
meal onto his rose bed. And, as the rain and hail fell in admonishing swipes from the sky, I gave in: ripping frantically at the
oily flesh of the brown wrapping paper, then at the fancy blue
gift paper underneath.

It was a fountain pen, my name inscribed on the clip, an
expensive one by the looks of it. Mont Blanc, too expensive to
send through the post. I wondered whether Sarah had taken
out insurance; it wasn't even Recorded Delivery. I thought
about the cost of it all, and the alimony, and the chaise longue
– that always came rushing to the front of the queue when it
came to Sarah and money. She earned more than me, yet I was
still making payments on an outsized sofa on which she had
the privilege of lounging. There was a card:

*Now there's no excuse, we will expect a letter a day
when you get to Canada.
Love, as always, Sarah and R and S*
– followed by a comparatively refined selection of the children's multicoloured kisses. And there was a smell, above the

alcohol of the children's marker pens, above the dry grime of the parcel's journey. Sarah, her face cream, the hint of tea tree: unerring over all those miles. I threw the card in with the brown and blue wrapping paper and screwed them all up in a ball. Gifts are always weapons, whether you like them or not. That's what they are.

Mistake number one: I took the case on in the first place. Mistake number two: I took it upon myself to check out the shed. Were these mistakes or moves of a higher order – fate, duty, destiny? Either way things were getting beyond me. I had a vague recollection of playing in the allotments as a boy, aggravating the old men with their barrows and rakes, throwing stones and turfs at the shed roofs and watching them roll down. I couldn't remember who I was with or if we ever got caught. It could well have been Richard, in which case they wouldn't have got anywhere near us; he never got caught.

It was worth a try, I wasn't going to find anyone by sitting around, I had to make an effort. The papa might have returned, might have moved to another shed, performed another immaculate conception. It was worth asking. All I needed was a nod of the head and a cross on the dotted line. The phone rang as I was tying my walking boots. It was Sarah. There was a hollow in my stomach, I could hear it rumbling as she asked, and I wondered whether she heard it too. Could Rachel and Simon come up this weekend? They were desperate to see me. She was lying. Had the present arrived? Did I like it? Really? Would I lie? When was it I was leaving? Yes, I had already told her, but could I just tell her again? When was it? It would do me good, get me out and about, out of the country, no less. Ha, ha, ha! Well, how long would this last case take? The kids wanted to know. Says who? She would drop them off, Saturday morning. Okay? Okay. I slammed the phone down and filed the gleaming, silver pen in my breast pocket. A pin in the heart. She'd sit in her car, staring inanely, revving her farty old Deux CV engine. Smiling, smiling, smiling. How bloody quaint! She always stayed in the car, it would implode if she didn't, or else she'd lose some essential part of herself, some *petite je ne sais quoi*. Behind the windscreen: smiling, smiling; keen as a cat to get off.

Sure enough the old men at the allotment knew our father, at least, they put me on the trail. The police had been after him as well. He hadn't been seen for a year or so and unexpectedly he was a crusty: long blond knots and dreadlocks, they said, a hairstyle I struggled matching with 'love' and 'hate' knuckles. None of the gardeners could testify to having seen the tattoos, but the holly was the clincher. The gentleman they described used to sleep in the disused sheds, sometimes he lit a fire outside – they said he wasn't exactly traditional in his dress, wearing a sprig of the prickly stuff in his lapel or in his hat. We really had a green god on our hands.

From there it was a piece of simple deduction. The holly tree was no more than a hundred yards from the perimeter fence, its upper branches leaning on the roof of an old green wooden shed, which seemed, reciprocally, to be leaning on the trunk of the tree. This is where my canopy joke came into its own. Most of the shed's paintwork was curled and flaking, and a lighter green lichen crept up the walls and door. Couch grass had colonised most of the surrounding plot. Inside, the sawing horse, just as she'd said, accidental grooves crowding its apex, spent bark floating with empty cigarette packets in the embers of dry soil beneath. Birds clucked and fussed in the branches about the shed, some cranking up their songs in preparation for nightfall. And by the window, seed trays, the twin leaves bound together, breaking through to the light. The compost was moist, recently watered. Odd amid the dereliction, but before I could dwell on it another thought flashed up, too bright and loud to be ignored: *How love burns ... How love burns through the putting in the seed.* And still I didn't know its source.

The fading light from the window and door fell short of the shed's back wall. I turned and saw the triangle of darkness in the left hand corner. It looked like another room – where God had lived, where Janet had drunk his apple juice, partaken of his bread and cheese and celery, his last supper. And on the third day he spoke to her. I laughed but I was laughing at myself in disdain. What was I doing? Intruding, trespassing – in a disused shed? There was no reason for it, no professional reason; it wouldn't find its way into my report. I didn't need to be there.

I remember the rustle of the birds subsiding, the mating calls suddenly more plaintive, more disconnected and solitary in the stillness. It was nearly dark. I thought I heard the latch on the door but assured myself that it was merely the wind. Suddenly cold and scared I groped blindly for something, anything – a weapon, just in case. I found the pen in my breast pocket and clutched at it in one hand like a dagger, a bunch of keys in the other. But there was nothing, just the stillness, so thick I could feel it on my face like an oily mist, so still it seemed to last forever. I lapsed into it, and some other lines came to me, again from nowhere, just then:

The sturdy seedling with arched body comes
Shouldering its way and shedding the earth crumbs

And I caught the sticky smell of chicory, the sweet Camp coffee, glimpsing again the crevices of his face, those old-skinned, unshaveable corners, beyond the reach of any soap or flannel. I knew suddenly it was my father, that he'd read or recited these words to me when I was a child, though I didn't know the author or correct order, how old I'd been or whether he'd read them to me many times, or how I'd managed to drag them up from the depths. Only the echo – *How love burns . . . How love burns through the putting in the seed.*

Still, I held the pen out in front of me to ward off whatever might be there, not thinking how ridiculous I might look: a Mont Blanc fountain pen, my last line of defence – against what? A ghost? God? But now it was no longer evening or late afternoon, it was suddenly night, and there was a new equality about the light. The triangle in the corner was no darker than the rest of the shed and searching into it I found I was now able, perversely, to see. Or so I thought. The hair first, dark and twisted, curling ever so slightly into the shadow of a shoulder; then the eyes, illuminated, grey and bright, and the hands, bloody and red. How could I see their colour in that light? Yet that's what I saw most vividly – bloodied hands. Then no more but the flash, the rush towards me and the teeth, cold white like ice, slightly crowded. Snarling? Or was she smiling? Was she really there? I cowered, the pen lost somewhere in the dusty soil about my feet never to be found, at least not by me; my hands around my head, down behind the sawing horse, waiting for the rush to hit me, for the ice to bite. I waited and waited without looking up, like paper crumpled up in a ball, creased and ruined; for a minute, forever.

It was a little bird, that's all. A thrush or blackbird; when I opened my eyes I still couldn't make it out for sure. But a little bird that was all it was, trapped by my entrance, desperate to get out; it flapped against the window for an age before I finally stopped cowering. Eventually realising, I pushed the door ajar and backed off so it could escape.

I walked home along the river, unconvinced about anything. It didn't matter what I saw in the shed. What did matter was this feeling of being bitten and shaken, as though someone had not only stolen a secret but was now taunting me with it, waving it in front of me and shouting: 'I have it, I have it, it's no longer yours'. The river, in spate, seemed to be sucking everything towards it. I wondered why the embankment houses hadn't collapsed into their daffodilled gardens, how the whole lot hadn't slid down into the murky current. The sandstone wall alongside the path flaked and crumbled into the puddles, exposing a fleshy stubble to the encroaching moss and ivy. The wall seemed already to be on its slippery way. The torrent was nearly at the level of the path, carrying branches full of aborted buds in its wake; at one point a young sapling sailed past in its entirety, roots and all. Everything seemed hopeless. Fathers, children, moving, staying – it all felt like a waste of time. Nothing would work. Futility was too big a word for it: that was something grand, off in the past, to do with wars and trenches. What I felt was much less worthy. I couldn't find a good enough reason to believe *anything* was worth doing. There was a gap – behind the belief – a chasm that swallowed me and whatever will I possessed. What made it worse was the feeling that a reason *did* exist somewhere, it *was* possible to believe and I'd once known how. But my memory failed me – and it would always fail me. I'd never get back to that feeling of knowing the reasons for doing things. I'd always be stepping into the dark, which I knew in itself took no little hope, if not faith. But I wanted more than that, more than blindness and darkness.

Having to deal with a woman who claimed to have met with God – had a child by him no less – didn't help matters. And there I was searching for this deity, this vagrant, this tramp, groping round the unlikely nooks and bleak back-ways, thinking deep down that I didn't care whether the father was alive or dead, and secretly believing that no one else cared either. A black shining seepage oozed down the arch of the railway bridge, some of it running down the brickwork in rivulets, some dripping off into the air about me. All the dark, dank way home I thought of my father and his lines – *How love burns through the putting in the seed. How love burns . . . love burns.*

CHAPTER 3

5) Chronology of Main Events Since Child's Birth (cont):

*10.11.86 – Mother and child reunited. They move to
another guest house on Portland Street; mother and child
relationship is seen to improve; mother is seen to be coping
much better. The support and observation policy are subsequently relaxed.*
*13.12.86 – Mother again mentions a 'presence' in her room.
She is involved in an altercation with the landlady of the
guest house in connection with another tenant.*
*23.12.86 – Holly received into voluntary care (S.2. Child
Act 1980), mother again goes missing (temporarily).*
*5.3.87 – Holly remains in foster care. Mother returns to the
C. Clinic. My inquiries commenced at this point.*

The morning after visiting the allotment I dropped by at the
clinic, using the excuse of having to pick up some paperwork.
I'd been seeing things in the shed, a trick of the light, nothing
more – but the seedlings had been watered, someone had been
caring for them. I needed to find out if it was her. I had to
know, but didn't stop to think why I had to know. I checked
with the duty nurse.

— No, Janet's still here. Why?

I mumbled some bureaucratic excuse. The nurse confirmed: Janet was still being diagnosed or treated – whatever they were doing with her they were still doing it. She couldn't have been watering the seedlings in the shed – the nurse said there was no Section Order, she was in the clinic of her own free will and could feasibly come and go as she pleased.

— Quite a few of them go for walks during the day. Some even make it into town. But Janet never goes.

Hadn't been going recently anyway, according to the nurse, whose strawberry-blonde hair clashed violently, at least in my estimation, with the blue of her uniform. She caught me glancing at her black-tighted legs and smiled knowingly, as if I was too old even to be her father.

— Janet's more inclined to paint, over in the Therapies Room. There most days.

The nurse pointed off down the corridor, adding with the same, speaking-to-geriatrics loudness.

— She doesn't get on with the ping pong, that's what most of them do, if they're not watching the box. Table tennis or cards. But Janet doesn't do games as a rule, far too sophisticated.

Even at that volume I couldn't make out where the irony was pointing, whether ping pong and cards might be more sophisticated than what Janet got up to, or the other way round. Picking up the file, I took my leave of the ward and headed to the main entrance. But instead of going straight out I followed the corridor – and the nurse's directions – down towards the Therapies Room.

The corridor terminated at double glass doors which opened out onto a patio. They were wedged open, allowing a fresh, spring breeze into the corridor, rustling the notices pinned to a board opposite the last door in the passageway. The door was labelled 'A213: Therapies'. I stepped out onto the patio and gazed through the window into A213, unobserved. The first thing I saw was a black guy, hooded top, young, eighteen or so, bopping his head to a walkman, sitting low in the chair, trying as hard as he could to ignore the fact that he was being bawled at by an older man with big jowls, a maroon dickey bow and waistcoat – some sort of catering outfit by the look of it. The older man's skin was lighter – Mediterranean or even Middle East I guessed, but you could tell they were related by the way they were with each other, and something about the curve of the shoulders and the startled, petal-shaped eyes. This, I later learned, was Guillermo and his father.

In the other corner was a little, creased man with red corkscrew hair and a smudge of a beard. His skin so white it was almost transparent; he looked young and old at same time and could have been anything between twenty and sixty. This, it turned out, was Marius. Both hands in his pockets and a blue rinse of cigarette smoke about his head. He was on the edge of his chair in front of the TV but he was looking over towards a table by the window. The sun on the glass was blinding and I moved round on the patio to escape its glare, trying to catch what he was looking at.

As soon as I saw her I realised. I was there and I hadn't meant to be there; I hadn't made a conscious decision – let's go to the clinic and see if I can set eyes on her. No, I was there, gazing gormlessly through a coruscating window, before I knew where I was. The clinic was on the fringes, like a subbranch of the general hospital – it was designated to give respite and intermediary care. There weren't supposed to be any long-termers, so it didn't have the feel of confinement you get in the bigger institutions. Beyond the patio there was an expansive lawn running down to a flimsy looking fence, reinforced with just flowering forsythia bushes – starred yellow rags clinging to the skeletons of cold winter twigs. Beyond the fence and hedge was the river, with a red rowing boat tethered to the near bank, bobbing in the dappled shallows.

Back inside, Marius had gone, but the family argument was still raging: Guillermo sank even deeper in his chair, his father having removed his bow tie waved it about in an angry flurry, looking bizarrely as if he were trying to send messages by semaphore. Janet was painting at a table, across from a man wearing a neatly pressed check shirt, its empty left arm pinned down from the shoulder. This, they later told me, was Alan. The nurse said he'd lost his arm in the Falklands, and that Marius was prone to call him 'the one-armed bandit'. There was a rivalry there apparently. But at that moment I found myself chuckling, picturing David Janssen, hot in pursuit and hotly pursued, I wondered whose wife had been murdered. Little did I know. And I laughed too as I caught sight of Janet's picture, not making out the content, only the storm of red. I could just see the label on the heavily squeezed, almost expired tube of paint – 'Vermilion' – as she dipped her brush and daubed another red line on the paper. And I laughed as I caught sight of myself in long shot: a cloud passing briefly in front of the sun, allowing the vast window glass to reflect momentarily its near vicinity. I wasn't quite in the bushes but near enough: a peeping tom, stalking a mad woman. She couldn't have got to the shed to water her plants; I'd been scared by a bird, a little tiny bird. But even if she had been in the shed, who cared if I'd looked like some kind of idiot, there with my shimmering pen? The pen I no longer possessed. Now, that *was* something I should be concerned about. The pen was worth something. I noticed Alan's painting was all black – together they made quite a combo.

I was about to go when I saw, just before the sun regained its full glare and again blocked the reflection in the window, that I had two bodies and two heads. At first I thought it was caused by a peculiarity of the angles and light, and perhaps the warp in the glass. But as I checked again I could see that one of my heads had long, curly hair. And on that curly haired head the beard had been reduced to a few chin whiskers and a thin, soft moustache. And the face was thinner too, the cheek bones higher, the skin much whiter. I looked closer and realised that Marius – the man with the ginger hair, very similar in hue, if not length, straightness and style, to my own – was standing right by my side, his hands still in his pockets, his face attentive. I turned and guessed he must have seen me peering in through the window and come out to investigate. Either that or he was just coming out to escape the row, to get some fresh air. Whatever his reasons, he'd come out of room

A213 and into the corridor and through the glass doors and out onto the patio without me noticing. No 'hello, how are you' or 'nice weather', he just looked at me and nodded with a smile toward the glaring glass. And we both squinted and bent to get a better view.

By now the two painters had really joined forces, each having run out of paint, they were squeezing what they could from the empty tubes into a communal saucer in the centre of the table, throwing the discarded tubes by the window – mainly Vermilion and Cobalt Blue, but some Ebony as well. Then the unmixed reservoir was filled with a little water and the contents of a quarter-full Crimson Lake Janet found under the table. They smiled at each other for an age before taking the plunge. She was first: using her index finger, more of a paddle than a dive. Testing the feel. He wasn't far behind. Their fingers touched in the middle, wrapping around each other in the centre then letting go just as instantly, like Flamenco dancers, twisting the strands, the reds and blues and blacks. Their other fingers joined in: glancing, dancing, and, without knowing why, I realised I felt uneasy. Because of the mess, because of the visible feel, I didn't know what it was, but my palms were damp, my feet were edging on the spot, as if very soon they'd be making a move of their own. I remembered the interview, Janet touching my knuckles, showing me where love and hate had been tattooed. I remembered it as if she'd just done it, I could feel the trace of her fingertips on the back of my hands. My curly haired friend made a noise next to me. I tried not to hear, I tried to concentrate, and get to what it was that was getting to me.

And then with his index finger Alan painted a circle on her paper and she painted a line coming from the circle out to the edges of the sheet, and he painted another circle around the first and she another line, each again and again, fast but controlled like surgeons, until the paper was filled with a giant web of purple-black, with red veins woven into its daubed gossamer. I looked at her palms and wrists, the vermilion recasting them as tortured screams, and I thought of the shed, recalling the fear and the sight of the bloody hands. Had I really seen them? Had I seen anything? But more than these doubts, much more, I realised I was jealous. That's the nearest word I could find for it. As though whatever it was I thought I was missing it was suddenly tangible, through the window, drowning there in the union at the centre of the table. In the vermilion, in the ebony, in the cobalt lake, I could see it, though still I couldn't put a name to it. This had nothing to do with Janet or her one-armed friend. It had to do with me, something that was teasing me, playing with my senses like the fragrance of an un-recallable dream. I had the scent of it; I knew it and didn't know it all at the same time.

As I looked up I saw that Alan, clenching his one fist, wasn't smiling anymore. He'd stopped painting and mixing. He was crying. Janet got up and, skirting the table, put her arm around him, careful to avoid his empty sleeve and careful too not to put her bloody hands on his prim shirt. Was that the first note of admiration, the first admission of anything about her that was positive? Suddenly she appeared like a nurse ministering – no, more like an angel: quelling his tears, stifling his pain. She was in charge. As if she had some sort of magic to hand, some power in her touch. And now Marius too – not to be unheard any longer – croaked beside me.

— Him Up Above has given, Him has taken away.

I thought at first this was some grotesque reference to the missing arm, but I was guessing and really didn't know what on earth he might mean. As I turned to look at him, I realised his coiled locks were springing about like galvanised wires; the communion in the saucer or Janet's comforting embrace – something had obviously affected him as well. His hands were now both out of his pockets, one holding up his gaping, estuary-wide trousers, the other busy in a different way. Yes, his right hand, with its swollen blue veins, clinging and concealing, pushing and pulling, a succulent tentacle round his bright pink cock. Right in front of me, as if I wasn't there. Or maybe it was just for me, his all-important witness? Even his face showed signs of blotchy colour, his slit eyes glistened with near-exultant intent. He smiled horribly, a confederate's smile, before nodding then looking back toward the window.

Later I learned this was not unusual; Marius was 'always at himself', as the duty nurse put it. At that moment I couldn't help but take it personally, to feel like his accomplice. I was after all watching with him; I was after all excited by what I saw through the window; I was transfixed, aroused, tantalised, hooked. I fled, and in so doing ran into that very same strawberry-blonde, black-tighted nurse, as she ushered the remonstrating father away from his son. She glared at me reproachfully – what was I doing still here? Hadn't I left twenty minutes ago? Cajoling the father, who was now carrying both his bow tie and waistcoat, along the corridor, she told him in her shout-speak voice.

— Come on now, Mr Brown, you know visiting time's over. Guillermo will never get to feel better like this, now will he?

But she was looking at me all the time, as if to say: you're actually the naughty old man in this; you're the daddy who should really know better.

CHAPTER 4

Brief Social History (continued):

*8. The mother, Janet Burns (aka Janet Greenaway),
was born in North Wales. The family (she was the only
child) lived together until she was 7 years of age when her
parents separated, her father moving to S.; Janet and her
mother remaining in North Wales.*

*9. Later that year (1972) Janet Burns was received into
foster care, as her mother was receiving inpatient psychiatric treatment for clinical depression. Her father was
unable to care for Janet at that time.*

※

I would be seeing a lot more of her pictures, those intricate
lines with their vermilion webs: the morbid effect, like a
bloody mould spreading over the paper. K could never understand why I didn't like them; the pictures really did something
for her. All I could ever see were daubs: no delicacy or finesse,
just smudged paint, kids' stuff. Rachel and Simon could do
better; at least I hoped they could.

One thing was for certain, whatever anyone might think
about Janet Burns' artistic ability: there was nothing in the
paintings that was going to offer real enlightenment; nothing
to help me come up with what I really needed. It was my job
to reach an end. I was a prophet, of sorts. I looked into the

various pasts – the births and childhoods, the trials, separations, court appearances – and through the supernatural powers of my pen (and typist) I invented the future. Yes, I too was a god. My recommendations were barely contested. So, what was the problem? A little digging and weeding and the reports wrote themselves. The mother didn't want the child; the father was nowhere to be found. The case workers had spread some fertiliser of their own, tried nurturing the tendrils – parent skills, observation and training, all that pandering – but to no avail. The climate was hostile, the ties torn. End of story. So, what was the problem?

I phoned the police to see if they'd ever heard of our father. Hate and love were commonplace, even rasta mops. It was the arboreal theme that rang bells and sure enough he wasn't in heaven. Far from it.

— Holly, you say, sir? Sounds very familiar.

— You know who he is then?

— Wouldn't go that far, sir. But I do remember something about a certain gentleman, a traveller I think you'd call him. Of the new age variety. He used to pester the cafes and restaurants on High Street for leftovers. As I recall he was known to wear a sprig or two about his person.

— And is he still around?

— That I can't say, sir, not for certain. But I suspect . . .

The duty sergeant thought he was inside, arrested a while back – locally, but he was wanted elsewhere. The sergeant couldn't remember, he'd get back to me. I imagined this dreadlocked divinity getting into deserted warehouses, sneaking into old, closed down factories, sleeping on building sites where he could find wood to burn. Breaking and entering: more than likely that's what it was.

I decided to await Rachel and Simon by looking through the Schedule 2 Report and case notes. Up until then I hadn't had chance to find out who Janet Burns really was. It turned out Janet herself had been adopted – in 1976, aged eleven – by a Mary and George Greenaway (that had been her surname on all the documents before she changed her name). I checked

through the notes but the name 'Burns' didn't occur anywhere – it was neither the name of her birth father nor her
birth mother's maiden name. And yes, they had been married,
and in a church – well, a chapel. Janet was born in Wales, and
spent the first part of her life in a village up in the hills. Then
it all fell apart – her father moved away. After her mother died
Janet went to live with him but encountered the usual problems with steps – mother and siblings. There was some controversy about which Authority should deal with her, but she was
fostered, and eventually adopted, by the Greenaways.

I took note of their address and phone number. I'd have to
check them out, just in case, but guessed they wouldn't want
too much to do with the illegitimate offspring of their adopted
daughter – child of God though she may be. You didn't have to
read between the lines to see the problems. There had been
more than a few visits to the clinic. Janet had attacked a man
when she was sixteen, while in hospital having her appendix
removed. Nothing serious – a few scratches, a bite or two. It
didn't draw blood or go to court. There'd been a bed shortage;
the man's wife was next to Janet and was in a coma. The man
came in every day and applied make-up to his wife's face. That
was Janet's justification for the attack. According to the social
worker's notes, Janet said that the woman told her in the night
that she didn't want him to do it. This was a woman in a coma,
and she never regained consciousness. Janet had to be moved
to another ward.

There were other episodes, hints that she'd been violent
with the Greenaways, and that they'd only just managed to
cope with her. She'd left home at eighteen and, by the look of
it, just drifted since. She didn't have a habit though, at least
not according to the testimonies in the report – those of the
social workers and the Greenaways. As I was reading I pictured
her framed by wisps of smoke, a vignette; the line of her face
sometimes dissolving as the light hit her features. I coughed
at the thought, tasting the sticky fumes on my lips. It seemed
so familiar, like the smell that hung around my mother, yes,
but something else, there was something more. I knew what

it meant but . . . but . . . somehow a part was missing – as if it was a memory I wasn't yet able, for whatever reason, to fully receive.

As Janet hadn't gained any contact with her birth father I didn't feel obliged to get in touch either. With no legal requirement, one father seemed quite enough to be going on with. Besides, I wasn't reading the case notes to find out what I had to do: that was the problem. I realised, as I heard the Deux CV pulling up outside: I couldn't just put her down and close the deal; it wasn't a possibility. *No such thing as a last case*. And something nagged. I dialled the case worker – let the kids wait outside for a while, let Sarah steam behind her petite windscreen. It wouldn't do them any harm.

I was immune to the orphan thing, the pull of the urchin: please sir, can I have some more, sir? And the glory trail that follows: oh, reader, reader, I married him. All that costumed nonsense, bringing a tear to the world-weary eye. I'd seen too much of the flip side, what they could do to the people who took them in. Orphans – more likely as not they'd rob you and slit your throat, emotionally if not literally. Sometimes both.

I'd been on the pitch too long; I was beyond sentiment. I was beyond a lot of things, things I didn't understand, things I'd just missed or was just on the edge of knowing. I was starting to sway with it all, as if the edge might be precipitous. The Deux CV beeping its little French horn didn't help, neither did my children knocking on the door in their inimitable rat-a-kick-bang way. Of course. What was I doing? Social workers weren't behind their desks on weekends. I left a message on the answerphone and, as I replaced the receiver, just for a moment, recalled Janet Burns' picture: the drip of vermilion along the lines of the web, as though something was bleeding, something was suppurating, deep down. And I knew it was true: something *was* bleeding, something *was* leaking. I stared into thin air, searching for what it might be. Then I heard.

— Dad! Dad – are you there? Dad! Open the door.

When Sarah and I split up she'd wanted me to stay in London

– for the sake of the children, of course, never for her own convenience. But I was already chasing shadows. Yes, it had already begun, even then. Before then, before all possible beginnings. I thought for a time that maybe the answer did lie back home, back in the past, before I even met Sarah. I used my mother's health as an excuse. In reality I was hooked by another possibility: the childhood memory of a hill. Just a knoll when I revisited it, with a few craggy pine trees on the top – unimpressive against the hills to the South and East, pitiful against the black mass of Welsh mountains off in the West. But you could see it from miles around in the plain. I remembered walking there with my father: thinking we'd never get to the top, thinking it was a mountain itself, an impossibility, and that my father was mad for suggesting we try. It was like a miracle when we made it, sitting and eating our picnic among the spindly trees. I think we were the only ones there – Edmund Hillary and Sherpa Tenzing – but I can't remember exactly, or how old I was. Seven or eight maybe. Nine even. Just a memory, to go with the odd sightings of his ghost. But it seemed to have something in it, some secret or possibility that was worth investigation. As good a reason as any to leave my own children behind.

Of course there was more to it than that. Sarah said I should move south of the river, Clapham perhaps. But Richard told me they needed people back home: case workers, welfare officers and these new posts – *Guardian ad Litems*. It was 1984; there'd been a run of debacles and inquiries: kids being murdered and abused by social workers, according to the tabloids. The government, looking for a quick fix, had invented a job, or revamped an old one; someone to keep an eye on things, give a voice to the little ones – autonomous, away from the coal-face, but requiring a certain amount of experience and authority. It was tailor made: my old home town, but a fresh start. Richard acted like my father sometimes, guiding me in the right direction. He'd told me to beware of the reunion, the last fling: all very well at the time but it just screws you up if you take it to mean anything – you, the kids, everyone. Get away, as far as you can, as quick as you can. That's what Richard had said – the Family Court solicitor and on his third happy marriage.

I didn't listen. When I'd moved out, but was still in London, sleeping on a friend's floor, I called round for lunch, knowing the children would be at school, knowing that Sarah knew I was coming. We took a walk on Hampstead Heath, intending to talk of the grimy things: how to split the albums and books, whether to keep up payments on the chaise longue. Only we didn't. Talk. We ended up holding hands as we walked. Near Parliament Hill we stopped under an oak tree, the old acorns popping under foot. We kissed, and almost as soon as our lips touched Sarah reached down, undoing my zip and sliding her ice-cold hands round my shrivelled scrotum. I wondered then, who else she'd done that to. She'd never done it to me before. I was sure of that. When we got back to the house and the chaise longue I didn't think twice. Until afterwards, when she got dressed to fetch Rachel and Simon from school, shouting from the bathroom that I better go in case they saw me. They were my children for God's sake! It was my chaise longue.

This happened a few times and I never managed to remember what would follow. We always went for a walk, and always ended up on the chaise longue. Why not the bed? I couldn't work it out, not then. I wanted to stay for when the kids came home from school; I wanted to stay until they went to school the next morning. And yet I had been the prime mover. I'd wanted the separation, the divorce – more, or so I thought, than Sarah. I'd always wanted more. In truth I hadn't known whether it would be greater or better. I just wanted change, something else. I was guessing.

In any case, we soon started arguing again, but it was all toothless, almost nostalgic. The future imminent, the past gone, we couldn't hurt each other anymore, not together. All that was left was a strange sofa of dubious pedigree; at least, that's how it seemed. Richard had been right. When the job came up I was out of London in a flash, using my mother as the final, compelling factor: I had to live near to her, being the only child, the next of kin. What a joke! But part of me smiled at the thought of occasionally forcing Sarah off her French recliner and out of London: a small revenge for unzipping my trousers with one hand while waving good-bye with the other.

This weekend she hadn't even moaned about having to drop them off. It was by rights my turn to collect. But she'd seemed almost pleased. She was going to pick them up on Sunday as well. Unheard of. And no explanation.

— Where is your Mummy going while you're with me?

Simon grunted; he was never much help. Rachel was older, quicker off the mark.

— She's got a client, a conference centre.

— The one on the farm? Same as last time?

— Yes.

I thought as much.

— Is she staying the night?

I stopped myself just short of asking if she had a friend with her. I knew the farm, she'd stayed there during their half-term – it was a few miles out of town, to the West, in the hills, the real hills. It had a shop in town – organic produce – and a reputation: a hippy colony, still there after all these years; thriving by all accounts. Sarah was never very forthcoming about her work, so I was clueless as to what they might want with a graphic designer, eco-friendly and cotton-tighted though she might be. I pictured her briefly: drawing bright yellow sheaths of corn, jars of lentils, baskets of wholemeal buns, and lettering the labels for hand-potted crab apple chutney. I made a joke about Mummy becoming a farmer. Rachel and Simon looked at me as if I was mad, not for saying it but for laughing.

CHAPTER 5

Brief Social History (continued):

10. After her mother committed suicide in 1974, Janet went to live with her father and step-mother.

11. She failed to adapt to the new family setting (her step-mother had two children from a previous marriage) and after several periods of foster care her father agreed to her adoption. She was formally adopted in December 1976, residing with her foster parents of the previous six months (Mr and Mrs John Greenaway).

12. She lived with Mr and Mrs Greenaway until she was 18, but maintained good contact with them until the discovery of her pregnancy when she was aged 20.

13. In March 1987, she changed her surname from Greenaway to Burns. Her daughter Holly's surname was also changed. There is no obvious reason why this name was assumed as it bears no relation to her own birth father, her mother's maiden name or Holly's putative father. It may have some obscure connection, however, to Janet's birth mother.

14. Janet Burns has been receiving inpatient treatment at the C. Clinic, S. General Hospital, on an intermittent basis since January 1986. A diagnosis has not been ratified. She has received treatment there on previous occasions.

I'd arranged to meet Richard in the park, knowing he had a new little boy. Younger than Rachel and Simon, yes, but at least a fellow child. I was always short of things to do with them when they came up. Rachel wasn't too bad, she read a lot, but Simon was a whinger. He got on well with my mother.

I'd become untuned; I no longer knew quite how to do it, not easily anyway. It was wavelengths and habit, I guessed. There was no pattern to our being together, only a strange, tawdry novelty and that soon wore off. The only thing we had in common was a dislike of burgers. The park always seemed as good a bet as any, yet Rachel was growing out of it fast, leaving Simon increasingly without a playmate.

Richard was late, the breeze and rush lashing his blue tie up so it settled like a scimitar on the shoulder of his russet tweed jacket. He apologised for his tardiness as he made the introductions, letting the paisley-clad toddler down from his arms. I was forever confused when it came to Richard's hordes.

— I thought you had a Ben already?

— No, perish the thought.

As the two year old ran to play with Simon and Rachel in the sandpit, we took the opportunity to stroll around the as yet bare laburnum arches.

— So, Philip, what appears to be the problem?

I groaned, as I always seemed to with Richard.

— My last case, I had to get one didn't I.

— No such thing as a last . . .

As I say, it was one of his phrases. He said it all the time, only sometimes, like today, elaborating.

— They haunt you. They'll never go away, even when you've stopped. Goes with the territory. Can't just leave it in the pub or on the ninth or eighteenth or thirty sixth. Not that sort of job. Too many stories.

We'd been in the same form and house – grammar school, nothing grand. Local lads, both of us; only he was proud of it, he was rooted, a part of the community. If you counted up all his kids, he could almost form his own. He caught the latest in his arms then swivelled round so Ben returned, running, to the sandpit, discarding items of clothing along the way. It looked so easy, so jolly, it always did with Richard. Meanwhile there was piteous old me: Simon running up and burrowing under my jacket for protection from Rachel, who was hissing like a goose to get at him. The red mop, a replica of mine, didn't help; it made her look angry, even when she wasn't. Trying to be casual, I whipped my jacket off and swung it over a shoulder, not only exposing Simon to the pummelling fists but catching him round the ear as well with the jacket's trailing arm.

I knew I should say something to stop the screaming and fighting – play a game, comment on the flowers and cherry blossom at least, say how beautiful they all were. I remember trying – pointing up towards the branches – but no words came out. Rachel and Simon stopped momentarily anyway, laughing at my silent rictus, no doubt thinking it to be a weird-Dad joke. I knew I'd become strange to them, and they to me. When I left London I'd been relieved, and it wasn't just because of Sarah. I wanted to see them off to school, yes, but I also had a feeling about them. I'd had a dream – well more than one, but there was one in particular. Throughout it Simon was standing in a doorway smiling, his teeth showing, as if he knew a secret about me, a secret I didn't even know myself. I woke up shaking, convinced he wasn't a child anymore. From now on, no matter what expression he might have, no matter how much he might behave like a child, I felt that deep down he was smiling like that – all thin-lipped, with his teeth gleaming. He knew what went on in my darkest recesses, the places I didn't even know about myself. He knew and the world would never be the same again.

Rachel was in the dream too. There was water everywhere, I didn't know whether I was inside a house or out on a marsh. I was paddling around trying to find my bearings, or a sign to tell me the way home. And that's when I saw Rachel floating among the lilies and algae – like some Ophelia, only she wasn't dead. I tried to speak, to shout at her to get out of the water. But my throat wouldn't work. In close-up her face transformed. First it became Sarah, and her arm was the only stable form or shape, reaching out of the water, beckoning me. And I was going to her, I was sinking into the water with her. Then, as I approached, the face turned into my mother. She was telling me not to be so silly, touching my cheek, mocking. And all the while Simon was standing there by a door; those thin lips, those glinting teeth, smiling darkly.

At the time I blamed it on London and my caseload. I'd seen firsthand and far too often how in-the-family-horror thrived where the roads, and car crime, were bad. But it wasn't as simple as that: some part of me was scared of Rachel and Simon, as if they might do me harm . . . or me them. Now I watched them as they chased each other back towards the sandpit, Ben desperately trying to get in on the older-kid action. I remember him trying to impress, kicking at the fallen cherry petals so they gusted up like snow. Some things are so banal you can't help but remember them. And, as we strolled, Richard tapped into the mood of my bleaker thoughts, as only he could.

— Do you want to fuck her, this Janet Burns, is that it?

Richard had a way with what he called the 'unconscious paperwork'.

— No, I do not want to . . . to . . . for God's sake! We're not all like you. She wants the father to adopt.

— What's wrong with that? I thought he was a benign sort of fellow. What was his name?

I didn't laugh, why should I? If I hadn't known Richard for a life time . . . If only.

— The father's in prison, at least the police think he is. They're getting back to me.

— Case solved. Adoption the only possibility – and, if I might say, most probable from the outset.

— Yes, but . . .

— Yes but that's too simple isn't it? Your last case, and it would be closed, solved, the end. Goodbye job, goodbye children, goodbye England. Have you ever thought of that, eh? You're procrastinating, dear chap, you're putting it off.

— There's no such thing as a last case.

— Ah, yes, I might say it but you, my friend, are living it.

— And what's that supposed to mean?

— It means you probably do want to fuck her.

Despite the ugly, self-congratulating chuckle, he might well have been serious. You had to know him – some other catch phrase he'd come up with about probabilities and possibilities. If you didn't go for an appetising bunch of the latter you'd end up with a very predictable and boring lot of the former. And if you didn't identify any possibilities at all, then you'd always be shocked and surprised by yourself. I could never remember it exactly. Like a joke, but he used it as a formula. And it worked. He was good at his job, good with his children, good with his wife, even his exes.

Richard was the wrong person to talk to about difficulties or for any sort of confession. But a child's scream stopped us in our tracks anyway: another of those everyday, prosaic memories. Piercing and unforgettable. As was the sight that met us as we rushed to the call. Richard had almost fallen and was well behind me. Over at the sandpit Rachel had Ben's arms strapped to his side so he couldn't move a muscle, while Simon poked at the two-year old's eyes. Not surprisingly Ben was howling: enough to raise the fire brigade all on his own. I shouted as loud as I could.

— What are you doing? Stop it this instant! Do you hear? Rachel, let him go. Simon, stop doing that!

They obeyed reluctantly, stepping back from the trouserless two-year old whose hands immediately rose to his eyes and then rubbed frantically. Rachel started to cry as she spoke.

— We didn't do it on purpose.

I grabbed each of them by the arm.

— Looked like torture from where I was standing.

Simon freed himself and backed off as he spat out the excuses.

— I was aiming at her. She put it all down my back.

Rachel cried in earnest and I tried to explain to Richard.

— They've been throwing sand and some of it went in his eye, they were trying to get it out.

My children weren't really barbarians and torturers, though I was experiencing difficulty believing it. Having reached the scene just before Richard I tried to tend Ben's sand-scratched eyes, merely causing him to cry even louder. I too found myself holding his arms by his side in an attempt to keep them away from his face, and as I knelt in front of him I experienced a hot flush in my thighs, just above the knees. It was a few seconds before I realised the heat was also damp. Ben had not only removed his tartan trousers in the sand pit but everything else as well. Scrambling back out of the way I just stopped myself from shouting at him. I felt my arm rising again, like in the interview with Janet Burns; I was going to slap him, at the very least, whether I wanted to or not. To stop the noise, stop the bleating, stop the torrent. Luckily Richard got there first, whisking him up into his arms just in time.

— Never did like big nasty men did you, eh?

The toddler stopped howling, and leaking the second his feet left the ground. Richard apologised and sniggered in equal measure about the damp patch on my trousers. Rachel had taken over in the bleating stakes. Ben peeped up from his dad's shoulder, staring across at her as if she was mad.

For my part I started shouting and hugging, all at the same time.

— I don't know what's got into you two. You know sand's dangerous; you came here to play with him not blind him.

Rachel was the sole beneficiary of the hugs. Simon neither cried nor moved from the edge of the sandpit, well out of striking distance but still raging and full of blame himself. Rachel nestled into my leg as he shouted at her.

— It's your fault, it's all your fault ... It's her fault, she never gets told off, it's always me who gets it, she's such a goody goody, that's what you think, but she isn't, she's a ...

Louder and louder he shouted: she's a this, she's a that; louder and louder, like a banging drum. I couldn't take anymore. Couldn't he see? Surely he was old enough; he'd done wrong and must take the consequences.

— Stop blaming. Stop trying to hurt your sister. Stop shouting. Just stop blaming everybody else, stop blaming everybody but yourself. You're nothing but a baby. Stop shouting. You're acting like an idiot, an imbecile, a . . . just stop shouting.

And yes, *I* snarled, *I* shouted. Not stopping until he was silenced, apart from the usual revving sob. I remember that, and where he stood – stock still, off on his own at the edge of the pit, a cherry tree behind him shedding the occasional flake of spiralling blossom.

It's difficult to remember everything, but I do recall thinking it was definitely over now: the recriminations, the tears. I turned to Richard, to apologise properly. Ben was taking longer, even more transfixed peeps, aimed exclusively at Simon. I didn't dare address the toddler directly in case I set him off again. It all fell still and quiet for a moment; Rachel must have been clinging closer, trying to avoid the wet patch on my thigh, but I didn't notice at first. Simon cracked the lull.

— You always take her side. You're going to marry her.

He squealed it out and Rachel stuck to me, grabbing hold of my trousers and an excruciating pinch of skin, as he carried on.

— You're going to marry her. You fancy her.

I thought briefly of the dream – Simon's thin lips, his teeth. And he was smirking now, over at the edge of the sandpit, framed by the branches of the cherry tree: it looked like a doorway. I realised what was happening. And I could do nothing to stop it. Nothing except what I did – flinging Rachel off into the sand, I brushed my trousers down and straightened up.

Unfair I know. Later I might rationalise: these things happen between a father and his children; storms soon pass; afterwards you can laugh about it; those accidents with sand, piddle, bad dreams, pinched skin. But now I hated them both with a vengeance, as if they'd both pinched me, both shouted and bawled and scraped at the same nerve.

— You're as bad as each other. You came here to play with him. And what do you do?

Soon they were together, shoulder to shuddering shoulder, united on the edge of the sandpit. Simon, having helped Rachel to her feet, was now spokesman for them both.

— Who wants to play with a baby anyway? You always pick on us, you always blame us. We didn't want to play with a baby. We didn't . . . We'll have to do enough baby s-s-sitting . . ..

And there it came, stuttering at first, but gradually gaining in daring and coherence.

— We'll have to do enough baby sitting when Mum has . . .

Still unfinished but symphonic in its clarity. Rachel stopped nodding and tugged, whispering, at Simon's sleeve.

— You weren't supposed to say anything about it, not yet.

It was too late now. Much too late. Silence, not even any sobbing. No more shouting, just quiet, real quiet, broken only by Richard's studious and deliberate gathering of Ben's paisley outfit from around the sandpit. Richard's silences roared at the best of times.

— Your mother's going to have a baby?

I think I asked. I must have. Automatically, without thinking. I remember staring at them until each in turn nodded, at least twice, I remember turning back from one to the other. I needed absolute confirmation. And I remember feeling it coming, the second question, but somehow I stopped just short. It took all my nerve.

Richard walked away, dressing Ben on the far side of the pit. He may have made some excuse about having to go, I can't remember. He went out of earshot but he knew all right, if not before, certainly now. I wondered who else knew. I wanted to ask the question more than anything, I felt it coming again. But if I can look back and get any credit from our day in the park it was from that. Just that: I didn't ask, I didn't force them to tell me. I didn't comfort them, I couldn't; yet at least I didn't ask.

But who was the father?

I had no number for Sarah at the conference centre on the farm. I could have looked it up or tried directory inquires – even hippies have phones. It all seemed so much bother, and in any case I didn't want to phone, I didn't want to see her or talk to her. What was strange about it all was my indifference. I was curious, emphatically, I wanted to know, and I was going to ask her when she came to pick Rachel and Simon up. But I didn't really care. It didn't fill my head like it might have done.

The Deux CV pulled up outside, and I told the children to wait a second. They'd got their stuff together in a sombre pile by the door. We never really recovered from our outing to the park. The plan was to leave them in the house, just for a minute, and I would pop out to the car and ask. Quick as you like – no tension, no build up, no sooner asked and Sarah would be gone, on her way. No time for argument, no time for a scene. And it saved on the phone bill. It was only a courtesy after all, I didn't need to know. I'd just nip out. Who's the father? Quick as you like, and they'd be off on their way. But the phone rang just as I opened the door. Fatally, I stopped to pick it up: before I could remonstrate Rachel and Simon ran outside with their bags, desperate to get away. Within seconds Sarah was waving and hooting and they were driving off down the road.

It was the police – the duty sergeant, apologising for ringing on a Sunday, only he was due a week's holiday and couldn't trust the message would get passed on.

— It's your Hollyman, sir.

— My Hollyman?

— Yes, the fella from the allotment. I think I've located him.

Janet Burns' face flashed before me, as the sergeant told me what he'd found out. Her lineaments shaded in a red light, the eyes filling with dark, kohl-edged tears. It was as if I knew how she would take the news. Our father was in Kent – on remand.

— His own wife and child, sir.

41

— He had a wife and child?

Yes he did. The daughter would have been eight next birthday. It would be hitting court, and the headlines, in a few months.

— Hadn't been back home for years apparently. Only a week back in the fold, sir, that's what they say.

A week back with them and it happens. He can take no more.

— His bare hands, sir.

The hate consumes the love. Wasn't there a Robert Mitchum movie, the inscribed hands tussling with one another?

— Strangled both of them, sir. His own wife and child.

I needed to meet with this dubious god, just to seal the adoption. But in effect he was off the list. *Pater non grata*. No longer a possibility.

CHAPTER 6

2) Process of Enquiry – those interviewed and spoken to:

Holly Greenaway or Burn – subject – three times
Janet Burns (aka Janet Greenaway) – birth mother – three times
Mrs Peggy Greenaway – maternal grandmother (with Mr Greenaway)
Mr John Greenaway – maternal grandfather (with Mrs Greenaway)
Mr and Mrs Bowlby – adoption candidates – three times
Mr Andrew Berry – putative father
Ms Ann Wide – social worker, S. Adoption/Family Finding Unit
I have spoken over the telephone to:
Ms Mary Bell – social worker, S. County Council
Ms Sheila Hampton – social worker, S. County Council
Probation Services – HM Prison Canterbury, Kent

ॐ

The weeks that followed were a blur. There were a few court appearances to mop up: straight forward Care Orders, the bits and pieces that had always kept me going. Physical and emotional neglect – I could write them in my sleep. In one case the judge praised the thoroughness of my report. It was gratifying to know I could still do some things right, but the case in question had hardly presented a challenge. The mother had a dependence on a particular brand of whisky liqueur – bought it by the crate, using her child benefit. Together with her boyfriend she'd also been dipping into her uncle's Parkinson's medication, using it as an LSD surrogate. During one episode, witnessed by a social worker, the boyfriend claimed the woman's eight year old daughter was the devil. He forced the girl to brush her hair off her forehead because the curls looked, as he put it, 'like fucking great horns'. All I had to do was give a flavour, the court lapped it up.

There was a day when I'd have joked about it with Richard, taken the plaudits in the pub afterwards. Now I steered clear of Richard. That silence in the park and the way he'd responded when I had confided in him – I should have known: he was never someone I could turn to, not with the sort of misty, off-the-road problems I had. There was no one I could turn to. And there was no time to lose either. The letting agents came round measuring rooms, wanting to take an inventory of furniture and fittings for when the house was rented out. But I wasn't ready, not yet. I avoided the phone. No Sarah, no kids. I needed to keep a clear head.

I tried to clear my desk. I went to see the Greenaways to check they didn't want to adopt or foster Holly, though I was fairly sure they'd had their fill. They were getting on and must have been fairly old when they adopted Janet. The rules were different back then. I don't know what it was about seeing them that reminded me of my father, but something struck a chord. Maybe it was the ivy swarming over their slate-roofed semi, or the monkey puzzle tree filling the tiny garden. More likely it was the music coming from inside. K said later that it was like bubbles rising to the surface, these things about my father. It was bound to have come up sooner or later, whether I wanted it to or not.

On the phone Mrs Greenaway had talked not like a mother but as if to a policeman of a crime she'd witnessed, with a hushed 'I knew all along' tone. They would and could have done more but were never heard. They tried to help Janet, but she just wouldn't listen. But for this, but for that. It was the pleading tone of one who once cared but who could no longer. I knew what to expect.

30) Interview with maternal grandparents

30a) I met with Mr and Mrs Greenaway at their home on the 20th April 1987. Since shortly before this interview all contact between them and Janet Burns – the birth mother – has ceased. I understand this is because of on-going and apparently irreconcilable, differences. Mr Greenaway described Janet as 'emotional' and 'difficult' and I understood from our conversation that this impasse had existed for some time. They enjoyed their last brief contact with Janet two days before this interview.

30b) Their views on the proposed adoption are as follows: "We're all for Holly's adoption – we would like to see her settled and have a secure future. I'm sure that the family [the adoptive family] are younger, they'll do a better job than us."

They weren't keen to talk and gave me the impression that, even with willing, couldn't tell me anything I didn't already know. They were career parents, Janet the last in a long line of fostered and adopted children. Tens of the former, three of the latter, even two of their own. They'd had enough. Mr Greenaway sat like an embedded rock in his chair, a deep grease stain on the headrest. Without shifting legs or torso he rustled in the overfilled pockets of his brown, fluff-worn cardigan, gradually gathering the paraphernalia necessary for the packing and lighting of a pipe. Something was boiling away in the kitchen, the steam stealing over the half-open door into the room where we sat. Before the pipe was lit and the mists of deep-sweet virginia wafted airlessly around us, I thought I detected the creeping sniff of liver and onions. Mrs Greenaway sat in her apron, palpably resisting the urge to run to turn things down in the kitchen. With her compact perm and lips pursed tight, she looked intent on getting it over and done as quickly as possible. She listened to my questions but kept her eye resolutely on the TV screen over in the corner. Satellite dishes weren't long out and the Greenaways had just got one – it hung in the ivy above their front door like some broken-winged bird. It was so new they didn't switch the TV off while we talked, not even turning the volume down. Instead Mr Greenaway gave me a guided tour: instruction booklet, the remote control and what seemed like most of the channels. For the rest of the time we were entertained by a camera sweeping over valleys and mountains, plains, rivers and cities, accompanied by music that someone somewhere considered appropriate – Dvorak for the Rockies and prairies; Gershwin for Manhattan and any clumps of three or more buildings.

— The Landscape Channel. Our favourite, isn't it, John.

Mr Greenaway nodded without looking at her. It made me feel giddy. It was all a waste of time; I could have got what I wanted over the phone. We swooped over the Grand Canyon, the camera taking on the eye of an eagle, as Mrs Greenaway finally relented, scurrying away at some heightened hiss from the kitchen. Her husband didn't turn from the screen as he spoke.

— We don't know who it was, so it's no use asking.

— I'm sorry?

— The father. Holly's father. Janet won't tell us who it was. We don't know him.

Scrutinising the side of his face as he sat, still fixed on the TV, I saw that his front teeth were bucked like a rabbits and stained treacle-brown by the pipe. I wondered about his relationship with Janet, how on earth they'd managed to sit in the same room together. I pictured the gut-scraping cumuli of tarred fumes. And then I remembered their connection.

— You never saw him at the allotment then, at the shed?

— The shed? What's that got to do with it?

He was shocked enough to give me a glance. I realised he didn't know. Mrs Greenaway returned with a pack of family snaps. Neither of them knew.

— John doesn't go to the allotment anymore, not these days, not with his legs.

— So, Janet didn't tell you about the shed and who the father was?

— I've just told you she won't tell us ...

— No, I mean ... I mean ...

And I explained as subtly as I could, a little shocked myself: they knew nothing about the father of their adopted daughter's daughter.

— God? What do you mean, God?

But they didn't look too surprised, all things considered. Just battle weary and resigned. They'd been through this sort of thing with Janet before, I could see. Mrs Greenaway sprayed the photos out on the coffee table, as if to prove they were a proper family and did those family things, like having picnics and going on holiday. There were a lot of children of all shapes, sizes and ages. Initially none of the faces seemed familiar, though in one or two I saw a resemblance to the Greenaways. Then I saw her. The red bikini, the ribs protruding and the side-off stance; she was just seventeen, a beanpole. But the same look: straight at me. Mrs Greenaway saw I was staring.

— Yes, that's her. Cornwall that was, wasn't it, John?

I had to look away; I had to look back. And I had to get the Greenaways off my trail.

— What about boyfriends in general, has she ever had a stable relationship with a man?

Turning even more towards the screen so I couldn't see even a profile of her face, Mrs Greenaway let out a disdainful cluck as her husband explained.

— When she lived here she brought lads back for tea once

or twice, but they were more of a joke than anything. Make you laugh just to look at them. One said he was a musician.

At this his wife just couldn't keep quiet.

— Musician indeed, ha!

— Peggy saw him playing a whistle in the precinct. Didn't you? One of those little tin things, what are they called?

— He had a hat out in front of him. Begging!

— Yes, we had to tell her. What are they called?

— We were always having to tell her.

— What are they called, woman?

— Flageolet.

— Flageolet, that's it. That's what it was.

— And did Janet see him for long?

— Who?

— This musician.

Mrs Greenaway didn't seem to notice my eagerness.

— If he was a musician, I'm Ginger Rogers.

Neither her husband.

— No, she was never serious about any of them.

Mrs Greenaway shuffled the snaps, burying the red bikini deep in the pack. Meanwhile on the TV violins soared as the camera flew over peaks and ridges, cellos and bassoons took over as it plummeted down into valleys. I felt too queasy to recognise what I was asking or why.

— And did you disapprove as well, Mr Greenaway?

— Disapprove?

— Of the musician.

His wife turned to me and wouldn't let him answer.

— I didn't say that. I didn't say I disapproved of him.

— But from what you said it sounded as though you didn't think much of the fact that he was a musician or that he busked?

— I didn't say I disapproved. No, I didn't say that.

She looked for support from her husband who was searching deep and long into the mists of his re-ignited pipe. He shook the match out.

— It isn't that we disapprove, it's just she always picked such strange lads.

— Of course we approve. Anything musical . . .

She gestured towards the screen.

— Of course we approve.

We were now all looking at an anonymous Mid-West vista of prime prairie, honeyed yellow oceans swelling and swirling almost in time with the fading gusts of the New World symphony. I had to get away.

— You know she's decided to have Holly adopted. I have to clarify certain things about Janet, her state of mind when making this decision. And I'd very much like to hear your opinion. What do you think of Holly being adopted?

— If you're asking us if we're interested . . . if we'd be able to . . .

I had to inquire despite the odds but I could tell from the defensive bark in Mrs Greenaway's voice, the tear of last resort in her eye, the one that would never quite roll down her cheek. She was upset but she wanted Janet and Holly and the whole story wound up with as little inconvenience to her and her family as possible. She stood, as if about to return to the kitchen, but instead turned to Mr Greenaway, with a look that said: 'you tell him, tell him to tie it up as tight as he likes, tell him to tie it all up and take it away'. And he too was beyond asking, beyond giving. Once he'd had time for Janet, but not now and not again.

— We're too old. It isn't that we don't care, it's just . . . well . . . Holly's such a young child, a baby.

— Yes, they're very demanding.

— You don't need to tell us. No, it's just . . . it's just . . .

As I got them to spell it out I stared at the TV and golden deciduous forests; a glorious sad stream of still frames ebbing into bleak, leafless mid-winter. Obviously alarmed by the boyfriend conversation, Mrs Greenaway wanted to press a point.

— You know about her mother I suppose?

— Of course he knows, woman. He'll have it in his notes won't he!

Yes, I knew about Janet's mother, I didn't need them to excuse themselves.

— Bet he doesn't know it all though, John. I bet he doesn't know her father wasn't her father. That isn't in the notes is it?

Sitting down again Mrs Greenaway's mouth cracked like an old glaze. It was a few seconds before I realised she was smiling, and it was all because she'd caused me to take note.

— So, the man Janet's mother married and divorced wasn't actually Janet's father?

— No. He just married her to make it respectable. Nobody knew who the father was. Like mother like daughter.

This was the burning bit of evidence; giving you all you needed to know about Janet and her mother. This pinned them together forever, according to Mrs Greenaway. But how did she get to know about it?

— I've got a cousin, married someone from the same village. They said Janet's real father was an older man, married they say.

She stared at me as if to say: 'what do you think of that then, eh?'

— My cousin, she says there were a lot of stories but she knows for a fact that the one on the wedding certificate, he wasn't Janet's father. Reading between the lines, I think Janet's mother wasn't one to keep herself to herself.

I cringed as she said it, crossing her legs before pulling down on her skirt and apron. It wasn't my place to play defence advocate but I just couldn't stop myself.

— Were you close to Janet, Mrs Greenaway?

— Yes, they were.

— Maybe it would be best if your wife answered.

— Yes, I suppose, yes, we were close, weren't we?

— Would you say you were closer to Janet than Mr Greenaway.

— Yes.

— And when was the first time she attacked you?

That made Mr Greenaway finally look up from his TV. But

he still managed to strike a match and re-light his pipe before saying anything.

— Janet's never attacked anyone.

— No, she's never attacked me, why would she do that? What does it say there?

She peered over at my folders as I searched through them. I could have sworn there was something somewhere, I'd read it, an account in the case history, an episode. I rifled through the papers but found nothing.

— Whoever told you she attacked me? We had our quarrels, who doesn't? But she never attacked me.

The swell of indignation and outrage rose steadily as I scanned the papers in front of me, finally falling on the word 'attack' – but realising immediately that it wasn't about Mrs Greenaway.

— Forgive me, I've confused the hospital incident with . . .

— What hospital incident?

— It says here she attacked a man, a male visitor on her ward, when she'd been admitted for an operation.

— Her appendix.

Mrs Greenaway said it with an air of admission and fell silent. It was left to Mr Greenaway, now safely back staring at his fuggy screen, to elaborate.

— Hardly an attack. A scratch on his face, a little tear in his jacket. And in any case he brought it on himself.

They recounted what I'd already read: the man visiting his comatose wife everyday. Janet reacting. Mrs Greenaway finally joined in and fell deadly serious in her re-telling, as if this had something directly to do with her.

— He never ever said a word to his wife, just fussed around the bed with the lipstick and the eyeshadow.

Mr Greenaway was less contemplative, he laughed mockingly as he spoke.

— Eyeshadow, ha! What would she want with any of that, she was half dead.

— Rouge as well, and blusher, like she was a doll.

— And Janet attacked him?

— Yes.

There was a pause during which Mr Greenaway tutted and tapped the bowl of his pipe into the ashtray. Like a knock on the door it seemed to wake his wife.

— Yes, she attacked him but he was very good about it.

— Didn't want to take the matter any further, that's what made us think. He must have made a gesture. Provoked her.

But Mrs Greenaway was still shaking her head.

— The nurse said she was pummelling and scratching . . .

— You weren't present then, when it happened?

— No. Looked like she was trying to kill him, that's what the nurse said.

I thought for a moment that Mrs Greenaway was going to cry, as Mr Greenaway packed a new bowl and began to proselytise.

— A man without a wife, you see. A man without a wife, and a young girl. Attractive, you see, Janet's always been attractive.

— How old was she?

— Fifteen. Just fifteen.

— He made a gesture, woman, that's what happened. You can bet on it.

— No, he didn't look the type. He wasn't the sort.

— Difficult to tell nowadays.

— Everyday, rain or shine, he'd always be there, nothing would stop him.

— Now, there's something strange about that if you ask me, putting make-up on a woman who's half dead.

— Would you do it for me?

I groped around for the necessary paperwork. Best get out of here as soon as I could, get them to sign what they had to sign, get out and let them argue in peace. But just then Elgar started up and a memory came to me. I felt suddenly as if I was in a dream, flying up with the rooks and crows in a clear blue sky, up high over the top of a pine-coppiced hill. For once I could see clearly. The Cello Concerto. Amid the blue-brown fog of Mr Greenaway's exhalations there was a new, acrid stench coming from the kitchen. Mrs Greenaway shot up to try and save whatever it was. Mr Greenaway grumbled.

— What are you doing, woman? Open the window, what on earth have you done?

But I was busy remembering another man's voice, equally gruff, and growling too. *Whenever you can, count.* From long, long ago, snapping and admonishing: *Whenever you can, count. Whenever you can, count.* That's what it said. So utterly familiar it was like having him there in front of me. My father – not a poem this time, just a mantra – something he always said when I was practising the cello. *Whenever you can, count.* It was a rare time when he'd put things aside to help. *Whenever you can, count.* More times than not he lost his temper and ended up shouting at me, and for good reason. The screeching. I only played for a couple of years before giving in to a dearth of talent. But he must have been around more then. I couldn't recall.

Mrs Greenaway escorted me to the door, her husband still stuck in his chair, contemplating Norwegian Fjords judging by the twittering flute. She shook my hand limply, an icy trickle in her touch. Nothing had warmed her, neither the resolution of Holly's fate nor her travails in the kitchen. Sad, bitter or just impervious, nothing could touch her any more. I looked at her briefly but couldn't catch her eye.

— Sorry about the smell, it was the broad beans, they'd boiled dry.

CHAPTER 7

27) Interviews with Birth Mother

27a) All of the interviews with Janet Burns (the birth mother) were conducted at the C. Clinic.

27b) In some parts of the meetings Janet Burns appeared lucid and fully cognisant of her situation. She talked affectionately about Holly. On other occasions she appeared not to know who Holly was. How much of this was due to the medication she was taking at the time remains unclear, but in my considered opinion such episodes should be taken very seriously.

27c) As I will proceed to adumbrate (and the psychiatric reports fully document), Janet Burns appears to be fixated by Holly's putative father and, indeed, by the nature of their meeting.

27d) Concerns about Janet Burns' mental health continued to prevent any concerted reconciliation with Holly during the course of my enquiries.

27e) As the Psychiatric Reports show, the diagnosis and treatment of Ms Burns' condition have not yet stabilised, so a prognosis is proving difficult. Given the nature of Ms Burns' hallucinations and her tendency to 'forget' Holly's needs as a child, I am of the opinion that she has made a wise decision in apparently forsaking the hope of future

reconciliation. She would appear, somewhat paradoxi-
cally, to be putting Holly's welfare first.

27f) As well as the aforementioned problems with regard
to her health, Janet Burns also went missing for periods
during the course of my enquiries and was consequently
unable for some time to sign the adoption forms in the
appropriate fashion. This is by way of explanation of this
report's late presentation.

My father was a doctor. He died the year after I got married. Coronary thrombosis – nothing unusual there, or in the fact that we never got on, though we didn't spend a great deal of time in each other's company. He held research posts in a couple of the medical universities when I was small. Then he turned to GP-ing: ten years of locum jobs until he finally got into a practice. I'd left home by then.

Sometimes the locum work was nearby but often it was out in the sticks. My mother used to stay with me, he used to go off on his own, sometimes for months on end. He had digs. Sometimes, when I was older, I stayed with him for a week or two at a time, while my mother had what she used to call 'a little holiday', all on her own at home. I came to think that when he got into a practice it was a shift that upset *her* plans; she preferred him as a locum. He was a few years older and was, I always thought, eminent and well regarded in his field – though I never quite worked out for sure what that field was. His university work was so many years before I became conscious of such things, and it seemed to count against him when he tried to get a foothold in the local practices. I remembered the arguments, the rumble from the back room – what he lightly called 'setbacks', and my mother trying to explain: 'they're all against him, dear'. When I got to the age when I could consider such things I assumed he was too well qualified. I was vaguely aware of his immodesty, secretly liking if not fully understanding it; whereas my mother ignored it, waiting, typically, until he was dead – the day of his funeral to be precise – before protesting to me about 'that ugly vanity'.

I came away from the Greenaways with *Whenever you can, count* ringing in my ears, and a momentarily revived picture of my father – singed ginger sideburns framing a ruddy face, with thick Dickensian waves in his hair. Call it vain if you like, but that certainty had its attraction. I wondered when he had changed, what had caused the decline. It comes to us all – but as I thought of him it felt as if that was the thing that was making me stumble – growing old was the difficulty – and I didn't deserve it, not yet. I hadn't even had chance to be vain or immodest, I wasn't old enough; I hadn't picked up the knack.

Was that the problem? Was it really all there was to it? No more than a man approaching middle age and hitting the panic button: stop the world I want to get off – this one's immortal, beyond the processes of time. Can't you see? I haven't been given my due, not yet. And was that the meaning of Janet Burns too: a greying man's pitiful, wanton, wished-for fling? I hadn't thought of her for at least – well, what was the point in lying – but after the call from the police and seeing the Greenaways, I had some questions to ask of her. The proper little investigator: if she couldn't even tell her own family about the shed and the miraculous conception, who was this deity she believed in? How strong was her faith? What sort of god was he and what was he worth? Two strangled bodies, a mother and child. The perpetrator: Holly's putative father, Janet's supposed Saviour. So where did she get the conviction from, now or ever? That's what I wanted to ask her. K called it the 'melodrama of faith' – but I wanted to know the mechanics of it, how she could be so certain and come to believe in someone who could do a thing like that. How could she know? Because Janet, despite whatever other illusions she might have cast, despite the look she gave me and all the doubts she caused, she had, unmistakably, given the appearance of knowing.

My phone message wasn't returned: I eventually discovered that Holly's case worker, a Ms Ann Wide, was on holiday. I used this as an excuse to postpone my last visit to the clinic. Instead I met up with Holly and her foster carers a couple of times.

It's often difficult giving a voice to a child not yet old enough to talk, yet Holly was obviously doing well. She was a pre-talker but one of those who doesn't articulate the usual range of da das and ga gas. She had a voice but it was unconventional – some might say perverse. She liked putting her new upper front teeth on her lower lip and blowing as hard as she could. This produced a challenging range of 'F' sounds of varied pitch. It wasn't difficult to see that the ginger-mopped, freckle-faced monster was and would be a lot happier with her foster parents than she had been with Janet. What was more, they were keen to adopt.

Case solved. Maybe Richard was right, maybe I was procrastinating. But if I had last minute nerves why did I have this idea in my head that sitting on the plane would constitute some sort of miracle, and that actually getting to Canada would be like arriving in the promised land – free of the past, free of all the old possibilities? There wasn't a doubt in my mind.

I was taking the post of researcher for a Canadian mob called The International Child Care Foundation. My brief: to establish the background and history for State intervention in child care provision. Remit: ostensibly international but in reality British and European. They had another person working on the same project in an American university and were due to appoint someone else from the subcontinent. The ICCF wanted at least one of their busy bees to work from HQ. I drew the lucky straw. The prospective outcome: a child charter, a bundle of recommendations that might be implemented universally, irrespective of cultural context and political regime. Some hope! But as Sarah so generously put it – it would get me out of the house. After weeks of scrabbling through the job ads, it had boiled down to this or staying put, and once you start running it's difficult to stop. I'd run home to my mummy, only she didn't want me. My hometown didn't either – or me it. Richard wanted me, but only because I was a reliable stooge. That's what I'd always been to him. I'd done the running back to Sarah. Now there were only recriminations and misgivings. I had enough of them to pass around.

I had ghosts too, people who'd come and gone, a horde of them in the night: old girlfriends, a strange mother and dead father, colleagues, school friends, even teachers. I was missing my whole past and everyone who had ever shrugged a shoulder in my vicinity. I was weepy with it. I missed myself, or at least, I was struck with what I thought to be an insight – it was over, I'd never again see all these people as they once were; I'd lost them, forever. I'd never again sit on my mother's lap, or even talk easily with her – and this despite praying as a child that I'd die first, before her. I'd never again walk up a hill with my father, no matter how small the incline. I'd never kiss Sarah like the first time, or even walk again on Hampstead Heath. It was over – intimacy, fondness, caring, hope – none of it possible.

What was the point? Without these things what did anything mean? What could I do and where could I turn? I could think of my career, think of the things that had kept me going through thick and thin, and try not to think of old dreams; think of being able eventually to get away from this way of thinking. What could I do? I could go to Canada.

I finally met up with Ann Wide two days after she returned from her holiday. It looked as if she'd suffered a reaction to her family name. Tanned but painfully slim, she was one of the few local case workers I hadn't previously had dealings with: she was newly qualified and persisted in calling me 'Mr Eyre' and 'Sir'. Who was I to stop her? But I didn't learn much that I didn't already know. Everything was in black and white in the notes. And I'd waited and waited for this confirmation, while

Ann Wide had cycled round a Greek island in search of rare flowers. Didn't that tell me something? It might have done, except our conversation did reveal something that didn't feature in the reports.

In the case notes Janet's psychiatric social worker had given a typically vague definition of her problems – no detailed symptoms or prognosis. But the thin Ms Wide had met with this social worker and discovered that Janet suffered from regular hallucinations, specifically since giving birth to Holly.

— She sees hands.

The thought of it amused her.

— They just float around the place, looking after her, apparently. If she has a problem they sort it out. She was in this bed and breakfast place the Department had found for her, a mother and baby suite. They had some Scottish workers staying there as well. Shop fitters, I think she said. Anyway, one of these shop fitters took a shine to her and knocked on her door late at night, after he'd had a few. She said he was trying to break in. But the hands appeared out of the patterns in the wallpaper and shored up the jambs. Saved the day. Like guardian angels.

She laughed at her inadvertent joke – yes, I too was a guardian, ha, ha – then straightened on seeing no smile on my face. I didn't connect this story of the hands with 'love' and hate', or with Janet's fingers grazing my knuckles, not then. But I did recall what I'd seen in room A213; the fingers touching in the saucer. And what I'd seen in the shed, or at least what I thought I'd seen: the bloody hands. I was struck with the realisation that I might be a hallucinator as well. No better, no worse.

Seeing my face and my silence, Ann Wide's expression changed. I shivered and felt something in my eye as she asked.

— Are you all right, sir?

CHAPTER 8

6) Basis of Guardian ad Litem Report

6a) This is a shorter report than normally compiled as, during the course of my enquiries, it became apparent that Janet Burns (the birth mother) may agree to the making of an Adoption Order.

6b) Matters were complicated, however, by Ms Burns' suggestion, and subsequent insistence, that the putative father should adopt Holly.

7) Interview with Putative Father

7a) It was some time before Mr Andrew Berry (the putative father) was located. Due to the circumstance of his situ-ation (i.e. being on remand) and his consequent state of mind, only one interview was sought.

༝

I travelled down south the next day – two birds, one stone. Sarah second, but first: our father.

His case still hadn't come to court. He'd been on remand for a year already. The rasta locks had been refashioned, half shaved, half pony-tailed, but still a central theme of barbed, blond knots. Not red, like Holly's. No holly in the lapel now either, but the hate and love were there on his knuckles; the letters were the only unabashed thing about him. Didn't they do a dance in the Mitchum movie – the story of good and evil; hate, the hand that had murdered Abel; all that biblical nonsense? These particular digits looked feeble, rushing like cornered ants up and down on the prison table. The index and second fingers on the right hand were nicotine-stained from nail to tattoo. The other fingers were delicate, almost articulate, as if they'd like to play an arpeggio if only they had a piano.

We went through the formalities. I explained about Janet. Yes, he remembered her. Yes, they had a relationship. No, he wasn't the father. Pardon? He couldn't be, they didn't . . .

— Excuse me? You just said you had a relationship with her.

— Yes, we did . . . but we didn't . . . we didn't . . .

— I'm sorry?

He was blushing. Most ungodly. Unmurderly. It took him a while to come out with it.

— We kissed and such like, yes, we kissed. But we didn't . . . She wanted to, yes, she wanted me to. She was young, she didn't know. I've been down that road. That road leads to nowhere.

— So, correct me if I'm wrong, you're saying you didn't have intercourse with her.

— No. I did not, thankfully. It must have been . . . I don't know . . . it could have been . . . it must be some other man, I don't know.

I asked him what he meant exactly – 'could have been' – but he refused to say more, blinking down at his hands, tremulous. He peered deep into himself and mumbled something, but by this time I'd given up. Being forced to talk about it evidently made him shake. He wasn't really blushing, it was more agitation: that's what talking about it did to him. It turned out he'd been brought up by his grandfather, a vicar or priest of some sort. All death and damnation. I checked with him that should Holly turn out to be, by any random quirk of nature, his daughter, would he have any objection if she were adopted. He looked at me quizzically and answered in the affirmative, not taking up my suggestion that he could be lying. I was trying to cover all eventualities and avoid having to make a return trip. In the absence of my sadly missed tape machine I got him to sign a statement. That was that. Our father no more – or at least one down, one to go. I was going to call in on Sarah unannounced.

On the way out of the prison I discovered I wasn't the only one to notice the Hollyman's peculiar state of mind. The prison officer who escorted me through the numerous metal doors and clanging gates informed me that our friend was not the sort to last long inside.

— Too intelligent by half.

— You think so?

— Just got to look at him. Some of them get what they deserve, no repentance, a place in the pecking order, that's all they're after. But him . . . he'd been away five years. Doesn't look old enough does he? Seven she was.

— Who?

— His daughter. Did for them both.

— So I'm told.

— Both of them, with his hands.

The officer almost smiled at this, as if it was an achievement to be pondered. I pictured the reddening face, the nervous knuckles dancing on the table top, the nicotine rust, the red and blue tattoos. The officer had obviously thought it through.

— But what I want to know is why did he go back? He's bright, you can see it. Nothing lacking in that department; he must have known it would happen, and yet he still goes back. Now why is that?

At this point I had to disabuse the prison officer. I wasn't the psychiatrist he thought I was. His insights had been wasted on a mere lay person.

✢

Rachel answered the door.

— It's Dad. Mum, it's Dad.

But there was no surprise in her voice, only a strange kiss, full on the lips. I tried to ignore it, dipping straight into my pocket for the bribe. Sarah too seemed unsurprised, barely greeting me. She cringed at the slam of the door as they ran out.

— You really shouldn't, they eat too many sweets.

— I wanted to talk . . . alone.

— Thought you might.

— They told you they told me then?

She giggled.

— Is it that funny?

— It has its funny side.

— Really? Why didn't you phone?

— Why didn't you?

— Who is he?

— Who's who?

— The father. Who's the father?

— Philip, you sound like my dad, God rest his soul.

— Well, who is he then?

— I don't know.

She giggled again. Nerves, she declared – nothing to do with me, in the sense that she wasn't laughing at me. She said she felt like one of my cases, the subject of a Care Order, a fallen woman. It was all so inappropriate, the way I made her feel. So it *was* to do with me. I was appalled.

— You don't know? You're thirty-seven years old and you don't know!

— Well, I know who *they* are. I know the possibilities.

She put her legs up on the chaise longue. Now, of all times!

— What the hell do you mean – *possibilities*?

— I mean there are two possibilities, two possible fathers, both have been informed, both are, though surprised, happy at the turn of events. They're both very supportive.

— What?

How was it possible at a time like that, faced with such

news, confronted with such grotesque realities, how was it at all possible to say anything other than 'what'? Yet the strangest thing worried me most – the fact that some day soon, somehow, I'd have to relay these revelations to my mother. Along with everything else. Gradually clearing the backlog, she was due to be my next port of call. I'd told myself I had to tell her about Canada before the week was out. But now this. I'd have to be selective with the details.

Sarah's child, it transpired, had been conceived at The Ranch, the hippy commune – organic farm and conference centre. No surprises there, except the way in which my dear ex-wife had adhered so unquestioningly to the house rules. No couples allowed: inhabitants, whether they be permanent or just passing through, are not permitted to sleep with the same partner for more than two consecutive nights. Of course this only went part way to explaining Sarah's predicament. She had a will of her own didn't she? She was a grown woman; she knew what she was doing. I couldn't help but wonder how they policed these rules – video cameras; a rota by the kitchen sink?

— That's never a problem. It was a unanimous decision, been in force for more than ten years now. Everyone's agreed.

— Men more than women, I'll bet.

— No, not at all.

— Well, why make the rule then?

Sarah said something about legislating for the future, just like marriage had done for lifelong mating. But she was growing indignant, said I had no right to be asking some of the things I was asking.

— I thought you'd be pleased for me. Aren't congratulations traditional on these occasions?

Tradition was the last word that came to mind, and as for a pat on the back for old time's sake . . .

๑๛

Some people put their mothers in a home. Mine was uncontainable. She resented it when I visited, she hated me for returning to the fold, or two streets away – the nearest I'd dared. Independent. That's what she was and that's what she intended staying, son or no son. K would say she was finally asserting her own wishes after a lifetime in service to men. K never met her. She'd always been the same. Husband or no husband. Even so, I didn't expect what was coming.

— So, sailing the Atlantic, eh? Get you out and about.

Yes, she used the very same phrase. When we were married Sarah and she always were in cahoots, and there was more to come: sitting there on the sofa with her cigarettes, acting as though there was nothing wrong. But I could smell it again, even above the Peter Stuyvesants. Never drunk, only port or sherry, but it was worrying, not least because she invariably gave the impression of waiting for me to leave so she could resume: sitting there on the edge of the sofa, her piled grey hair feathering down over the Yin Yang earrings. Never a welcome mat.

— I'm not exactly a recluse, mother.

— No, dear – but you know what I mean.

— But what about you? Who will ...

— Don't worry about me, I'm happy as I am, it's you we worry about.

— We?

And sure enough there was no coincidence in this urge to get me out of the house.

— Sarah was just saying the other day ...

— Sarah? When did you see Sarah?

— She calls in every now and then, and occasionally I have a chat when I ring Rachel and Simon. I told you.

— You didn't.

— What does it matter?

— Then you ...

— Yes, I know her good news.

— She told you?

— I think it's wonderful.

— But what ... think of Rachel and Simon.

— Absolutely wonderful news.

65

No, my mother never read from the right and proper script. And today she was intent on resetting the scene entirely. She told me, without pause.

— Your father had one you know.

— Had one what?

— A daughter. I'm pretty sure it was a daughter.

She went on to explain why she'd never told me before. Because she hadn't wanted to hurt me, she didn't see the point; then she'd just plain forgot, if that was possible. And now?

— Now, I don't see the point in not telling you. You're a grown man. It was a girl. I'm certain. It was a long time ago. I'm sure it was a girl. You're father had a bastard.

She hiccoughed, then explained how my father was the real bastard. She had two hairs coming from a mole on her cheek, a beauty spot grown old. But she was still beautiful, even I, her son, could see it. Her eyelashes still long and dark, her cheeks finely sculpted. But more than anything the eyes still shone, the spirit was still bright and firing. She looked dismissive rather than angry.

— He paid the mother off. An abortion, but she couldn't go through with it. Kept the money and the child.

— When? When was this?

— When he was away, working.

She hiccoughed again, but this time her lips curled. A nasty taste. I knew that look well enough.

— Slip of a girl. Old enough, but only just. We went to see him just before it all blew up, do you remember? Lovely spot, romantic, up in the hills. You stayed with him for part of the summer.

— Did I?

— You were sixteen, no seventeen. Don't you remember? What was it called?

— What?

— The village, the name of the village. One of those long Welsh names. Back of beyond, cut off. Country girl, the way he liked them.

There was more – but I didn't want to know. It was bad enough having the problems I had: longing for something in my past that I couldn't quite put my finger on; yearning for some part of my life as if I was already dead or dying. And now this. My mother rambled on about divorce, how it wasn't so easy then; it just wasn't done. I protested that it was, indeed, done. We weren't talking about the thirties, or fifties even. This was the nineteen sixties, first half admittedly but things were starting to pick up. She screwed her cigarette out in the ash tray and lit another. I coughed. The horrid intimacy, the commingled gloom: I pictured Janet Burns; the shed and those bloody hands in the half-light; the hands that made me feel deep down as if I shouldn't have allowed myself to see them. And I thought of the Hollyman – our father – pitiful, there in prison, having killed his own wife and child; barbed hair, barbed hands.

A cloud of smoke rose between us. I saw the garden through the window. The laburnum was in flower, poisonous yellow pods dangling seductively. And it struck me: could laburnum cause a coronary thrombosis – easier than divorce, easier than forgiveness, at least for her generation? A little holiday, at home, all on her own: that's what she had liked most of all. A keen gardener, she knew all about laburnum, she was capable. The smoke began to clear as I opened the window. No, I knew she didn't do it, could never have, but she was culpable nonetheless. She was to blame.

— You never told me. Why didn't you tell me? Why?

— Because ...

— Don't you care?

— Of course I care. Say what you like about me, Philip, but don't you ever think that. You want to look to a different quarter with that question, dear. Of course I care.

I remember the smoke curling out through the window into the garden, and I remember sitting on the sofa unable to say anything more. The past is like that. It happens over an eon, it happens down in the unfathomable depths. If too much rises to the surface too quickly it gets twisted, becomes melodramatic and improbable. It takes time to digest. While I remained incredulous and gawping, she started talking about something else. Mrs Lovett, my neighbour, was having a hip replacement – tittle tattle, under the circumstances quite inappropriate, but it was just like my mother and her reactions to life.

— Ah, the Lovetts. She always looked the type. Plastic parts. Lives forever but doesn't live at all.

There I was, going to her with what I thought to be fearful news – emigration, impending births – but I came away with the surprise of my life. There was no beating her. Never. I saw it in a photo of my father on the mantelshelf on my way out: the wave in his hair, the singed sideburns. But now there was more, thanks to her. Now there was something I'd never ever bargained for: a lascivious glint in his eye.

This is where the possibilities started to pile up. I was too overwhelmed to comprehend any of it. My world was being turned on its head. Where do you start when your beloved, or even not-so-beloved, ex-wife, the mother of your two only children, falls pregnant, identity of prospective father uncertain if not unknown? At about the same time you discover your own long-dead and sort-of-loved papa was a cad, fathering at least one illegitimate offspring. You have a half-sister somewhere. Your own mother appears oblivious. Your ex-wife is positively amused. Your children are at best indifferent to everything, at worst a threat.

At times like this the past becomes a free-for-all where anything might have happened. Everything comes and goes in a flash: ten year's history, a lifetime, yesterday and the day before. And I was longing for some unidentifiable element of that past, some ineffable stillness in the chaos and rush of love and procreation. A moment, that's all I wanted, all I ever wanted. Where could I go for salvation, eh? Where could I get my fix from now?

She was in room A213. All alone, or so I hoped.

CHAPTER 9

39 The Birth Mother's Health (continued):

39a) One of the symptoms of Ms Burns' mental health problems consists of visual hallucinations. She sees images of two hands and has repeatedly stated that these hands are those of Andrew Berry, the putative father. When asked how she knows they are his hands she invariably testifies that her hallucinatory hands have the same tattoos – love and hate – inscribed on the knuckles.

39a) Janet Burns' health deteriorated considerably on the discovery of the whereabouts of the putative father. Janet was shocked by the revelation of the circumstance in which Mr Berry now finds himself, though those treating her believe disclosure of Mr Berry's supposed crimes not to be the only factor causing the worsening of her condition.

39b) As the Psychiatric Report terms it:
". . .[Janet Burns'] reaction to the discovery of the existence of [the putative father] highlights the likelihood of previous delusions. In part she reacted appropriately, and as anyone might given the extreme circumstances – a person with whom she was once intimate had been accused of homicide and infanticide. Yet accompanying this appropriate response she reacted as if prior to the indisputable discovery of [the putative father's] existence she had been convinced of his non-existence – i.e. his non-material existence. Janet Burns had hitherto believed him to be God."

First I had to negotiate the nurse with the strawberry blonde hair. She was in a chatty mood and it took me longer than I expected; desperation made me brave but acquiescent. She looked up from her desk, the blinds casting the soft and misleading lines of a smile across her features as she told me some local gossip, how Janet was doing, yes, but all about the others too. No clinical details – she was too cute for that – just snapshots; telling me about Alan's phantom limb pain and about another woman who couldn't control her arms, how she'd just been transferred up to the 'loony-bin proper'. There was Marius Pritty, of course, as if I needed telling: his penchant for administering his own therapy and how you had to keep an eye on him no matter how aesthetically unpleasant that might be.

Mostly she wanted to talk about Guillermo, as if she had a mother-crush on him. This was more life history than snapshot: how his mother had gone home to Belize to bury her own mother and never returned. Worst crime in the world according to some: a mother deserting her child. Guillermo's father was Spanish, but with some Portuguese in him. He had worked as a cook on the tankers in the Gulf of Mexico and the banana boats out of Belize. That's where he'd met his wife. They moved to England a year before their only son was born, changed the family name to Brown, according to the nurse, and bought the lease on a railway cafe in the Black Country.

— Close to the canals and one or two derelict factories, but nothing much else.

— You've visited his home then?

She didn't bother answering, I never discovered how she knew so much about Guillermo. Later I guessed it was just that she wanted to know, that was enough in itself. Desire could provide no end of facts. At that moment I was hopping on the spot, desperate to get on down to A213. But all the suddenly-friendly nurse wanted to do was talk about Guillermo's mother.

— When he was ten she started writing to him, told him

how she couldn't leave her own mother's grave untended. She asked Guillermo to follow her back to Belize.

— Evidently he didn't go.

— He showed me a letter. No wonder he's screwed up.

The nurse explained how Guillermo took pleasure in showing everyone the letters and photographs his mother sent, trying to tempt him.

— She sends him herbs as well . . . no, not those sort. Proper leaves, stuff to make him well. He carries a nugget of rauwolfia root around in his pocket. Keeps his spirits up, that's what he says. Hasn't done him much good though, has it?

— I wouldn't know.

She didn't take the hint. She told me how Guillermo hated his father, but couldn't leave him, no matter how tempted he was by the photos and his mother's enticements. The nurse was proud to have spotted the inversion.

— It's like he can't leave his father untended.

— Really?

— He's always running away, and then he always runs back. His father hasn't ever remarried you see. Not even divorced. And there were no beatings. It's something else, and something more than just adolescent rebellion. Guillermo told me, he hates his father's shape.

And the nurse related what Guillermo had told her, about his father's tight collars and bow ties, the fleshy layers of his stout, sea-cook's neck. His dimpled knees and callused elbows and the voice that cooed its pigeon English like a 'hissing idiot'. Guillermo called him that when he was really angry, the nurse had heard him, and she could see that's what really made him mad: the way he stood so humble in the world, so humble and so proud of it. That's what Guillermo had told her, that's when he hated his father most: when he was serving his high and mighty customers, his commuters, his businessmen and grammar school boys.

The nurse had barely a word to say about Janet. I suspected she'd tagged her, subconsciously at least, as one of those women, just like Guillermo's mum: the ones who leave their children. Finally she appeared to realise that I was waiting and pointed off in the direction of A213, her look vaguely sarcastic: you already know where it is, don't you? But she was helpful too; if we needed privacy she said to go out in the grounds or take a room further up the corridor.

Janet was alone apart from Marius, who was on the far side of the room by the TV. The first time I'd noticed just how handsome he really was. What had the nurse said? 'Ugly as sin, a phrase tailor made for his like'. The sheet-white skin and the kink in his nose were more unattractive than ugly, I thought. His eyes were crowded, his mouth tight and pinched. It was hard to imagine a big smile. I felt almost sorry for him – that uneasy sort of pity it's impossible to dwell on.

He was watching TV but looked disappointed we weren't staying. Janet brought a rolled up painting along, together with her tobacco tin. We walked out into the grounds and I told her the state of the case. I was about to submit my report, recommending adoption. I asked if she still felt this was what she wanted. She looked at me, suddenly lost as if we had a previous agreement: childcare wasn't on the agenda; there was something more important we should be talking about. Had I forgotten? It could have been my imagination, but I'm sure she smiled. Not like I'd seen her smile before; she looked at me as if she was looking on an old friend, someone she could confide in, someone she trusted and knew intimately.

All the questions I'd wanted to ask her flooded in: about God and conviction, about faith and betrayal. How did she believe? How did she manage it? But I couldn't, not then: I was here to do my job; I was here to go through the motions. Though eventually I did ask one thing that wasn't entirely in the rule book.

— Where did the name Burns come from?

She told me about a memory of her mother reading to her as a little girl – her birth mother, not Mrs Greenaway. The only detail she recalled was that there was a girl in one of the stories whose surname was Burns. She couldn't remember her first name or anything else about the story.

We paused to rest, sitting on a bench overlooking the now withering forsythia blossom, the fresh leaves burgeoning. Beyond the fence the sloe bushes were just yellowing, the hawthorn coming into leaf. She rolled and lit a cigarette. The swell of the river had caused the current to be perplexed, flowing concertedly in one midstream direction but torn between at least two, whirling between calm and rush, in the shallows and elbows. The rowing boat bobbed and turned uneasily like a gelding on its rope. The cigarette smoke smelt different, and I wondered whether it was because we were outdoors. Now it was fragrant, balmy even, like wood smoke in the night.

It was one of those days: the earth rising to the surface, muddying the water, overflowing into the sky and air. The world was in spate. The earth appeared to be glimmering with the density of its own substrata. She wanted to talk more about her mother.

— I've always had two memories, sometimes they get mixed up. I don't know whether they're real anymore, I've played them back so many times. They're pictures . . . in the first she's just standing by a wall of white and blue tiles, like the swimming baths, only there's no towels, costumes or water. I'm eight, maybe nine. She looks lost, she can't see me; it's like she's searching, looking for me. I want to shout out – it's all right, Mum, I'll get the costumes, I'll get the towels – but the man pushes me out to the door and somebody grabs my hand. I can't stop turning back. I'm eight, maybe nine . . . You know what happened to her don't you?

I nodded: yes, I knew. But I couldn't comprehend the ease with which she was talking about it. And to me of all people: the one who had laughed like a crow. I was consumed by more questions, ones I'd never considered before. When did she realise her mother had killed herself? Did she always know because of these early memories or did she forget? Later, I realised these were the questions I should have asked, had I been civilised.

— The second memory, she's ironing. I've seen this one a thousand times, she's standing there, pressing backwards and forwards. And she's reading to me. On the ironing board there's a book, while she presses the shirts and blouses. All I know is there was a girl called Burns.

And she explained how she wanted to take that name, to remember it always, because it was one of the only things she had left. The only thing her mother had given her that she could keep. But as she spoke I felt something twist inside of me, a barbed knot; I was being duped, at every turn. A siren sounded, I didn't believe her. She was lying, I was sure. How could anyone iron clothes and read at the same time? It was a joke. She was some Circe playing her tricks, turning my life into a dark magic den, and all who knew me into swine: my mother and father, Sarah, my own children. It was coming clear – Janet Burns was the cause of it all. I was certain. I knew. She was the problem. And I knew I had to be careful, otherwise I'd succumb as well.

Janet's mother had read to her. So what? Maybe she was telling the truth, and maybe it was the same with our father. Our man with the holly had said something, probably about sinning and sex, something he'd got from his lay preaching grandfather and, hallelujah, she sees him as some sort of divinity: a man refusing sex, a saint. This was possible.

The other possibility was that she didn't believe at all. There was no conviction. I'd been deceived and it was all one big joke – our father, the surname, everything. Janet Burns was just like the rest of them: a cynic and fraud. She was playing a little joke on me, just for the sake of it. I tried to remember Richard's dictum about probable and possible – and though I couldn't get it literally, I knew, yes, anything was possible. In this day and age, in this climate, in this country, I knew what was most probable. I looked at her squinting as she re-lit her nub end. I looked at her and knew. She was a trickster. I told her.

— What I don't get, what I can't understand ... what sort of god is it that kills their wife and child?

— What?

— Their own flesh and blood.

— What do you mean?

— You don't know?

She didn't, nobody had told her, and as I explained it all – him going back there, with the love and the hate in his eyes, returning after five years, slaying the innocent, his own blood, his own love – I saw her crumble. The smile slipped first, then the rest of her. Down, down, into an unimaginable, unending pit. And I smiled, because I thought I'd shown her. So much for Circe; this is where hateful jokes lead; this is where wilful evasion gets you. That's all evil and hate really are – a refusal to play the game, a cynical disbelief in the institutions of life. Now, if she'd just co-operated from the start . . .

Suddenly she was crying and my arm was round her shoulder. I saw a hand on her head, the pink knuckles wrapped in black strands. Entwined, like shining, fragile eggs in a nest. She was sobbing into my chest. Was that my hand? Was that her hair?

— I'm sorry, I thought you knew.

But this was all subterfuge. I felt her warmth, the conviction of her body heat. As much faith as I or anyone might need. If it wasn't for Marius poking his ghastly, ghostly head around the tree behind us, who knows what might have happened.

As it was, with the red corkscrews bobbing over our shoulder, she made her excuses and left without blaming me, without seeing my madness, my faithlessness – even quietly insisting on handing me the present she said she was going to give me anyway: the rolled up picture she'd brought with her from A213. Why did she start giving me paintings? I didn't unfurl it until I was in the car. Her signature scrawled at the bottom in deep red slashes, next to – *for Mr Eyre* – in black.

CHAPTER 10

45) Conclusions

45a) The birth mother – Janet Burns – and the putative father – Andrew Berry – have both now given formal agreement to adoption. Blood tests to verify parentage did not prove necessary.

45b) The adoption applicants, Mr and Mrs Bowlby, have been through the rigorous accreditation procedures of the Family Finding Unit and have been approved as adopters by the County Council.

45c) As the appointed Guardian ad Litem, I, Philip Eyre, do offer my considered opinion therefore that an Adoption Order should be made on Holly Burns forthwith.

I told no one of the arm around the shoulder, the pink knuckles wrapped in her hair. The eggs. The nest. Who could I tell? Richard – to be faced with 'I-told-you-so'? My mother, Sarah? No. More than a month later, the day before my flight, the mayflower past its peak and the meadowsweet beginning to swaddle the riverbanks, the duty nurse phoned to tell me the story as it had unfolded. She thought I might need to see Janet again, or so she said. My guess was she just wanted to gossip.

My work had long since been done. The report written, Holly was all but adopted, the court hearing had come and gone without a hitch.

The nurse said that Janet had run away with Guillermo, up the river in a stolen rowing boat. She began chuckling as she told me, building up a crackle on the line:

— But they were both voluntary patients and didn't need to escape. They could have just walked out of the door. Can you believe . . . running away . . . uh . . . uh.

It sounded like she was choking. Yet when she had calmed herself there was more than a hint of bitterness, as if she blamed Janet for leading her beloved Guillermo astray.

— As for the boat, no-one seemed to know who it belonged to, so there was no big stir. The blankets they stole were written off. In any case Guillermo was back within a week – no blankets or boat. But he'd saved her life.

— Whose? Janet's?

— Yes. On their way up river he'd left her in the boat, moored it up while he climbed the embankment to the road to see where they were. She jumped in the water apparently. He just got back in time. Pulled her out.

— Is she alright?

— Sectioned, for her own safety.

In 'the loony bin proper' according to the nurse: the old psychiatric hospital, on the far side of town. Apparently she'd left something in her locker addressed to me. The nurse said she would send it on. Another painting: no names or signatures this time just a crimson river, bloody and red. In fact it was Guillermo who took it upon himself to send it to me. I don't know how he got the address, but by then I was long gone. The agents, on my behalf, had installed tenants in my old house and it was they who forwarded it to me in Canada. Guillermo enclosed a letter, the first of his epistles, telling a little of the fateful trip up the river and how the hands had turned on Janet, how love and hate now stalked the one they'd once protected. The hate had taken over, just like in the Mitchum movie. What had I done in telling the truth about her Hollyman? If I hadn't, somebody else would have. She would have found out eventually. From a distance it was safe to reason.

PART TWO

CHAPTER 1

And then there was Kismet.

She told me the name came from the East, from Turkey along with her father, and before that from Persia, old as the hills. From two words: qisma(t) – meaning portion, lot, fate; and qasama meaning to divide. It was pronounced Kismat or Kismut, even 'Kiss Mine' back when she was at high school. Destiny, she told me, was the usual definition. Some people give this name to their home or holiday bungalow, but who would confer it on their daughter? Too loud, too garish, it was over the top and in that way it suited her. By default or design, I never could tell, it had fractured – occasionally Kim or Kimmy but usually just K, all on its own, no 'ay'. That's how she signed her letters and notes, formal or otherwise, as if she'd tried to change her name but hadn't ever fully escaped her parents' will.

Some generations go for fate, some don't. I couldn't match such big words to the thing I was missing: the gap, the erosion. That seemed mine and mine alone – produced by me, solvable by me – if it could ever be solved. No-one knew what it was like, that was its essence. Untellable. Ineffable. All those universal truths – souls, spirits, destinies – seemed like they always had: hogwash, imbibed only by the desperate and gullible. K was neither of these things. At the start, if not entirely taking my mind off matters, she certainly transported my body to a place it hadn't been in a while. All that nonsense about never having sex again, well . . . I was wrong. K, Kim, Kimmy, Kismet – my future, my path, my portion, my fate. As Richard was apt to say – I was due an adventure.

We met at the end of my first month at ICCF HQ – a labyrinthine building known locally as 'The Institute'. I thought of it as more of a badger set, with long saturnine passageways converging on a constellation of offices and labs. K's lab (yes, she was that side of the divide) was just along one of the Stygian corridors from my office, her field – Deprivation Dwarfism, the study of emotional neglect on physical development. Unsurprisingly she wanted to move on. The scope was narrow, her boss, a Professor Slater, was vertically challenged himself – she called him the 'duckbutt jerk' and joked about his private experiments. Insulin and growth hormones had a limited attraction, they were getting outdated. So, what did she want with me?

It was a Friday. It was lunchtime, in The Institute's cafeteria. I was pawing over a sad, best-forgotten bagel and some thick, molasses-black coffee. She caught me gazing out of the windows, casting an eye on the slate roofs of some nearby houses: huge three storey affairs, brickwork with painted red timber cladding, balconies off the upper windows and around the porch. Yet they seemed strangely familiar, out of place even. The white balustrades were everywhere. I'd got used to those, and the glass towers and high-rises, I'd expected all that. Not slate roofs. K soon put me straight.

— 1842, just after the great fire in Hamburg, Nathaniel Matthews, some English big shot entrepreneur, went on a tour to North Wales. That was the fashion, don't you know. Stopped off at a place called Blaenau Ffestiniog. Guess you know it?

— No.

But I was impressed with her pronunciation.

— The greyest place. The wettest, meanest place, but to Nathaniel Matthews that drizzly old grey, it glittered. It shone like diamonds. He looked at those rocks pointing up to those doom-laden clouds and boy, he let out a scream. He ran down the valley screaming, he ran all the way down to London, still screaming. He saw how he was gonna change the world. He'd struck gold all right. He saw how he was gonna *roof* the world. Hamburg first, New York by the turn of the century, not to mention the little old backwoods places like here.

She laughed, but I was taken aback by what I later came to see as her didactic mode – and by the suspicion that I, being of the old world, should already know what she was telling me. History – wasn't that all we were good for? I played coy:

— You seem to know a lot about it?

— It's the transformation of hostility, don't you know – the barbaric enmity of the land. Sheer drops, bone-aching cold . . .

— Here in Canada, it surely gets colder than . . .

But there was no stopping her.

— . . . and that damp. Guess you know all about that? Ancient tradition, in France and Spain they found Neolithic axe heads coming from that same part of Wales. Exporting hostility, the name of the game, the only thing Natt did different was to turn it into shelter. Quite an innovation, eh? And wouldn't you know it, while Nathaniel Matthews Esquire became a very rich man indeedy, those slate quarriers still felt that old wind chill factor, struggling away to keep a roof over their heads. Now there's irony for you.

— You've been there then?

— Backpacking, bearer of the old maple leaf, that was the fashion, don't you know. Stopped off at a youth hostel, fell in love with the guy who ran the joint. Up in the hills, buzzards and ravens. When I was young.

— How old are you now?

I didn't want an answer. It was intended as a compliment. All I knew was that she was younger than me, not a great distance but enough to let me know it in a race. I was impressed by her stamina, her loquacity. Especially when she started talking about her work – no more than a week and a dinner date later.

— All blood reaching the pituitary gland first stops off and has a bathe at the old hypothalamic media eminence. All cells sojourn for a while at what you might call an emotional resting place. Rejuvenating the spirit. You should know all about that.

— Should I?

She was forever putting me on the spot.

— Spa towns, that's what you're famous for. Bath, Buxton.

I didn't realise until a few weeks later that this wasn't her didactic mode at all but something else altogether: she was parodying a research article. A straight-faced gift she had – irony – an affinity with the old world.

She had family connections too – a (dead) Jewish mother – 'second generation Canadian of East European stock' was all she'd ever say – and that Turkish father (alive). Was Turkey in Europe? It was certainly old. At first she didn't let out much about him either, other than the odd snarl and growl. He ran a business importing tobacco and coffee – not to mention esoteric monikers – from his father's homeland. But I suspected his daughter's name might just as easily have come from the Vincente Minnelli musical. We were, after all, on the baseball side of the park.

If I'd ever asked her she would no doubt have backed me up on that one. According to K, facts, names, they were all inventions, passing testimony to incoherence and never to be relied upon. One day she told me the story of Piaget's nurse, but with such evangelical verve that I soon realised this was the nativity scene at the heart of her faith. Piaget had a vivid memory of his nursery nurse being attacked by an assailant while walking him in the park. He was convinced by the detail of the memory, even though he was still in a pram at the time. The nurse was awarded a gold watch as some sort of compensation for the ordeal. But years later the nurse returned the watch, saying she'd made the whole thing up. Piaget had not only believed the nurse's story but invented images to go with it, even though the incident never took place.

According to K and her disbeliefs, history was fickle and should never be trusted, even though she was prone to come up with the odd date and episode herself. She said I, in my new job, was being paid to invent the history of copulation, 'boring *fucking* facts', as she put it the first time she ventured into my office, peering like a preacher over my shoulder at the date-filled computer screen.

— History's dead, long live history!

I tried to argue, saying that you could pick the facts up and put them in a new place, somewhere they haven't been before. I told her history was never dead. I nudged the keyboard trying to demonstrate but only managed to lose my screen, as K grabbed a pile of BMA reports and threw them up in the air as she went out of the door.

— Look, I've put them in a new place. Look, they've come alive.

K came to have real grievances with my work, but from the very start she had a way with entrances and exits, and a way of making me blush and feel guilty, not to mention angry and small. She made me want to argue and fight, but she dried the words right up, there on my tongue. According to K even our meeting, our being together, was disputable, an accident, a freak of nature. It was a coincidence that was neither bound to happen nor not to happen. I was stuck on a notion. Weren't we destined to meet in that old fashioned, romantic way? At the time I thought that we sort of liked each other. I asked her.

— If sex is an accident, then we don't choose to . . .?

— Oh, we choose, up to a point. That's what choice is. Collisions. Pure accident, thank god.

— Sounds like Chaos Theory?

— Older than that. The Epicureans, the random swerve of atoms, don't you know.

But in my lexicon atoms and swerves didn't trip off the tongue one after the other. She was a crank, and I had other reasons for thinking this. She had a penchant for red and black, in combination. A vermeil dress guaranteed black tights, and vice versa. At first this went unnoticed. I was attracted, and no doubt at least in part by the colour of her clothes, but I didn't perceive a pattern. When I did eventually remark upon it K said I exaggerated, said she liked red and black, yes, but so what? Most of my clothes were brown and grey, 'cord and crap', according to her. She said the difference was that she could see beneath the surface, she could see the 'random swerve' that had brought us together. When she talked like that her eyes glistened like spring dew and I could see she was reaching out, yearning for something from me, something I didn't know about.

I just wasn't used to it. Despite Sarah's more recent waywardness there had always been something reassuring about her cottons and calicos. K's clothes gave me a puritan's guilt. The different feels and weaves – it felt risqué just picking them off the floor. I was a little older (only a year as it turned out) but I was like a little child in front of her, helpless and compelled. I tried to feel older, to rationalise: her mother died when she was ten, her busy father lavished compensations upon her. She was used to getting what she wanted, excessive drives and desires all too freely gratified, a genuine case of parental deprivation. Could this explain her reluctant line of research? But none of it really made sense; none of it quite explained her effect on me.

When we first undressed, the lights of the city dappling the walls of her bedroom, I became transfixed by her moles. The one I'd seen previously in broad daylight, to the left of her nose but not quite middling her cheek, was echoed by a larger and even darker mark, plumb centre beneath her umbilical scar, but above what she insisted on calling her *petit bois*. She told a tale about where the label came from – a French teacher and a camping trip in Quebec – which I didn't quite understand. It looked more like *une grande forêt* to me, deep chestnut and thick – even her forearms were well downed, and two long interlopers sprouting from her left nipple. I imagined it all to be typically Jewish or Turkish or Canadian or . . . That first time, she caught me staring and was excited rather than embarrassed. Typical K. She remarked on how bald and white I was.

— Like a baby, apart from that red hot face, and that singed old thing.

She tugged at my beard, and later on that first night, as we lay peering out at the butterfly shadows from the flickering candle, finally legitimized by the covering duvet, she whispered.

— They say it's like the death of a small civilisation. Was it like that for you?

I thought it was one of her mad jokes and laughed, pondering her diminutive description of the most recent demise. Irony was going to be a problem wherever I lived. She remained straight-faced. She wasn't talking about the sexual act.

— I mean divorce, separation. Was that what it was like for you? Leaving your family? I've got nothing to go on.

I told her yes and no, I told her I didn't really know, that sometimes it felt like that, and that sometimes it felt like a relief, like the civilisation wasn't that civilised anyway, or that it was just too civilised. I didn't admit to feeling as I did in her presence, that at that particular moment when she asked, all I could think of was her lying next to me. That's all I could remember. The miracle of amnesia; was that love? Losing your past. She asked if I'd had a lot of affairs.

— No.

I was indignant in a jokey sort of way. I stroked her thigh. Whatever my doubts and guardedness, I couldn't stop now, even less talk about such things.

— What about when you lived with . . . what was her name . . . Sarah?

— Nobody. I haven't slept with anyone else for . . .

— But you're divorced, right?

— For reasons of incompatibility.

— Nobody?

I shook my head. And she smiled.

— Just like a virgin.

And she was right, that was just how I felt.

She'd had her share of live-in lovers, and live-out ones too by the sound of it. But she'd never had kids, never wanted them, at least that's what she said. And I believed her, I had no reason not to, until one morning, late in the summer, the glow beginning to fade. We lay contorted in the sheets, exhausted and silvered in the early light; I caught a glimpse of some cracked white lines on her creamy, cappuccino skin. Stretch marks. I was shocked. Why hadn't I seen them before? They could have come with age I know, but just at that moment I didn't think so. I asked, but not the right question.

— Why don't you like Slater? Is it just because he's a man?

— Why bring him in here? He's my boss for Christ's sake.

A rat had crept in the bed and was wagging its tail between us. Maybe I was onto something here. What was really wrong with Slater? Was it just the wild-west moustache? In fact from Philadelphia, at first glance harmlessly repugnant, you wouldn't want to *be* him; he was one of those people who appears friendless but who is really very well connected; arrogant isolation was really a front. K knew this well enough, so why did she react like she did?

— He's got that stupid, husky, Nam Vet voice.

— But he's too young to have fought in Vietnam?

— You know what I mean.

— So, what's wrong with straight white males? After all, you seem to quite like them.

By this time we were lying suddenly still, the rat having fled. I forgot about the stretch marks, our ankles crossed on top of the contorted sheet, my hand resting, a ghostly negative, on her dark breast.

— Why did you have to bring him in here?

— But he goes to his men's groups, he's getting hold of his emotions.

— Exactly! Re-segregating. He's only interested in researching women.

— But most children are brought up by women.

— He's obsessed with single-parent mothers.

— Everyone's got to specialise, and it does seem rather topical.

— Stop defending him!

And with that she turned her back on me again and moved away across the bed, my hand flopping down onto the strangled sheet.

— I'm not defending him. It's just you can't criticise a man just because he's specialising in women's issues.

— Why not, I'd criticise a woman if she was dealing in shit and she was getting it wrong. But then I wouldn't get chance to say a damn thing, there'd be a whole bunch of y'all taking turns.

She often fell into southern belle mode when angry: a seamless ironic slippage that came naturally to her, especially when engaged in man-woman talk. Sometimes it irked me. On this particular morning it made me laugh. My hand reached out and traced her vertebrae past the white-line scars from old summers, past the thick down at the base of her spine.

— What have you really got against poor old duckbutt Slater? I'm sure he doesn't deserve . . .

And as I touched the broken white lines, like tracer flak, following them one by one, she turned, smiling, and kissed my shoulder.

— Guess I just don't get on . . . mm . . . with his gnomish ways.

I traced a figure of eight on her stomach and laughed.

— He's not tuned in to the random swerve of things then? Not one for bathing at the hotel hippopotamus?

Laughing too, she pushed me off the bed.

— Go for a walk!

And she muttered something about never being able to understand anyone who wanted to walk about in parks.

I brought her coffee before leaving like an obedient dog, but didn't ask about the stretch marks, not then. I forgot.

CHAPTER 2

I walked every day, as I'd done in England, only with more
trepidation. The parks were further away, the street bums
more numerous and importunate; the opalescent office towers
were bigger, intimidating, ganging up over the sidewalks
like sun-glassed bullies. I seemed that much smaller in the
world. Sometimes I took the sub-way; sometimes I walked all
the way to wherever I was going. Sometimes I went down to
the beaches on the lake, or took a tour of the harbours. That
tended to depress me – the jagged glare on the water, like
so many shattered mirrors, the stench of sulphur, saltpetre
and the unending lapping, like disdainful applause, up off
the sour-faced, tide-stained quays. Before I met K I'd taken a
long week-end up north and got the same feel and smell then:
hiring a car I'd headed up towards a place I'd spotted on the
map, Vermilion Bay. I was taken by the name but it was way
over on the Trans-Canada, almost in Manitoba. Distance was
just a different entity here; I only made it as far as Sault Ste
Marie. No buffalo roaming up there, just potash and chemical
works; the stink of stale eggs heavy on the breeze.

The park I liked best was on the northside and was remark-
ably English: oaks and birches scattered in among the maples;
begonias as big as bugles; neat little flower beds; even some
pansies and violets arranged in reds, whites and blues. But
it had buffalo as well. And that's what I wanted, and needed
even. Just like I needed the snow shoe-ers and street skiers
when they came in the winter; it fulfilled my puerile expectations, it made me feel at home.

In the park I always stuck to the path, avoiding the characters lying on the grass, dossing on the benches. Every town, every country has them; here there were just more of them than I was used to. One always sat on a bench by the park gate, his laces snaking over the tarmac like some extravagant piece of street art, his boots looking like they'd stay right where they were if he ever got up. I called him Grey Owl, after K told me one of her stories about a renegade trapper who had joined an Ojibway tribe and turned his hand to saving the beaver from extinction. My bench bum had the right sort of lank, jet hair, even if he looked like he was having problems saving himself. His eyes were a dead grey like frosted glass, and he had a creased adolescent face, like a paper bag that had carried too many cans back from the drugstore. Sometimes he sat with a blond boy who looked like he wanted to grow a beard. I thought he must be Swedish, just by the Bjorn Borg looks, then one day I saw him on the subway downtown and heard him shouting, trying to sell dope to passers-by. Just goes to show how wrong you can be. He had a big Irish brogue: fecking this, fecking that; no Scandinavian manners at all.

Once I brought K to see the buffalo. She insisted on driving in her vintage VW Beetle. Subways and walking were things you only did downtown, don't you know. She said the bison looked sad and lonely in their pens. I said that at least they had each other. She said it was possible to long for more than just company. It was the fur I liked most, the way it hung loose, falling away from the crusty old torsos and bewildered tails, like relics held together by rust, with the horns poking out of those huge, minotaur heads. Even their smell was big, everything but those tiny, glistening eyes – the smallest imaginable intelligence, like single raindrops in a storm. K said it was barbaric to pen them up. I knew she was right, but still it got me mad; she didn't see the significance. You might not be able to see them running free – those times were gone – but you could at least imagine, you could remember. That's all these two old beasts were – sacrifices to our memory.

The buffalo riled K; she couldn't understand why I was

interested in them and not in 'more important matters'. Like my supposed sister. There I was walking around in parks while out in the world somewhere was my father's long lost daughter. I could have walked past her in the street. Why didn't I care? As a boy I'd desperately wanted a sister or a brother, a confederate in the war between the man and woman in my life. The truth was now there didn't seem a need. Inquiries would probably turn up more disturbing facts: she might be dead, or worse, she might be a social worker. What was the use of finding out? I had a capricious interest: hiring a detective and spying on this so-called sister appealed. But I didn't want to meet her. Never. What did it matter to me if my father was a dark horse? He was dead and buried, who cared? K, evidently. On the way back to the car she asked about Rachel and Simon, if I could imagine them not knowing each other. I told her they'd probably be a lot happier, she hadn't seen them together. She looked admonished, and I felt sorry for her. An only child, no children of her own, she could never know the dynamics, the ups and downs. I'd been cruel to point it out.

That night, after visiting the buffalo, we lay in bed, restless; I contemplated the stretch marks in the flickering dark. Maybe she wasn't so ignorant after all, maybe . . . but still I didn't ask. Realising I was awake, she turned and picked at the sparse ginger hairs on my wrist, slowly making her way up my forearm, she asked tentatively. K was curious about a lot of things. I couldn't work it out, either then or later, whether she wanted to know the answer or really just had to ask.

— Do you still want her?

— Who?

That was the first slip. Admitting there was a range of possibilities.

— Who else? Sarah, of course.

— No.

But I answered too quickly. Feeling obliged to say more, to exonerate myself, I joked, or at least tried to.

— The best times are those that aren't . . . aren't consummated.

It came out like an edgy sermon, like the frail advice my father might have given his patients, or at least how I imagined him to talk. K wanted clarification.

— You mean the times you didn't . . .

— Not necessarily.

I felt disturbed, I wanted her to stop and not say what she was going to say. I wanted to change tack and tried to take charge of the joke. Yes, I could be ironic as well.

— Our skins may have touched, our lips glanced. All too briefly.

— You couldn't get enough, eh? So you do still want her.

— No, no, no.

I knew she was wrong but I didn't know what I was trying to say, whether I meant what I was saying or if it was still a joke. Suddenly I couldn't understand myself.

— It lingers on, the doubt, the promise of something more, and yet the knowledge too, the disappointment and knowing, knowing what's to come.

— You mean . . .?

She held a finger erect then let it droop pitifully. I got mad.

— No, no, it's more than that, stop reducing everything to sex and genitalia. Love, that's what it's about . . . Love is about finding happiness in non-fulfilment, sex or no sex. That's irrelevant. What matters is the longing.

— Sounds pretty sexy to me. So, you still want her?

I pretended I didn't hear.

— Love is a journey, it's never arriving.

— Ah, so that's it, I thought as much. Coming, not coming; keeping it in. You've got a thing about control, has anyone else told you?

I laughed despite myself, I heard the chuckle but it didn't sound like me. embittered and barbed like the rattle of an old train on rusted rails. Her nose curled, her dark ever-falling hair shading her eyes. She didn't move to pin it back, no matter how much I willed her to. I wanted to like her; I wanted to love her as well. But I just couldn't help myself.

— Love, by definition, is unrequited.

She looked up in the stillness, not smiling anymore, pinning back the curls with crimson-nailed fingers, staring into my eyes, searching, suddenly hurt. I'd only been playing her at her own game. Couldn't she see? No.

— Thanks buddy. So, we don't love each other because we fuck too much, eh? We have too many orgasms, is that it?

Why did she have to do this? I turned my head as she carried on.

— Absence makes the heart grow fonder, presence makes the cock crow, eh?

There was no way out; now just the turgid silence, long and unending. I could say nothing. I could do nothing. I didn't have to. Out of the quiet she reached over; no words needed. She knew, rubbing the sheet, pulling it back. Was she mocking? Was this ironic? Or did she mean it? I was getting in a real mess with irony. She was in control, again. That was all that mattered. I wanted to run away but she had hold of me, I had no meaning. And her smile resurfaced, brimming and full of know how.

— Maybe I get the best deal after all.

And as she bent over, just then, I remembered Sarah unzipping my trousers on Parliament Hill. How far had I come? How many thousands of miles? I remembered the chaise longue, I remembered, I remembered . . . and K, with her head half-risen, half-looking, said it. I remember now, her curls dropping slowly one by one, interrogating echoes, as she pronounced the words.

— Are Rachel and Simon *your* kids?

She had a way of reading minds. Not literally, not the surface, but getting down in the nooks and crannies. The things you couldn't even see yourself.

— What's wrong? I only asked.

She stroked me but to no avail. I tried to look away, to avoid her eyes. But then I realised she was still smiling. She asked again.

— What's got into you? People remarry; they have kids with

different people, that's all. I only inquired. Because you never talk about it. I only inquired.

And she stroked me one last time, then patted me with her other hand.

— Heh, does this mean you love me?

And she laughed. She laughed.

CHAPTER 3

The beginning of the end. Destiny was, after all, nothing more than a matter of getting ahead so you could look back. K, Kimmy, Kismet. She was an improbable possibility. Or was it the other way round? There was still the sight of her, the pull of her, the fall of her hair, and those eyes. This wasn't something I could easily walk away from, but a part of me thought I'd taken the first step.

I resolved to go for more walks. I spent more time, even the odd night, at my own apartment. Basic though it was, and full of the building's intestines – major waterways and corrugated heating ducts – it retained a certain charm. Mrs Wong, who lived on an upper floor, was fair and pleasant enough as a landlady, kindly taking in parcels and larger items of mail during my sometimes week-long absences. Over the summer months I hadn't had chance to personalise the rooms but now I made, what was for me, a real effort. I stuck pictures on the walls, picked up some pine cones from the park and arranged them on the half-filled book shelves. I put candles in wine bottles, bought fruit for the table.

Autumn came and with every postcard, fax and phone call Richard threatened to fly over and visit. We made a few trips out in K's Beetle to the surrounding country; art and craft centres mainly, and a variety of vegetarian cafes where egg plant and ratatouille were always on the menu. Once or twice I managed to get her out of the car and we walked through the gilded woods. I was dazzled by the tomahawk hues, enchanted by the Mohican glamour of it and started collecting the silvered twigs and red and golden leaves. On these trips I felt like

I'd really landed; those child-like expectations were coming into their own. My walls began to glow. I clip-framed some of what I collected, hung and dried some of it in mobile-like clusters. A friend from The Institute visited and he said my decor was positively feminine. I thought it was more Longfellow.

When winter closed in the decorations became just sad reminders of the world as it once was, before the skin of snow and ice grew over everything, before the ear-severing wind blew into town freezing eyelashes blindly together, crusting stalactites onto nostril and beard hair. As the noise from the pipes increased with my co-tenants now hibernating indoors, Mrs Wong's thousand a month started to look extortionate, no matter how much hospitality she extended. For a week or two I watched the chain-tyred cars struggling through the salted, brown-grey sludge. I watched the skiers and shoe-ers on the sidewalks and blocked avenues where the snow stayed white for a little longer. But the novelty soon wore off. I began spending more time at The Institute, exploring its dark corners and dingy corridors. And, despite my resolve, I spent more time at K's apartment. It was modern, came complete with janitor and intercom, a waste disposal unit, relatively silent heating and plumbing, and a splendid high-rise view of the lake. And it was still just a block away from The Institute. Each floor had its own lobby, tiled in highly polished, pastoral ceramics, like a Mediterranean bank, with immaculate free-standing ashtrays that no-one ever used. I'd sold it to myself, at least for the winter. When the snow began to melt – that's when I'd make my move. I'd sort this business with K out once and for all when the wind died down. That was my plan.

Besides, there was a twenty four hour grocery store at the corner of K's block. Not quite a supermarket or a deli, it sold warm bread and sad looking zucchini-stuffed peppers, but, best of all, it sold loose hazels, peanuts and cashews, and had a machine at the checkout where you could grind your own butter. I'd become addicted. K looked at me as if I was a little boy when I came back with my nut butter tubs. Even her janitor looked at me strangely, as though I was doing something illegal. I soon realised that was just his way. He was called Harry, though his real name was Eddie. Everybody called him Harry, if they called him anything, because his predecessor was called Harry. K said the name went with the job. He was big, two hundred and fifty pounds plus, and never said much. He rarely looked at you, face to face. More often he stood bowed forward and all you saw were the beads of sweat on his bulbous forehead; he was always sweating even in the cool of a 20-below night. He wore a perpetual, and so I thought meaningless, smile. His father once had reason to call at the building and he had exactly the same build and expression: both sets of eyes caught like the buffalo's in the park; tiny dots of inscrutable intelligence swamped by a sea of flesh. Harry's destiny was there for all to see; where he'd come from was where he was going.

I didn't convey any of my observations to K. She'd once passed a remark about Harry being one for my chopping block; this being just one of many swipes at what she perceived to be my work. 'State intervention in childcare' inferred a whole host of sins, according to her, not least the cleansing of the stock. She told me how the Nazis were extremists, yes, but it wasn't a phenomenon exclusive to right wing or state dictatorships. She told me where to look if I really wanted to see some State intervention. One day she pulled out some extracts from what she told me was the Brock Report. She kept a kind of scrap book. Written by a 'bunch of aristocratic inbreds', she said, ranting about how they had recommended three and a half million voluntary (she laughed at that) sterilisations. She told me how the Fabians were in favour, and the Women's Labour Movement too, they were all in on it, left and right. 'You caring, innocent Brits,' she said. The only thing that stopped them, according to K – and this brought on her ironic laugh – the German invasion of Poland.

Another time she pulled out a photocopy of an old Morning Post article from the thirties, a survey they'd done, finding that most people in Britain were in favour of sterilising mental defectives. I asked her what a mental defective might be, feeling like one myself. I didn't tell her my father had been a Fabian; my mother probably still was. She told me about calls to give Jewish refugees IQ tests to see whether they should be allowed into Britain – and the States too. The Carrie Buck case had blown it into the open but they'd been 'cutting the tubes of ill-educated single mothers' for decades. Sweden had been doing it too, right up into the seventies. These were just the things we knew about, according to K. No wonder she wanted to get away from insulin deficiency; she had a whole thesis waiting in her bottom drawer.

But she was barking at the wrong man. What she was talking about was a far cry from what I was actually working on. Child benefits and tax concessions were my thing: just money, that's all. I had to undertake some research, review the past, but there was nothing dubious. The 'Endowment of Motherhood' project and Lloyd George's 'Brat Allowance', how Major Darwin wanted to give family allowances only to tax-payers, that was about as dark as it got. I'd been instructed to steer clear of 'universal entitlement', and had become a little perplexed as to how and when the terms had twisted from 'benefit' to 'allowance', from personal entitlement to state beneficence. But this was the height of any controversy. I had to look at precedents: breeding encouragements and disincentives; ways of discerning who to give the money to; good parents, bad parents; children worth having, tykes not worth the time of day. It wasn't anywhere near as glamorous as conspiracy fascism and secret sterilisations.

Not long after the New Year the wind chill factor broke all records; freezing rain brought down spirits and power cables across the province. And K bought some dope. This was not something she usually did; comfort for the cold, she called it. She smoked and baked like there was no tomorrow, and in one Sunday afternoon haze she told me all about her friend, Peter.

— I knew him in high school, and kept in touch. I think we may have been intimate once . . .

— You can't remember?

— Or twice. You know how it is.

— No, I'm sorry, I don't.

— Anyways, Peter was a guy I knew at high school and he was in a car wreck. In a coma for five or six weeks, they didn't know if he was gonna make it. But he pulls through and he can't recognise members of his own family. Well, he knows them but he doesn't believe they're really who they say they are. He doesn't feel they're real.

— Sounds right up your street. Memory lane!

I laughed briefly but soon realised I had started something.

— Now you mention it, my guess is he had problems in the temporal lobe, the amygdaloid synapses, gateway to the emotions.

— Not stairway to heaven?

I played air guitar to accompany my joke but was ignored.

— That's how we know things, we feel them. His problem was he had lesions, scar tissue. Around about the amygdala, that's my guess.

She pointed through the tangle of dark curls into her head, explaining about an almond-shaped clump of cells that was all to do with making you laugh and cry. You had to do one or the other when she was like this. Dope makes me smile, inanely I suspect. It makes me eat a lot and act stupid. I can't smoke it, I have to have mine cooked. I eventually collapse. But on occasions, with a select band of people it works a different magic. It makes them buzz, so they walk or work or talk all night long, without pausing for breath. K was like that.

When she talked about brain exploration she did so with a passion. This wasn't cold function-spotting, this was marching off into eternity, way up there in the media eminence; and it always put a mysterious, knowing smile on her face. She made me feel spiritually dumb when she talked synapses, as if I was her student or patient. And it made me resist.

— So, doctor what did you prescribe for this friend of yours?

— He joined this group, guys with the same sort of problems. One guy, he couldn't put names to faces. Felt like he knew them, tip of his tongue, but he just couldn't get it. How do we know things? We name them.

— But Doctor, Doctor, you just said we know things because we feel them.

I pleaded like a school boy trying to disrupt the lesson, but she was on the trail of something. No time for scoundrels, you could see it in her eyes.

— Yeah, both have something going for them. But if we can't name things then we can't know them. He could feel he knew who his wife was but he couldn't put a name to her. So he didn't know her, no matter how many times she told him who she was. I had a friend whose mother got Alzheimers, same thing happened: he'd go visit and her face would light up and then fall flat. Her own son, she knew he meant something to her but she didn't know why. He said it was like seeing a bird shot out of the sky, that smile of recognition, the way it faltered and fell.

Suddenly I didn't feel like joking any more. These stories reminded me of something else, or someone else. A while ago; it seemed like an age: before the sleet and sludge, before the wind, none of this under-floor heating. But there was, like now, a smearing of white everywhere. This was blossom, not snow; the sloe in full flower, the hawthorn coming into leaf; cow parsley covering the banks and verges; the rowing boat bobbing in the current. An English spring, the grounds of the clinic, that last time I saw Janet Burns. I remembered saying something to her about the blossom and flowers and Janet telling me that Guillermo knew all the names. He could put a name to anything, she said – daisies, clover, stitchwort, campion – knew them all, but he didn't know anything. That's what she said. I asked what she meant and she said he didn't know the feel of them, he didn't know what *she* knew.

Now, I looked outside K's apartment, just as the snow started to fall again, obscuring the lake and almost illuminating the crepuscular gloom. I marvelled at the surreal light falling snow gives off, like dimmed lanterns in the dusk. I thought again of spring, the white of the blossom, the river in spate, and realised there was another echo in these tales of K's. It was to do with being close to knowing, almost remembering something, and then all of a sudden that something slipping away like it had never existed.

Janet had been right about Guillermo. He did like to name things, to describe and explain things. His first letter, when he forwarded Janet's painting, told me all about her suicide attempt, laid out her problems, the possible diagnosis and what drugs she'd been put on. He wrote without seeming to care that he barely knew who I was or that I'd encountered him as a psychiatric patient. I sent a card in thanks, not wanting to encourage him. So then he wrote to me on postcards, all sent on by my tenants.

According to his letters and cards he had discharged himself from the clinic, having reached some sort of pact with his father. At first he regularly visited Janet in hospital, and sent on any of her scarlet gift-paintings. Halfway through the summer he went travelling, taking a year out before university, much, I imagined, to his father's annoyance. The postcards started coming from all directions – Montpellier, Bordeaux, Portugal, Italy – I didn't really take note of the places until he reached a mountain village in Greece, and appeared, from the fuller, more excited content to have discovered something, maybe just the place, I couldn't tell for sure. He wrote the postcards without any response at all from me. Most of them took an age to get to me. After he left, Janet's paintings almost dried up but she did send the odd one – again via my tenants. He must have given her the address.

In one of Guillermo's postcards – from Portugal – he told me he was visiting the village of his paternal grandfather. He wrote of how he had come to know what his father meant when he said *saudade*, the only Portuguese word left in the family. His father used it as 'a kind of sad curse' – but now Guillermo knew he had been wishing for something better, a golden moment that never really existed. And this was what I felt now, late on a Sunday afternoon, looking out at the snow. I remembered what was wrong, as if I was searching for a thing that I'd never get back to, though I'd sometimes sense it, feel it, hear it, think it was near. It might have been almond shaped; it could have been any shape as far as I knew. I'd never get it, whatever it was.

K said there was another guy in her friend's help group.

— He suffered seizures. His amygdala was most likely affected as well, by the fits. But that doesn't tell you anything. He'd cry if he saw a bum on the street, like he had an overactive empathy gland. Lucky guy; came from a rich family.

— Lucky?

— Yeah, he used to see all this significance in everything, a grain of sand, a speck of dust. He'd cry at the sight of the sky in the morning. It was all too much.

— So, this constitutes good fortune?

— He'd make connections all the time and see significance in things you and I take for granted or don't see at all.

— Has this, by chance, got anything to do with God?

— Yeah, he sometimes thought he was God. Who doesn't? That's no bad thing is it? He thought he had the key to make things better.

— So did the Women's Labour Movement, so did Hitler.

— No, what I'm saying is that the world's wrongs, he wanted to right them. He didn't care about himself, that's what he lost in these seizures. But he got something in return, something more than what he forfeited. They'd call him feebleminded back then, degenerate, mental defective – you name it – despite an IQ of 160 and rising. He felt the world. And he wanted to change it. If only they'd find a pill to give us what he had. None of this seratonin nonsense.

Prozac was only a rumour at the time – the patent was out but not the product – just a warm, superior glow amongst the pharmaceutical types that sometimes hung out at The Institute's informal soirées. We all knew it was coming, and K didn't like it one little bit.

— No happy pills, no Brave New World, none of that lotus-eating shit . . .

I tutted; she'd not long finished sucking on a joint the size of a banana. But I didn't interrupt.

— What we need is a god-pill, now that would really make the world a better place.

We sat and watched the snow for a while, K rolling another joint, deep in contemplation of her utopia. I'd read somewhere that the Greeks believed Hermes, the trickster, mischievously passes through the room during every lull in conversation. This particular dope-induced pause seemed to last forever; Hermes appeared to be taking over. I nibbled vaguely at the hash flapjack K had baked earlier that afternoon, trying desperately to recall what it was she'd last said. I'd already eaten half a slice before Peter had even appeared in the conversation and remembered thinking then – that was my limit. My face tended to ache if I ate too many of her concoctions. It eventually sent me maudlin. Not K though.

— The Greeks thought it divine, don't you know.

Suddenly I realised I didn't know what on earth she was talking about.

— What? What did the Greeks think was divine?

— Epilepsy. Called it the sacred disease. Came from the gods, least ways that's what they said before the Hippocratic guys put in their dime's worth. Dostoevsky suffered, that's how he came by his big old empathy gland. Grand and petit mal. The Jews said it was down to demons, unclean spirits – only way to shake it was to do some sort of exorcism, stick the stake in. But some of the rabbis said it was straightforward. In the blood. O positive, O negative and O moonstruck. They banned marriages to women from epileptic families. Yeah, the guys were okay. Wouldn't you just know!

But I was still catching up on what she'd said.

— But you reckon . . . correct me if I'm wrong, what you're saying is . . . you're saying we should have pills to give us epilepsy?

— Why not? Not the physical part – we could do without that. Just a pill to hit the God-spot, make us good. Altruism pills.

— You'd never get anyone to take them.

— We know because we name, yeah, but we do enough of that, and where does it get us. That Linnaeus guy, what a fraud. Real name was Carl von Linné; classified himself first off; Carolus indeed. It was all invention in the end, not something you can pin a whole lot of faith in and say this is the truth. I reckon we could do with more of the feel sort of knowing.

We started to giggle, about how words were getting difficult, about the snow falling, about Carolus Linnaeus, about A tabs, and about Dusty Dostoevsky, not being able to remember his first name. She had a particular aversion to Linnaeus and had a fonder regard for some of the head doctors, modern and old. Luria and Broca were particular favourites. According to K, they weren't just about experiments and naming things: Luria felt for his case studies, and Broca might have measured heads with the best of them but in the end he believed in high school for all, no matter the cranium size. She had a thing about Galton though. He was the white-coated devil, the cause of much grief and suffering.

Before the laughter had calmed I asked.

— What happened to your friend's group?

— What?

— Did they get better? Peter and his friend. Did he get to know his wife again? And the other one. Did the Pharisees burn out the demons?

— Could say that.

— What happened?

— The group stopped meeting.

She didn't want to tell me but I eventually got it out of her.

— He killed himself.

— Which one?

She didn't have to say.

— I thought you said he was lucky?

Fits, madness, suicide. It was all too familiar. I glimpsed red, maybe a hand. I thought of the blossom, the rowing boat bobbing. I thought of it all and felt my eyes filling up.

CHAPTER 4

It wasn't long before K found out about it all. We were going out – 'Oedipus Rex On Ice', it was happening at a rink outside one of the malls. I had to call in to my apartment on the way so I could get clothes. She was mooching around while I trimmed my beard. The temperature had risen a degree or two, I was attempting to civilise myself and turned, scissors in hand. She held up a bright red picture. Vermilion. A river. She soon got to Guillermo's letter and postcards, and that first picture, with Janet's signature at the bottom.

— What are these?

The pipes were gurgling.

— Well, what are they?

I felt that I didn't need to explain, as though I'd already told her: all about Janet Burns, the clinic, the last case. She had forgotten. This was no secret; this was my past, part of my life before I met her. But I had never told her, apparently. At first she thought the bundle was from Rachel and Simon, who in fact had sent a grand total of ten words and three felt tip kisses in six months. I explained and was astonished at her reaction. Why on earth should K get upset by daubs of paint? Because, apparently, I was hiding them from her. And because, apparently, they weren't daubs at all; they were masterpieces. She didn't go so far as to say so but she plainly liked them. They were after all generally red and very, very black.

Holding the paintings up to the light and pinning a couple to the wall, she started firing the questions. Does she still send them? Why does she send them? And who's this guy, Guillermo? Can't she send the paintings herself? She does? How often? Medication? What sort of medication? What's wrong with her?

Finding the paintings exposed a naïvety. Until then K had held this strange idea of me. I was some sort of movie lawyer – I'd been denied witnesses; the poor, poor child in peril; evidence was sometimes destroyed; but I always came through in the end; the final peroration that brings the house to the tear-stained truth; justice with a big, big J. When I told her some real facts about how it worked she looked so young and unknowing. I told her that the court hearings were all clear cut; written before they'd started. I did some of the writing, yes, there was a little destiny-deciding, but hardly any of it was read out loud, and most of it was very boring.

After I'd done with all my explaining Dr Kismet recovered enough of her poise to come up with a diagnosis. She knew what was up with Janet Burns all those miles away. She even had a name for it: disaffectionate psychopathy – the inability to form bonds; the adult form of a childhood malaise. I was having none of it.

— She manages to form bonds with men.

K was onto me like a flash.

— Yes, I had noticed. The glazed eyes, like a frozen river. Not like when you talk about Sarah.

She smiled cautiously, her mouth quivering. It wasn't quite jealousy, but near. She continued.

— The fact that she can't form or maintain emotional relationships doesn't mean that she has no emotional need or function.

— You make her sound like some sort of animal.

— All diagnoses will reduce her to something. She isn't normal so she must be less. You should know that – no room in the medical glossary for 'more than' . . . even though her paintings say she's . . .

— What are you talking about?

— Well, she obviously has an awareness of God.

— Sure, a man who kills his wife and child!

105

— No, a higher consciousness; it's just the reality part that she can't deal with.

— She has babies, that's real.

— She only had one baby, for God's sake!

— Yes, literally!

I laughed as K glared. I couldn't believe how serious she was. She didn't come back to me about the glazed eyes and frozen river. She started lecturing about parthenogenesis and ovarian teratomas: some insects did it unaided but in the Biblical instance it was down to malicious mistranslation; Mary was no virgin, just a 'normal young woman'. I missed half of it because of the gurgling pipes – my neighbours were taking a shower – but gathered enough to know that the Greek patriarchs and Roman 'dickheads' were to blame. It was they who had tied Mary up with all sorts of 'pagan garbage'.

True to form, she came up with some study from the fifties, said she'd dig it out. K was always good for a study or two. Sponsored by the Sunday Pictorial, no less; she said that a 'world-wide search' for a virgin birth had come up with a German woman, then residing in the Welsh Marches. The woman claimed she was a virgin and unmarried when she fell pregnant. All the tests confirmed it. The woman had been in hospital for all of the year preceding the birth of her miraculous child. She suffered from a rare rheumatoid condition, so she couldn't possibly have conceived in the normal way. K didn't believe it for a minute.

— Yeah, you know what goes on in hospitals, in the name of science and patient care.

She told me the woman mysteriously disappeared shortly after the Pictorial's feature article.

— I guess being German in Britain, in the fifties, she wasn't exactly going to be another Mary in any case, now was she?

She made some joke about the German woman and Janet Burns being related, mother and daughter, granddaughter even, proud possessors of the teratoma gene; the secret of life tied up in their mutant gonads. But K was never far from the diagnostic trail.

— No, it sounds to me like Janet's problem is that she cares.

I laughed, incredulous. A second take of the paintings and all I could see was a mess of coloured lines. Might be a spider, might be a web.

— She cares so much, right? So is that why she gave her child away?

— What we all do now, maybe we've always done it, we stifle the feeling that everything is significant. We control the impulse to care, to be altruistic. If you felt everything you'd explode. We select and delegate, just like the ants.

I'd heard about the ants once too often. How some breed aphids for honeydew, how some keep fungus farms, how some master ants have parasitic dealings with their slaves. And I'd heard about the altruism, about the ultimate sacrifice: infertility. I'd also heard about the termites, ambrosia beetles, thrips and mole-rats. I'd heard it all – the great deeds – sacrificing one's reproductive right. Was this where she was heading? Was Janet Burns just an ant now? A caring sharing insect?

— She's mad for Christ's sake, she's lost it. Isn't that enough of an explanation in itself?

By this time I'd had it. K was talking about someone she'd never even met.

— Doesn't the fact that her real mother committed suicide have something to do with this? Her adoptive mother wasn't as supportive as she might have been, doesn't this all have a cumulative effect?

— Ah, we're on familiar territory now aren't we? Maternal deprivation. Or should we just say, mothers screw you up.

It was useless protesting. This was her 'matricidal malice' angle, her personal quest. The daddies of the world had had it too good for too long. I, of course, could say nothing.

Not long after the last snow K found something else – a piece of paper on which I'd scrawled: *Love burns with the putting in the seed*

I'd started writing things down in case I lost them, in case they vanished as quickly as they'd returned. As she picked up the paper K read it aloud and then came up with another couple of lines, which weren't written on the sheet.

— *The sturdy seedling with arched body comes / Shouldering its way and shedding the earth crumbs.*

I'd never told her of my father and remembering the poem in the shed. Her face said she knew nothing of what it might mean to me, but I felt invaded just the same. I asked where she knew the lines from.

— High school, Robert Frost, as I recall.

But it was mine, my property; it resided with me and my father, a private memory, nothing to do with her, or Robert Frost for that matter. Faltering only occasionally, she proceeded to come up with it all, the whole poem. Well, I guessed it was all there, I was no expert. I was too aggrieved to listen properly. I liked it the way it was, all broken up and anonymous.

— So, what is it? A mnemonic?

She waved the piece of paper around and I laughed in the hope the question would go away.

— No, really, I'm curious. How come you've got it written down?

I told her it was my father.

— It was a memory. I think he read it to me when I was a child. I couldn't remember anymore though, I've been trying to work it out.

I tried to sound cheerful and grateful that she had identified it.

— So, it's Robert Frost is it?

It didn't come off. She could see what the problem was.

— Daddies are always like that. Not there. Even when they're around, they always give the impression of not really being there.

As spring approached, patches of green miraculously reappeared in the parks. The grey slush got sucked away by monstrous machines, snow-combines harvesting the streets. I bought some over-boots and started walking again. All the time I concentrated on my father. Not just the poem, the cello practice or the crumbs at the corner of his mouth, not just his decline and the steady greying and failing of his red hair. I thought a lot about the walk up the hill, and the other times I'd spent on my own with him. I wanted words, trudging reassurance; I wanted evidence from his lips. To say what – that he wasn't such a bad father after all? I wanted something more; that's all I knew. I wanted evidence, not just the voice of some poet; I wanted his words and no one else's.

CHAPTER 5

What I knew and remembered about my father was never enough. The more I walked, the more parks I visited, the more streets and avenues I trawled, the less I seemed to know about him. And the less I seemed to care. He would always offer possibilities, but it was all so predictable, too probable. A man has an affair, there's an illegitimate child, it must have happened a thousand times, to a thousand sons. I wanted more; something original, something unique.

I walked up a hill with him once, a few decades ago, but that was the sort of jigsaw memory that screamed at you: 'the important part's missing!' And perhaps there was some crucial thing left out which would illuminate my whole life and complete the picture. Maybe he said he loved me, maybe he just looked as if he loved me, or liked me, or approved of me even. Maybe for once I saw beyond doctor and father. Maybe I saw his vulnerability, his real desires, his fears, who he really was. Maybe he confessed all. Maybe not. I just didn't know. More probably nothing was missing, the memory was complete. I remembered everything just as it was. The only reason I got this 'saudade' feeling was because I wanted there to be more to life than that: something more profound to it all than just a walk up a hill.

Wanting more got me into trouble; at least, it was one of the reasons. Maybe Slater, K's boss, saw I was on the look out for more when he grabbed my arm on one of those dark and dingy corridors, handing me a bunch of research articles.

— Take a look at these. I think you'll like them.

His voice gave me the creeps at the best of times: as deep as the darkest pit and still diving. Yet there was nothing strange in what he'd done; he knew in a matter-of-fact sort of fashion what everyone should be reading and researching, that was his way. You could call it professorial arrogance, though he must have been younger than me. He was a know-it-all and he knew it. Nodding and wishing me good luck, he caressed and tidied the tails of his moustache. But I still couldn't make out his mouth to see if he was smiling.

Judging by the style, the articles were all written by the same person. There was no way of telling for sure: the author's name and publication details had been tippexed out on some pages, snipped off on others. The first article talked about the need for negative as well as positive discrimination in population control: 'positive' meant encouraging the right people to have babies; 'negative' meant stopping the wrong people having babies, by whatever means. By the second article I'd got the picture. The third article contained a survey of the old terminology, morbid inheritance and feeble mindedness, that sort of thing. The buzz phrases, 'social problem', 'the homeless' – hadn't kicked in when the articles had been written, but the writer was aware of the incoming trend: external deprivation replacing internal deficiency. The blame was shifting though the problem remained. Somehow, someone, somewhere had to care, and in a bigger way than just providing more dry-out hostels.

A week after Slater gave me the articles K commented on how busy I seemed. I pretended there was nothing amiss. I took the bundle back to my apartment, better they be read in private. Compared to some of the statistics I'd had to plough through at least these were easy on the eye. Their tone seemed familiar even, and though I knew I shouldn't be, I was intrigued. The problem was big enough and old enough: if someone had a suggestion to make why not at least listen to them? I'd developed something of a personal interest. Whenever I went to the park on the Northside Grey Owl was always there, sometimes with Bjorn Borg, sometimes on his own. I'd come to invent the tragedy of his life. Of course, he pined for the woods, the beaver and the bear, but his eagle rock had long since vanished. So he drank himself into oblivion. Imagination was never my strong suit. The blond Bjorn, according to my version, was just an opportunist, and Swedish after all, merely learning his English from a Dublin lass who he'd no doubt left with child, back in London or New York or some other Irish colony. She'd be better off without him, given his habit, so apparent in the flaked blue, far-away eyes.

My speculations would only ever stretch this far. I wasn't going to go across and ask them: who are you? How did you get here? How did you stumble on such grotesque misfortune? If I looked at them too long they seemed troubled, no doubt preferring a couple of bucks in hand to my two bit stares. They looked at me as if they saw what I was doing, as if they were used to it and resented it. It was the only time the Ojibway ever seemed close to getting up off his bench.

I even dreamt of them one night: I'm in the park by the buffalo, sun-singed dust dancing up into the beasts' hunched collars and dung-scraping beards. I sit on the bench and fall asleep, and I start to dream; so I'm dreaming inside a dream, one of those you can't work out what to believe. And I wake up on the bench to find the Ojibway sitting next to me, and Bjorn Borg standing over me offering me what he says is a 'good deal on Colombian coal'. And then he's screaming incredulously at me: 'What? You don't smoke? You some kinda nutcase?' Then he's gone and his friend starts moaning about his 'sweet baby', his 'sweet, sweet baby'. He has a child he hasn't seen for years, the mother gave it up for adoption. Yes, I even dreamt childcare! Only the Grey Owl of the dream has developed a deep Bronx accent, and is ranting: 'A good fuckin home, she went to a good fuckin home, all that whore'd say. What kinda mother says that? Some kinda mother fucker, thas who, givin her fuckin kid away to fuckin strangers.'

It unsettled me for days. The articles didn't help; they disturbed me too. Some of them talked about Galton and for that reason alone I knew K should never set eyes on them. She hated Galton. But the strange thing was, the more I read the more I thought: I know this voice, this style of writing, this way of putting things. I was like Peter's friend, I knew who the author was but I couldn't give them a name. There was a simple and common enough case being made: ignore at your peril the fact that we're ruled by biology, chemistry and physics; being aware of this doesn't amount to a narrow determinism but to a glorious liberation. Hooray for scientists, boo to the cynics and doubters. But there was a political argument too, about basic human rights, like a woman's right to give birth. We shouldn't deny this, but we should be aware that this wasn't always a good thing. It could be a curse. I understood that well enough.

The jargon confused me, though I managed to work most of it out. In the past it was only possible to deal with those having a condition, not the passive carriers who weren't expressing symptoms. They thought it was going to take tens of generations to eradicate the rotten eggs. Then the new bio-chem boys came on the scene with their DNA. Problem solved. Was a day we just hoped to maximise genetic potential, making the best of a bad soup. Now we could proudly don the chef's hat. Man, as Galton guessed he one day might, could finally take charge of his own evolution. The articles talked grandly of eradicating diseases and impairments, with no mention of the flip side at all. There was a date on the last page of the last article. It was either behind or ahead of its time, I couldn't quite decide. 1962. This was the only means of identification; all other clues had been wiped. For their day the articles were hot and scary, and somebody knew it.

I hung onto the bundle. There was something about the voice, but I couldn't pin it down. I went up to Slater one day in the bagel queue and asked him who wrote them. He shook his head, as if such details were an irrelevance in the face of a higher truth. He asked, almost politely, if they'd been of any assistance. I detected a smile underneath the moustache. This was all Slater's doing. He didn't write them but they were his gift. He wanted me to read them. For a reason.

I hid the articles under the Buddhist meditation blanket Sarah had brought back from Thailand, not long after we split up. And that's where K eventually found them. No matter what beliefs they're wrapped in, gifts are always weapons. K herself had bought me a present that day: a Mervyn Peake print from *Treasure Island*. Long John Silver, one-legged and dastardly, clinging by his teeth to a rope, a knife and crutch in his hands. K said the illustration had a strange effect on her. She just had to buy it. The story's characters were familiar but she couldn't tell whether she knew them from films and TV. She couldn't remember whether she had read the book or not.

I kept quiet, wondering why she'd given me such a dubious gift. I thought it was perhaps another article of her faith: memory was hopeless, we could never trust it. I was getting tired of the theme. If we had no faith in our memories then who were we? It left us stranded. Small memories were a problem, narrow minds caused difficulties; but surely memory in itself was no bad thing? Then, as we were talking, she wandered over and picked up the Buddhist blanket, holding it to the light, admitting some flickering admiration of Sarah's taste, before looking down. There were the articles, lying open, with the name of her Satan printed loud and large at the top of the page. Galton. No further invite was needed.

She knew what they were after reading a paragraph. She flew at me, despite all pleas of innocence. She waved an arm at her own forlorn looking gift, ranting about how Peake died of Parkinson's, how he'd probably have been exterminated if some had had their way, and how the likes of Long John Silver would never have graced our nightmares. Goodies and baddies alike, never seeing the light of day; deviance, diversity, all scrapped according to 'poison like this'. I daren't tell her that Slater had given me the articles. I tried reasoning.

— Parkinsons, as far as they know, isn't a hereditary condition.

— No, but they'll be saying it is before long. They'll be calling it degeneracy, along with left-handedness, and red-beardedness. You should watch out, buddy!

She shouted something about insurance companies vetting for freckles in the family, and white-skin-only cloning. I tried to tell her.

— They're only research articles, and very old at that. Aren't you getting a touch hysterical?

— Ah, hysteria, well spotted! The instinctual response to evil; it's usually mad, female and deluded. Not necessarily in that order.

— Not all things you disagree with are evil you know.

She grabbed hold of the top article and pointed so hard I thought she was going to burn a hole through the page.

— Now, if it's hysteria you're looking for, here we have him. Galton, the perfect role model. Nervous breakdown at university, mentally unstable, that's what they said. If he was a woman he'd have earned the tagline straightaway. Guilt-ridden about his own infertility, brought the clap back from Africa, thought it'd dried him up. Poor boy! Fertility anxiety's got so much to answer for. Compensated by reading Who's Who in bed at night, got to sleep by counting the sheep who were following him. Counting, counting, counting. Him and his quincunx contraptions. Probability and deviation. Numbers. All we ever were to him, all we ever could be. A complete and utter madman. 'Whenever you can, count.' I mean, who'd have a slogan like that? Whenever you can . . . give me a break!

As soon as she said it I span straight back to my cello lessons, a new tape of my father starting up in my head. All these years I'd thought he was adhering to some simple, uno-riginal but firmly stated musical dogma. Something he might have picked up from his father. I thought it was meant for my ears, those of his only son; something he was passing down. I checked without letting on, without telling her anything about the cello or about my father.

— 'Whenever you can, count.' Was Galton famous for saying that?

I wasn't going to say anything until I was hundred percent sure, and even then I had a strong suspicion K wasn't the one I should or would be telling. Coincidence had to be ruled out, or at least probability ruled in, but it made sense; suddenly it was all making sense. I'd found what I was looking for, some words from his lips. Father, dear father. The familiar style to the articles, I'd known the voice. Father, dear father. I knew where I was now. Even the smile under Slater's moustache made sense. He'd known who'd written the articles all along. That's why he gave them to me. Written by an 'Eyre'; a patri-lineal pot-shot. My father, dear father. I was sure of it. This was how the new tape ran: my own daddy, a eugenicist, that's what his research work had been all about, all those years ago, when I was just so high. That's why he hadn't been able to get a job; none of the practices approved, he was a pariah. And now, suddenly, he was a kind of hero.

CHAPTER 6

Richard arrived with some good news, an offer, and a summer suit. It was barely April – the cruellest month, and so it was to prove. The supposed good news: Sarah had given birth to a baby boy, Arthur. A very spring-like thing to do. A very strange name. Mother, child and fathers were doing just fine. The offer: for me to come and give a lecture 'at the annual gathering of the clans' back home, the local County Child Care Conference later in the year. Richard was co-ordinating it and guaranteed me star billing. I tentatively agreed, though I didn't like his tone: how everyone was desperate to hear of my 'groundbreaking research'.

And the summer suit? This was obviously a follow up to the growing innuendo in his communications over the winter months. I almost expected it. He came alone when he was supposed to arrive *en famille*, blaming some stomach bug that he'd miraculously avoided. Besides the cream linen two-piece, there was an array of bright silk shirts. He was out for the kill and I guessed it was Kismet that had done it; just the sound of her name. I let him settle in for a day before setting him loose. We ate downtown at an Italian, meeting K inside, all politely slurping our taggliatelle and sipping our espressos, and all equally insistent on who should take the bill. Needless to say I ended up paying. We then took to the skies: a high-rise bar that K and I occasionally went to when we were feeling sufficiently cool. And there I go, talking as if we were a couple, two people habituated to each other's conscious and unconscious designs on the world. Goes to show there were times when I thought and acted like that. As for Richard, I didn't know what he wanted. I'd met a woman. Surprising for me, admittedly, but that didn't mean things were any different. I didn't possess a harem. What did he want from his paltry few days on the town?

The bar had a view of the lake and refurbished dockland, a jazz piano and sometimes a singer. Not tonight, just a pianist with a thick goatee, billed as 'coming all the way from Bombay', he played messy medleys of Gershwin and Cole Porter. K and Richard liked what they heard. They went to the bar together to contrive a cocktail. She was wearing a carmine halter-neck, Cuban heels and opaque black tights. It set off Richard's suit to perfection. Had I told him of the red and black? Had I told her of his promiscuity? Why had they gone to the bar? Why ignore the waitress? I heard them laughing as they ordered, Richard trying to pay, waving a fifty dollar bill in front of the barman. And K's hand going to his: keep hold of the money, they'll bill us at the end. That's what I presumed she was telling him, but her hand stayed too long, resting there, a rusty, downed arm against his bald, grey English veins. Or was it the other way round? I couldn't tell who was touching who, until, unmistakably the alabaster fingers clasped her gold-chained wrist, restraining it, pulling it down against her heart-scarlet waist. But staying there, staying there, when there was no reason to stay there.

They returned eventually, Richard in fine flow.

— Yes, all the folks back home are intrigued by Philip's work. You'll have to come over with him when he gives his little talk . . .

I noted the word 'little' above all others.

— . . . we like to keep abreast of things.

Richard looked pointedly and unashamedly at her neckline, as he said it, pulling the low, aluminium-frame chair back for her to be seated. A real gentleman. But what I couldn't understand was K's acquiescence. Her silence, her little-girl laughs. She was playing the game, they both were, and right there in front of me. That's what I remember: their elbows resting on the table and it rattling and squeaking with expectation. It reminded me of something: the illicit rhythm, the squeal of bedsprings dulled through the partition walls of a cheap hotel. They looked like soul-siblings finally reunited, and I was the gooseberry. They exchanged occupations, but I'd already told them all about each other. Hadn't I? They were playing coy. K enquired about Richard's hordes, without getting any specific response. And Richard teased.

— I don't suppose you have any children?

I pictured the stretch marks but K said no, without hesitation. I hadn't felt like this since I was young, and then it had been Richard as well. A girl from the far side of town. We were fifteen or sixteen. Night after night, four or five of us hung out down by the boat houses on the river: the lapping of the water, the willows weeping over the ripples, the unending splash and splutter of youth. It was supposed to have been me she liked. Richard got her. I felt a brief, ill-conceived relief, remembering, thinking this might be his compulsion. It might merely be a sad echo from our shared pasts. But no, he was definitely scoring points. He brought Sarah into it.

— I met one of the fathers, did I tell you?

K was hooked straight away.

— *One* of the fathers?

— I'm sorry, I thought Phil would have told you.

Yes, he started calling me Phil! I nearly retaliated: Richie, better still, Dick. K stuttered, realising she was in the middle of something.

— He .. he told me Sarah was expecting a baby but . . .

Richard just couldn't resist.

— She's living in a commune, father could be one of a number . . .

— Two, actually. One of two. And it's a community, not a . . .

He wasn't going to get away with it any more. But he wouldn't stop.

— In any case they have bizarre rules, don't they, Phil?

I think I forced a smile; it was hard to say how it turned out. Richard laughed like a chimpanzee, a big toothy rictus, not a sound coming out.

— What? The children have a choice of fathers?

K was now trying to help me out I think, but asking more questions wasn't the way to go about it. The pianist didn't aid matters either: 'Anything Goes' was just a touch too ironic for that particular moment. Richard was all but rubbing his hands.

— No, you're not allowed to sleep with the same person for more than two consecutive nights.

His voice slowed into a gravely drawl. He wasn't ridiculing, he was having a good old time; he was commending. Such a rule might be of benefit to the wider world, nudge, nudge. K was too surprised to stop herself.

— Sounds like a cult?

— Yes, do you think it'll catch on?

I left them to it, looking out of the frameless deserts of glass at the twinkling cityscape. A dull crescent moon flitted timidly between skyscrapers and cloud, failing to add any illumination to the man-made stars below. The lake, appearing like a black-green carpet, was embroidered with glistening white jewels of light. I searched out towards the dark horizon but just saw an iridescent bed, two jade-jet bodies silently swerving around each other. A man and a woman. The table rattled with the movement of elbows, another illicit squeal.

The next morning K explained herself.

— Flirting's convenient, whatever gets you through the night. It's easy. A way of being. Not a way of loving.

Unconvinced, I grunted my discontent. She didn't seem to hear.

— But it was good that it happened, wasn't it?

— What do you mean?

— It showed me . . . you care. You care enough to get jealous. Even if you do keep secrets.

I didn't know what it showed me, except that something was wrong. The moon's coy cameo, the stars all earth bound, and this ongoing doubt in spite of her denials and explanations. All I could see of the previous night was a flickering residue, the patina of light on the lake's surface and those bodies, like flames: alive, glancing, devouring. The hole was getting bigger.

CHAPTER 7

K was more than vaguely upset with me for not telling her the full story about Sarah. But why should I? Because of trust. Because of openness. Because the secrets were beginning to accumulate. What about the 'last case', Janet's paintings, and remember the articles under the blanket? According to K there always seemed to be something missing, something left out in the things I told her about myself. Couldn't she see that things might be missing for me too?

I still had my other secret, burning a hole in my head: my father-tape and the discovery of what I'd come to think of as his real job. I returned the articles to Slater, leaving them in his pigeonhole rather than delivering them in person; I didn't want to see the look on his face, looking for the look on mine. I tried ringing my mother to confirm my suspicions once and for all, but she was still away on one of her pilgrimages. The spring equinox: Somerset, Wales, or somewhere off west. I thought of telling Richard, but quickly decided against it. I considered giving him a note to give to my mother when he returned to England, but realised I didn't need to send anything to her. I just needed to ask her questions. Maybe she didn't know anything, maybe my father had worked at this secretly. Or maybe she did know, maybe she was in on it too and somewhere there was another stack of dynamite, with her name scribbled out on it. Whenever you can, count. If K knew where the catchphrase came from, others would know as well. My mother couldn't have not known; she wasn't stupid.

Sarah phoned, complaining that I was the father of her chil-

dren but I never saw them. I joked about how she was trying
for a monopoly on fathers. She didn't laugh.

— I phoned didn't I? They always go dumb on me. What am
I supposed to do? Fly over every weekend?

— No, but once every few months would be a start.

— And where would I stay?

— You could use the house in London, it's lying empty.

Hold on a minute, wasn't I helping to pay the mortgage on
that?

— Or your mother's. Or Richard's.

No, thank you. I'd sort my own arrangements, if she didn't
mind. She should look after herself. She had enough to deal
with. So, how was it with the baby? And why Arthur? Legendary
indeed! I didn't ask about the other males.

Before Richard returned to England I came to the conclusion
he was going through some mid-life tunnel (you couldn't call
it a crisis), and was nowhere near the dimming end-light. One
night in a beer hall downtown, he was almost unbearable.

— Did you hear about God's defence? Diminished responsibility.

He laughed, helping himself to my beer because his glass
was empty and the waitress was having a hard time.

— The Hollyman, that green god fellow, killed his wife and
child. Remember, your last case?

His peacock-blue collar wide open, anyone but Richard and
I'd have suspected a medallion to be lying in the undergrowth.
He alternated precariously between talking to me and waving
to the waitress, and it wasn't just for a drink.

— I ask you, if God isn't responsible for his own actions,
who is?

He croaked like a devil.

— The case rests on the fact that both his father and grandfather were violent. One a petty criminal, burglary mixed in
with the odd GBH, the other a lay preacher, for God's sake.
They abused him as a child, of course. We have to have a bit

of that nowadays. These criminal solicitors, they can get away with murder ...

Another guffaw at his own gag; and to my horror the waitress was leering back at him, giving as good as she got.

— ... turning psychopaths into victims over night. What was that judge's name? You know, the one who said we were all a pile of causes, couldn't be blamed for anything?

— You're the law man, Richard. It's no good asking me.

— Well, whoever he was, I think he's had his day. Perpetrators are perpetrators, in my book, victims are victims. No contest. If they think it's in the family then chop their bloody balls off. Prevention over cure, that's what I say. End the bloody line, stop the cycle, it's the only thing we can do, especially if they use that sort of defence.

By which time the waitress was refilling his glass, and his hand was helplessly stroking the side of the table adjacent to her thigh.

On his last night K came out with us and Richard shared an account of his first sexual experience, insisting we reciprocate. Of course his first time was with the girl from the far side of town. Yes, the lapping waters and weeping willows, and he wasn't slow to explain how he'd won her. K, after some coaxing, told us about Fergus, an 'older boy at High school' who after closer questioning transpired to be a man not a boy: not even a teacher at High school, but a lecturer at the local college. From the start K had aspirations. Then Richard started telling K about my first encounter as if he could remember it better than I could myself. I told K not to believe a word he said, to ignore his half-sharp barbs. We weren't away on holiday at the time, as he'd said; I'd been staying with my father in Wales, one of his locum jobs. I was seventeen not twenty one. It was a cave made by the rhododendron bushes behind the bus shelter, a really beautiful spot, not the back of a parked bus as Richard had said. And no, we didn't have an audience of 'coal miners' daughters'. It was in North Wales, there wasn't a pit anywhere near; and the other kids from the village had already gone home; they were a lot younger. I was a celebrity: an English accent, doing A-levels, a smudge of facial hair, and my jam jars full of scotch – Dutch courage, stolen from my father's cabinet. Turned out the girl was more used to that sort of thing than I was. And it was Jane, not Blodwen, as Richard had hooted. K asked the colour of her hair and if she was pretty. Richard asked for breast size.

K told me the next day that she thought Richard was 'cute, in a sad sort of way'. What did that mean? Less, apparently, than I took it to mean. But I couldn't listen to K's explanations anymore. Part of me was turning away. I couldn't confide in her, I kept hearing those illicit squeals; I couldn't tell her about anything, let alone what I suspected of my father. While my mother was on her tour of mystic tors, I walked and walked, going on a sort of spiritual journey of my own. I tried to seek out my father and imagine the consequences of my suspicions. I guessed my mother wouldn't admit anything straightaway. But eventually, when I declared all that I'd discovered, she would have to come clean. The truth was always hard to face down, even over the phone, even for her. I would tell the story I'd come across: the locum work, the reason my father had been forced to take it; he had been despised and cast out, by the BMA, the GPs, even maybe at home. Yes, perhaps my mother wanted to make the world a better place as well but not like he wanted to. And there was I, a child, the biggest irony of all. While Papa was trying his hardest to obliterate the very possibility of certain children entering the world, I was stuck between the two of them, wondering on odd self-sorrowful occasions, as all children do, how on earth these people ever managed to get it together in the first place.

If I felt uneasy at this new version of events, I was beginning to despise the old version: all those years thinking he was a good family GP, a boring old doctor; thinking he'd been too well qualified to get into a practice. This now sounded like a sick joke. I recalled all those sixth-form notions about his decline and why he lost the wave in his hair, why his face turned grey: bankruptcy, financial hardship, those nineteenth-century sorts of things that fathers suffered. All the time I was thinking there was something missing, something not quite clear. But I had never suspected anything like this.

As I ran this new tape, I got angry with my mother more than him – for not telling me; for allowing me to believe what I liked, with apparent impunity. I did some research but didn't find his name in any of the relevant lists: the numerous societies that had gradually dwindled after the war. Either he used a *nom de plume* or was wise to the dangers of such associations. There would have been a need for secrecy. After all, he was a spy of sorts, an agent for the future. Everyone has two families, the one they're born to and the one they find of their own free will. And this was his chosen family. Outside of it he was demonized, probably even by his own wife. It was, no doubt, his biggest infidelity, unforgiveable. I found it difficult to understand either my mother's reticence or loyalty. Why on earth had she stayed with him? I guessed she would say it was like that 'in those days'. Yet what was even stranger about it was that I found myself feeling not just a little proud of him: for doing something he believed in; for doing something as well as he could and for getting a reputation. I was sure he had a reputation. He must have been well regarded for the articles to have been published. Half the world and more considered him to be wrong, but at least he thought it through; he believed he was right, he had conviction. And he acted. If he was doing what he thought was right then he had to be worthy, no matter what anyone said. But there was no way I could ever explain that to K. I didn't want to try.

CHAPTER 8

It was in the bagel queue again. Slater was wearing shorts, sandals, and brown woolly socks. Taken aback by his appearance, I felt in no position to refuse the invitation to join him for lunch. He didn't mention the articles or their author. We sat overlooking the slate roofs, and I almost asked what *his* father had done for a living, but thought better of it. He seemed different, and it wasn't just the seasonally premature shorts. It wasn't long before he revealed what the problem was; the walrus moustache rolled up and down as he ate, shedding words and crumbs in equal measure.

— I'm going to have to find another assistant. I've got to replace her. There's no option, I'm afraid.

I was speechless: was he blind to my association with K? I wondered again whether he had assumed, knowing her, that it was over already, and I came to wondering again how well those two knew each other, as he elaborated.

— Someone like that, you just can't put your trust in them. Her heart isn't in it.

There was a glistening of the retina, an economy of facial expression; his forehead creased a little more than usual, that was all. He had always known she held certain views, views that might be deemed antithetical to any reasonable scientific purpose, but she was, nonetheless, thoroughgoing. He had once held out hope that she might pull through and become the assistant he thought he'd originally hired.

K and I might have had our problems but I was with her now, despite Slater's confederacy. Yet I said nothing. I caught a glimpse of his stubby fingers and suddenly thought of them stroking her thigh. I thought of K lying there by his side. I thought of her hair falling, and her smile. I hadn't thought these thoughts for some time; well, not of her with Slater. I watched him taking his tray and filling it with dessert. His calf muscles sloshed like milk in a pail, and on his return to the table I watched him again, the moustache riding the words, up and down. I added only the occasional 'yes' or conciliatory 'no' of my own. Burgeoning lower limbs, abbreviated digits and that lost-to-the-wilds mouth: how could she possibly, how could anyone? But what had she called it: the Nam Vet voice. Was that not the sort of barbed hate you get from intimacy? I said nothing in protest. K's heart wasn't in it, he said, she wasn't to be trusted.

I held it in for a while, a few hours, before realising: whatever loathsome thoughts I might be suffering they had to be put off. They might be justified, yes, but there was still a code of conduct. So, how could I put it? 'The man you work for just told me he's going to give you the sack.' That would make her look up. She'd want to know how I had possibly got so intimate that Professor Slater, the notoriously reticent and aloof, duck-butt jerk might divulge such confidences just in passing conversation. She would press me to find out if I really knew him that well. What did we have in common? Nothing that I could think of, no reason at all for him to tell me what he'd told me.

It was a week later. I'd built myself up; I was going to tell her, I was determined. We were headed downtown on the subway, the night was unseasonably warm. The train was sultry, our mood desultory. She held my hand; our palms were sticky. It seemed like a final gesture, both of us trying to cling on, as if we'd rather take a pace apart. I don't think I'm wrong in thinking it was both of us who were having difficulty. I'd been trying to work out how to tell her, rehearsing it in my head, seeing her disappointment, her rage, her relief even. It hadn't just crossed my mind: she might welcome the news. And all the time I was sensing there was more to this, I was in the middle of a thing I couldn't quite comprehend, something between Slater and K, something personal that went back a long, long way.

On the train she started talking about families: how screwed up most of them were, how even the cosy families had things wrong with them. She seemed to have some family in mind; some epitome of good rearing that was, in reality, completely off the rails. She said a few things about her own home life but it was plain that wasn't it. She was picking on somebody else's Ma and Pa and eventually she came round to it.

— When you were stealing that scotch in your jam jars . . . you were staying with your father, right?

— Yes, but . . .

— And he didn't smell it or anything, didn't notice his supplies going down?

— No but . . .

— He didn't ground you or put you in line even?

As far as I remembered he hadn't said a thing.

— I don't think he knew what was going on. I was seventeen after all.

I told her, trying to laugh about it; I remembered lying to him, trying all the time not to breathe out so he wouldn't smell the drink on me. What was so bad in that? Hadn't she done that sort of thing? Hadn't everyone?

— Yeah, Yeah, but leading a secret life, that's another deal altogether. Wasn't your padre pretty good at that?

She had some miscreant scent in her nostrils, whether I wanted to talk or not. She was onto something.

— Was that around the time he was having his affair?

— I don't think I'd go so far as to say he was having an affair.

— Okay, was that round about the time he was reproducing illegitimately?

I laughed despite myself; I didn't care to check dates.

— Did he advise you? He was a doctor wasn't he? Did he tell you to take precautions? You did take precautions, down there behind the bus shelter?

— It was a rhododendron bush, it was a cave made by the
. . .

— But you did, didn't you? Take precautions. Down in your rhododendron cave.

I might have a child just like he had, one I didn't know about. That's what she was saying. Did I see the girl again? What was her name? Did I write? Why not? And the way K spoke I could see what she was circling on; I could see it coming but couldn't do anything about it. Changing the subject or defending him was of no use. She was circling on him; it was my father's example, it was all his fault.

— Yeah, yeah, that's why you adore him.

— Who said I adore him?

— Okay, that's why you're obsessed with him.

— Well, I . . .

— He was always so far away, always on the horizon.

I realised now, whatever lay behind this, whatever guilt, whatever articles had been written or beliefs held, whatever I was trying to conceal or route she was taking, now that fathers were in it this was a fight of some sort. My first, instinctive and meaningless retort:

— Unlike *your* father I suppose!

She mumbled something about all papas being the same, before really taking up the challenge.

— I hate my father because of what he does to my mother.

She pleaded as if I was blind to the obvious.

— But your mother's dead?

— Exactly. I hate him for what he goes on doing to her . . . and to me.

I kept quiet: a hard won, professional suspicion, going hand in hand with this new, edgy hatred of her. Claiming the role of victim was all very fashionable; best reserve judgement until everyone was heard, and in the absence of all-party testimony it was always better to be cautious. But K could read my averted eyes.

— No, he didn't abuse us, not in that way. He just loves her too much.

— She's dead for God's sake!

— Yeah, tell me about it! I once asked him why he never

remarried. He said she was still the beat of his heart; everything he did was for her. This was when she'd been dead ten years. It's safer for him, even more after she died. She couldn't get out of the mould he'd cast her in. More putrefying than any grave. I can't see her anymore, I haven't got a memory that hasn't been wrecked.

— Most people would give a lot to sample love like that.

— Being faithful, huh . . .you believe it. eh? Unwavering fidelity, cutting out desire?

— Aren't you grateful? And what about your father? You talk as if he's got a choice in the matter, as if he does this devotional thing of his own free will. Don't you think he just can't help himself?

— Maybe, but you haven't seen his other side. The businessman. Ruthless isn't the word. See that part of him in action and you'd find it hard to believe a guy like that could do one little thing that wasn't of his own volition. He's programmed to exercise his will, no matter what. The opposite of aboutia, I don't know what they call it but he's got it.

All K's fathers were baddies: her own, mine, and of course Galton, the biggest, baddest daddy of them all. We got off the train and changed platforms, with fate, or the future or whatever you wanted to call it, shaping up like an ominous, black subway tunnel. We stood separately, as the frill of disturbed air and the swirl of her skirt alerted us to the next train's incoming rush. And as we sat down in the empty carriage, my mind still whirring with the impossibility of telling her what Slater had told me, still second guessing at her probable reaction, she let me know exactly how much *she* knew.

— Why didn't you tell me the articles had come from Slater?

— What do you mean?

— You know what I mean. I found them again, only this time they weren't hidden under any cute little blanket. No, this time they were just sitting there, plain as day. On Slater's desk. Well, why didn't you tell me?

— Why should I?

— Why should you?

— Why should I? What does it matter?

What was really going on here? Slater had just happened to leave them there, right where she would find them. He must have known how they read, and he must have known what K would make of them. I couldn't argue with her, she was right. I could do nothing but think of stubby fingers and stretch marks, milk pails and moles. I heard the age-old squeal of bedsprings and wondered at the game Slater was really playing, and how K appeared to know the rules so well. I tried reconstructing events, to work out what might have happened. She may have reacted there and then, as soon as she found them, gone into a rant. In turn, Slater probably couldn't cope; he would have wanted to wash his hands of her immediately. Later that day, still shaken by her outburst, he'd caught sight of me in the cafeteria, thinking he could confide, thinking I was some big buddy just because of something he thought my daddy had written a quarter of a century before.

Finding the articles on his desk confirmed a few things to K. It was true what she had said all along: I kept secrets from her and should never be trusted. To me it confirmed that I'd been right all along about being caught in the middle of the two of them. Pictures of them consummating their research were coming and going. I felt like I was getting blamed for something that had a lot to do with other people. There seemed to be a dance going on: Slater, K, my father, even my mother. But it had very little to do with me. I asked.

— Did Slater tell you who wrote the articles?

She didn't answer, letting her hair fall even more than it usually did, so one side of her face was completely obscured, the curtain drawn. The other side was scornfully half turned away, pretending to gaze at an ad above the train's windows. The ad was for condoms and she turned to me silently, knowingly. I repeated the question. Louder.

— Did Slater tell you who wrote the bloody things? Did he tell you?

I felt like grabbing her hair and pulling it back myself, off her face, making her look at me.

— Stop shouting will you. What does it matter already? No, he didn't tell me, okay, is that all right? Does that satisfy you? You interested are you, like to buy the next best-seller?

She looked at me with the twinkle of renewed suspicion.

— Yeah, why are you so interested in this guy?

And as she said it I felt relief and disappointment at the same time. I realised she didn't know. I smiled.

— How do you know it's a guy?

The empty carriage was sticky with the heat and the sweet smell of gum. She ignored me. I glanced at the ledges of the seats to see if I could spot any deposits. In the dull brightness the fluorescent tubes flickered and the hand-hold straps overhead flapped like out-of-time dancers as the train pulled round a never-ending bend. K finally pinned her hair back.

— You're just like your father.

Again my heart raced; Slater must have told her after all. More than he'd ever told me. And suddenly I didn't care; I wanted her to know, anticipating a cruel kind of glory. My defence was ready. At least my father had conviction, that's what I'd tell her. And there wouldn't be any irony when I summoned my mother's trusted old phrase: 'in those days'. I'd mean it. I'd mean it all. My father was worthy, he might have been wrong, but that didn't matter. He'd stood up to be counted.

I didn't get to tell her any of this though, or what Slater had told me: about her job. She started talking about about my glazed eyes, the frozen river. Jealousy, bitterness or just spite, it was hard to tell.

— You've got a lot backed up behind those eyes, a lot you want, a lot you're scared of wanting.

— Oh, really?

— Yeah, you're scared of yourself, of the whole damn world, scared of what you want deep down.

Without thinking I jumped off the train at the next stop, not seeing her again until it was too late. Not seeing the hurt on her face, the pleading, the fragile lines in her eyes, not until I remembered it all, a lifetime later. That night K was absent from all thoughts, banished from the kingdom. I dreamt of Sarah and Janet Burns, and I couldn't tell the difference between them. They had one and the same face. I tried to pin them down, to look this woman, whoever she was, in the eyes. And I felt an irresistible urge, a compulsion, to see her again, even though I didn't know for certain who this third person feminine might be. It was a 'saudade' feeling, part of my past that I missed desperately, a known intimacy that I'd never had.

I woke the next morning to find a letter signed by a Dr Kathryn L. Romme, from a psychiatric hospital back home. She wanted to talk to me about an old case of mine. My last case, in fact.

CHAPTER 9

It rained from then on. It rained in a way that made me feel homesick. I felt nostalgic for that kind of damp gloom. Rain wasn't quite rain here. How wonderful and unlikely: the things you long for. It was a way of life I wanted. The sound of the newly formed leaves dripping and twitching, isolated echoes colouring the day; the gentle pit, pat, plash on shuddering, slithering surfaces. The random slant and swerve of the droplets, each a world in itself, falling, falling and changing the world it falls upon.

The slate roofs suddenly took on an all too familiar and gory look, bleeding a deep, wet grey. This wasn't a simple yearning to return to a specific place or time. It was to do with a number of times and more than one place. Part of it was coming from K. The impasse between us was sending me hurtling toward some dark, where-have-I-come-from tunnel where I flirted with my past, looking on Sarah in a new and old way: she was my best friend, sadly, suddenly missed. I forgot about the deux CV with its silly little horn, the business about fathers, the nonsense about money. This was all to do with ordinary feelings: a walk along a mundane street on a mundane day, a sideways smile, unanimous clinch or touching of hands, a shared look at Rachel or Simon, an agreement, a pact. The amygdala, the almond, or whatever K had called it, was working overtime, and I couldn't help thinking: what a pity memory couldn't act retrospectively, not only bringing it all back but building it again upon these moments, these strengths. And what a pity every sharing ends in division.

First I wrote then phoned, both in the same week. Rachel

and Simon actually spoke to me without drying up, keeping to it as if they would have talked all night if I'd let them. Sarah too, as if she was really glad to hear from me. I'd heard Richard talk of post-divorce bliss but never believed him, thinking it – this fondness thing – to be just his luck or his way of rationalising failure. Now, after one phone call and one letter, I wasn't convinced it would last. Possibilities were hard won things, I knew that much.

I also knew that with K, no phone calls or letters would do the trick. I would have to face her. It was a Saturday, a morning, I went round to her apartment. I thought of ringing first, but no, I had to see her. Harry let me in, smiling as usual. Suddenly it crossed my mind that he was smiling because Slater was up there with her now; he was smiling because of the fireworks that were about to go off; he was smiling because this had been going on for a while, Slater and K; he was smiling because he knew, and that's why he always smiled and that's why I didn't. Yes, it was to do with intelligence, a different kind of intelligence. It struck me then, Harry knew, he'd always known. About K and her stretch marks, K and her child, about K and Slater, about K and Richard, about K and . . . what else did he know? What else was there to know? I wanted to turn back but no, I was going to tell her now, whatever. I was going to tell her. Except she already knew.

It was still raining. She handed me the letter, her contorted face like the drizzled window. *With great regret . . . research assistantship . . . funding withdrawn . . . after much deliberation and consideration for the needs of all research projects.* So, he got somebody else to write the letter, or maybe it really was a case of running out of money. Maybe I'd misread him in the cafeteria and there was nothing personal. I pictured his calf muscles; I pictured K lying beside him. Why didn't I just reach out and comfort her? Why couldn't I? I'd known it was coming, at least I could be calm and considered: that sort of comfort, just a hand, just a word.

She saw at a glance, wiping her eyes with a red silk scarf, the colour darkening so it seemed for a moment as if her tears were blood; her eyes all the time widening and clearing, the scarf eventually dropping at her side in a pool.

— You knew already?

Still, the thought dawning as she spoke.

— You knew . . . you knew all along!

At that moment, of the various possibles and probables, forgiveness wouldn't have registered very high on anyone's list. But it was true. After skulking off to see my bison in the park and returning still full of guilt, I was forgiven. The trouble was I got nowhere near being able to forgive her – for the pictures I kept getting in my head.

The rain dried to a fine mist but it never stopped completely. The image I held of my father had settled after all the recent revelations, both real and suspected. The Dickensian wave had long since vanished, so too the greyness and the old-man creases and crumbs. Now there was a vignette: a bleak and malevolent background, tendrils of rampant growing-in-the-grave hair, as red as it comes; the face like the crumbling façade of an ivy-clad house, one that had long since lost its roof. He was beyond dead now.

I couldn't help but think of the Lovetts and their childless, love-full marriage. When Mrs Lovett had gone in for her hip replacement I'd found her husband crying by the forsythia on the doorstep. The first time they'd slept apart in half a century. I wondered what my and their lives would have been like if I'd been their child. Would that have made a good story? I guessed not. And I started thinking about genes and my dad, whether I was a homozygous or heterozygous carrier; whether I would indeed get the disease K insinuated I already had. Being him.

During those arguments, K and I edging warily back towards one another, she told me again, as she'd said before, how distant I was and how I didn't seem to care about those closest to me – my children and my mother. I kept quiet, thinking it was her right to say whatever she wanted; she'd lost her livelihood, she'd been through a rough time. But that didn't mean I'd stopped seeing her in compromising scenarios with other men. Quite the opposite. After her bad news K started smoking. This seemed to wrap the sordid pictures in a familiar, jarring allure. The final ingredient. She smoked with long fingers held soft and straight around her lips, and exhaled as if she were kissing the world.

It was a day like any other: wet. Having finally bought an umbrella, I'd sauntered down the sidewalks and alleys, on the way back from the buffalo. The Ojibway had been lying all alone, wrapped in a plastic sheet on my favourite bench so I hadn't stayed long. I avoided the bustle of the main streets, cutting down the back avenues and circling round in as much as the grid blocks would allow. My mind was a blank, until I saw Harry, and his smile. Then it all came rushing in again. The pictures. Once they started it was hard to stop them.

She seemed relaxed, stubbing out a cigarette and asking if I'd join her for some hummus and pitta bread. She started eating heartily. It looked like she'd turned the corner; the paper spread out in front of her, the jobs page. It had become a joke already.

— What about this one? Research Assistantship: to work with Professor Amim on a project investigating the kinetics of upper-limb movement during tooth-brushing.

She laughed. Her crimson nails clustered to her mouth, her lips rolling over the pursed fingers then ebbing back, as she chewed an olive. We had to clean our teeth, someone had to find out how we did it. But I couldn't keep shtum any longer. I wasn't the only one with secrets. I started with Richard first. She gave her usual riposte.

— What about him? Okay, so we flirted. How many times do I have to tell you? People flirt don't they?

Then there was Slater, the walrus, the duckbutt who'd got rid of her. She was onto him though, she knew something about his family history, she'd let me know when she was sure. But I wanted to know about him and her, and *their* family. Was he the father? Was Slater the one?

— Why didn't you tell me you have a kid?

She wiped her mouth and reached for a cigarette. She wasn't going to get away with pretending she hadn't heard.

— Well?

She lit the cigarette and let out a blue rinse of smoke which barely dissolved in the waning, rain-smudged light from the windows. I'd eaten nothing, she'd barely begun, yet she gathered the plates and stacked them.

— Who told you? How did you know?

— Why didn't you tell me

— I *had* a child, once. Yes. I don't *have* a child now.

Her earlier lightness fractured, she returned to the table and tapped her cigarette pointedly, the grey motes crumbling like fallen masonry into the black ceramic ashtray.

— What else don't I know?

— I had a baby, a little girl, I was young, she got a good deal. They were nice folks.

— And?

— And what? There's no more, end of story.

— Slater.

— What about Slater?

— Is he the father?

— Are you crazy?

— But what about him?

— Give me a break.

— So you and Slater don't have a history?

— A history?

— You know what I mean.

— You are crazy.

— Then who was he, the father?

— Some guy or other.

— You sound confused, don't you know?

— What is this? I get the sack and . . .

— You didn't like the project, you said so yourself.

— That's as maybe. Being rejected in that fashion is a major life event. Most people would be sympathetic, but what do I get? A madman giving me the third degree.

— I just think you owe me an explanation . . . a child is also a major life event, or can't you remember who he was?

— Who?

— The father.

— Remember him, ha, that's a joke. The present can never live up to the past, or is it the other way round? In any case, good old padres aren't ever who you think they are.

— So you're not sure who he was?

— No, I know him, well . . . he was just not the person I thought I was making love to that's all.

— Sounds like it's not your memory that's playing tricks.

And I saw that old 'what-have-I-been-saying-all-along?' smile flicker across her face. Her cool had been clawed back, as she twisted the cigarette out in the ashtray, sending a last, valedictory wisp of smoke between us.

I started to cough. Desperate for air I rushed to the unopenable window, seeing the glass towers rise into the grey swirl above the slate roofs, and across the city a plane taking off, silently ascending, ever upwards like an importuning, inarticulate hand. So small in the scape of things, a child's paw. She emptied the ashtray.

— Why are you so angry? It was years ago, it's got nothing to do with now.

— And what happened to . . .

But by then I couldn't enunciate complete, original thoughts. K returned with the ashtray.

— Look, there's two kinds of determinism going on here. One, I have sex with a man and get pregnant. I'm not saying my own free will wasn't involved but what I am saying is that there's a biological factor which is straight material, cause and effect. And then we have the other kind of determinism, the perpetrator kind. The one you get to thinking you've got a free vote on. But it's all a trick, an illusion, you can't choose really. I couldn't be such a big determining factor in someone else's life. It was impossible. I was too busy determining my own. I couldn't raise a kid, not then.

Closing my eyes, as much with jealousy-fatigue as anything, I came out with a final, pitiful round of hackneyed accusations.

— So, it was just ambition.

— No. Why are you condemning me? What the hell's wrong with you? You must have instigated hundreds of adoptions. You know better than I do, there's no simple right or wrong. It's a cultural thing as much as anything. For God's sake, in Rome it was better to be adopted than to be brought up by your own folks.

I thought she was going to come up with a case study. Yet whatever she did, I'd got her on this one, I was sure of it.

— But we're not in Rome are we! There is a right and wrong about telling someone the truth. God knows you've put me straight on that one enough times.

— I never lied to you. I just never told you.

— And you think that's better?

— Look, you've made a bunch of choices in your life; you chose to be a father, you chose to be who you are. After a choice is made you can't go back on it and say that was wrong, strike it out. Life's already written, already history and no history's right or wrong. You can't go round telling me I'm wrong about part of my life.

But wasn't that what she herself had always preached? I didn't say anything. She was suddenly crying, the tears smearing mascara down her cheeks so she looked like some silent-movie heroine just got up from the railway tracks. I'd seen tears, when she lost her job, but I'd never seen this before. Frantically lighting another cigarette she fingered the rim of the ashtray.

— Don't you think I think about it? Don't you think I feel? What gives you the right?

I rushed out of the apartment just like I'd rushed off the train, just like I'd rushed off to see the bison after she got her letter. I didn't raise my head to see if Harry was smiling. Like two shy buffoons in the elevator, heads tilted timidly away; I knew he would be, and I wasn't. I knew Harry had been laughing at me all along.

CHAPTER 10

Two days later she told me who it was. Yes, Bleanau Ffestiniog: the youth hostel warden. He was a red-head too. She had a penchant, it was out in the open. And I wondered whether that was the explanation. Otherwise, what did she see in me? Coming back for more, and more: neither of us could just leave it. Exeunt and enter, over and over, this was the mad rhythm of our being together; a rhythm we couldn't seem to change.

I replied to Dr Romme courteously but without undue enthusiasm, wondering what she wanted to know about Janet Burns. According to the doctor's letter, there seemed to have been some problems. Holly was fine with her adoptive parents, there wasn't a difficulty there; it was Janet herself, something had happened to her. The doctor couldn't discuss it in a letter, but she would like to talk to me; would I be coming to Britain in the near future? I grudgingly gave her my number, asking if a phone conversation would suffice, saying otherwise I'd be back late summer for the Child Care Conference, hoping she'd have gone away by then.

Richard was right. Richard was always right. No such thing as a last case. Round about this time I got another postcard from Guillermo, saying he'd worked the grape harvest on Crete and had some plans to pick oranges on the Peloponnese; how he'd met up with a brother and sister from Marseille: Zinnie and Veronique; born in Algeria; true friends, he said. They were all saving; after the olive and orange harvests, they had plans: India, Thailand. He asked if I could keep my ears and eyes open for Janet. I was incredulous. What was I supposed to do about her from three thousand miles away? This particular card had taken weeks to get to me; Guillermo was probably in Timbuctoo by now. I wondered if he was going to make it back for university, and what his father was making of his travels. It filled me with a dry, fragile dread; it felt as if just thinking about him might induce something bad to happen. He might visit; turn his sights west and then there'd be no getting rid of him. A parasite. That's what he was. I didn't ask him to write me postcards; he was nobody I knew.

As for my other incoming mail, Sarah sent some school photos of Simon and Rachel which I placed on my desk with something resembling pride. And, of course, Janet's paintings had been trickling through. Literally: the last one had got soaked in the rain on its way to my door. That, too, had taken an age to reach me. I sat it on a radiator to dry out, not bothering to open it. I'd seen it all before: the envelope hand-painted, as puffed and brittle as a poppadom, indecipherable scrawl blotted on the seal. It rested there a week, or maybe two, before K spotted it.

— You haven't opened it?

— Why should I? It'll just be like the others.

— But you haven't even opened it!

— Okay, I'll open it, I'll open it . . .

The envelope almost crumbled in my hands, the picture inside bursting out: like a seedling unfolding its first leaves in one of those speeded-up nature shots. There was a gushing crimson torrent and a gorse-green cross with – 'Holly RIP'— printed in black on its apex. At its base a small rip in the paper. I wondered whether this was an ironic symmetry or just plain tattiness. I waited for K to pass admiring comment but she was busy chasing a photograph that had fluttered from the envelope. The snapshot was of Holly. K paused over it, checking who it was, before throwing it face down on my desk. Strangely she didn't say anything about the painting, and even looked as if it might have depressed her, or made her angry or sad or something. She looked lost, as if she'd been wandering alone and was shocked by my presence. Again I didn't reach out. I held the painting up to the light between us, thinking I might get an admission of Janet's artistic fallibility. But K said she had to clear her desk, that there was something she wanted to check out at The Institute's library before she lost her ticket. She kissed me brusquely, turning almost into the wall to avoid eye contact.

Later that day my mother phoned, sounding a little frail and jaded. But yes, she'd had a wonderful time on her tour. She listed a few hills and lakes, none of which I knew. When I eventually asked her about my father – her husband – and the articles, she laughed outright.

— What nonsense are you jabbering on about now?

— But . . .

— Have you heard yourself? Your father a radical? Ha!.

— So you don't think he wrote anything like that, he didn't belong to any of the societies?

— What nonsense. He could barely write his own name.

— Then tell me why he couldn't get into a practice, why couldn't he get a job. He was well qualified wasn't he? He had experience. All those years in the research post. What was he doing?

— Your guess is as good as mine. Some things just aren't for knowing.

She started chuckling to herself again at the thought of what I'd suggested, and was unable to carry on for a moment. I felt the possibility slipping. What proof did I have? What crumbs of evidence? There was a lot riding on this one. I felt the hole starting to grow again: if this tape got wiped there'd be craters, devastation; there'd be consequences. I sensed it. My mother gathered herself, but I could barely hear.

— I eventually worked out he was just one of those characters who isn't terribly, wasn't . . . despite the bluster and bravado, that was his cover, that's why he couldn't get a job. He just wasn't that good at what he did.

Yet another tale of dear old Papa: the failure tape. I didn't want to believe her. I couldn't.

CHAPTER 11

My mother died within a month of returning from her final pilgrimage. I never knew exactly where she went on her journeys, those times 'all to herself'. She came back crowing about Celtic-sounding valleys and rivers – Welsh, Cornish, sometimes Scottish – and what a bargain bed and breakfast she'd managed to find. Forests and hills rather than cinemas or theatres; there were never any cities or mention of friends. And when she returned she always looked like a different person; she had a glow about her, a brightness.

Not this time. It was her cleaner who phoned. Her heart; they said it was probably the Peter Stuyvesants that had done it.

— You'll be glad to hear it was in her sleep. I found her smiling in her bed.

— It's very kind of you to call me.

But a cleaner? I nearly asked her: shouldn't it be a doctor doing this sort of thing, a policeman or a priest or somebody?

— She looked just like a little child, playing hide and seek by closing her eyes. If you ask me she knew she was being taken, as though she'd willed it this way.

Cleaner she may have been but she obviously knew my mother well. I couldn't remember K saying much to me before I left. She bought a card and flowers, offered commiserations. But she was busy, still clearing her desk and checking out that one last thing in the library. I never realised it took so long to leave a job. I suspected she thought that losing your mother at the age of forty one was no big deal, given her own experience, but I didn't get to talk to her about it. It felt as though I took a breath and suddenly I was in the air, sitting in the palm of one of those tiny, importuning hands. My only memory: the rain finally stopping and the sun coming out, just as the plane took off.

It was a dry landing as well. Everyone was going round gasping and sighing, it was all over the newspapers: hosepipe bans and stand pipes. Winter and spring, hardly any rain all year, and now summer was kicking in there was a real drought. The fields and hedgerows were arid and sun-singed; the sedge had turned to bush. I hardly recognised it. My mother was dead and I had to dispose of the family abode – was that ever a home? – and now with these burnt browns and dusty swathes off into the distance, the colour of my own past seemed to be changing before my eyes.

From what my mother had told me over the phone before she died, I understood, if unwillingly: my father was no longer a possibility. No hero and only a dabbler: a man without any real principles, that's what she'd said; he didn't care enough about anything, only ever followed her into the Fabians, that's what everyone did 'in those days'. He steered clear of controversy. Surely I remembered that much? That's what she'd said: 'self-regarding, the best that you could say of him'.

I'd heard some of it before, the old back-biting and nastiness, but part of it was new. Gradually this third tape took hold. The other tapes – my father as good old family GP, my father as geneticist and radical writer – were fading fast. I checked it out with the papers I found in the house. They drew a blank. The research post was non-descript: an obscure corner of an obscure department; health administration, number crunching. He wasn't capable of writing what I thought he'd written. He said 'whenever you can, count' a few times to me when I was a boy; he may even have liked Galton. But as his dearest wife pointed out in that last phone call: 'what man of bloody science doesn't? They have their gods too you know.'

I still couldn't figure out why Slater had given me all those knowing looks or indeed the articles in the first place. Only later did I come to see. They were familiar, yes, but not because they'd been chiselled out of my old man's life's work and beliefs; in the end not because anyone at all that I knew had written them. That was too simple, most improbable. All along I'd been looking for an author, thinking it was someone close to home, someone I knew intimately. It was hard to admit, but later I saw: the articles appeared familiar because they had the trace of a long lost grammar; they were certain and sure. They had the hint of what I was looking for. Conviction. They gave the impression of knowing how to care about people. And I cared as well, at least I wanted to. I wanted to help, to devise long-term answers, to find remedies. I wanted to care and to do something: about Grey Owl sitting on the park bench with those frosted-glass eyes; about the children I'd come across in some of my cases; about Janet Burns and Holly; I even wanted to help Bjorn Borg. But it felt as if first of all I had to find that missing link, the dark shape that had been haunting me, and I had to find it before I could do anything. I had aboutia, the affliction that K was always talking about. Whatever I'd lost I'd have to find it. Until then I was useless.

The funeral was a farrago. My mother left strict instructions: time, place and music. The chapel's crumbling sandstone walls were still darkened with damp despite the drought. The muffled singing: 'The Lord's my shepherd I shall not want . . .' followed by all too prominent loudspeakers, crackling and squeaking: 'What a marvellous night for a moondance, with the stars up above in your eyes'; but both the Psalm and Van Morrison were outdone by a solitary thrush, singing on top of a nearby yew as we all trailed out towards the grave. Sarah, with her little one (Rachel and Simon came to the wake but not to the interment); Richard and the cleaner; a couple of distant aunts; one or two cronies; even the Lovetts turned out, walking sticks and all. There were no horses, only the steady clip-clop, clip-clop of severe heels, dissolving as people went off the tarmac and onto the grassy knoll near the hole in the earth where all life seemed imminently bound. There was to be an ash tree, no stone.

Sarah impudently threw the first handful of soil onto the coffin – this was my mother not hers! But as she did I realised: there was more that I could and should have asked that woman down there; questions that I couldn't quite formulate, even now while they nagged at my aching head. All about my father and this supposed sister of mine; even questions about Sarah and about Rachel and Simon, things she wouldn't by rights be qualified to tell me; I wanted to ask her about everything. Seeing Sarah like this was too much; with a bald-blond thing resting on her forearm, and that more-grey-than-black dress; the thin Indian cotton, too thin, too alluring. It wasn't funeral attire, couldn't she see? Fondness, I was discovering, was dependant on distance. And dearest mama, ten feet under: she'd be condoning Sarah and condemning me. Hadn't she always wanted a daughter rather than a son? I realised then, it had always been that way.

The children shocked me at the wake; both of them wearing Doc Marten boots, Rachel with a minuscule skirt and loud pink and black tights drawing every eye to the length and curve of her legs. How old was she? They both slumped on the arms of chairs, their laces untied, swinging insolently from their dangling feet. I was told it was the fashion, but it just reminded me of the Ojibway back on his bench near the buffalo pen. It set off a rush of irritations. I thought of the fathers and The Ranch. My children. I wasn't there with them; it was too much for me to be nice about. And there was Sarah, talking as if things were just the way they always had been.

— Have you seen? Simon's eczema has cleared up, must be the country air. And yours seems a lot better since you've been away.

The children waited morosely to grab at the dessert food, which they'd been denied until all the smoke-cured ham and organic cucumber had been consumed. My mother always planned meticulously. They moaned as if they saw me every day and I should be used to it, regardless of whether my mother, their grandmother, had just died; ignoring the fact that I'd been out of the country for a good part of the previous year and they hadn't seen me for months.

The Lovetts hobbled into the room briefly, each taking one of my arms and talking in clipped, duet style, as if they'd rehearsed the night before.

— We are so sorry, Philip.

— Your mother was a grand woman.

— One of the old breed.

— She had her way of doing things.

— Different.

— And we mean that in a positive sense, don't we dear?

— Oh, yes, a most positive sense.

It was time for talking opposites. Farewells are like that, forgive and forget. Objections dissolve. Almost. The Lovetts had been heard to say my mother was never the same after Greenham, and maybe there was something in that. They were obviously put out by the taped music in the chapel. It was a live recording, Van getting stuck on the line: 'I want to make love to you tonight'. I guessed it was my mother's little joke, together with the peace poem which punned on 'piss'. Despite it all Mr Lovett seemed to want to tell me something.

— Philip, I wonder . . . there was one thing, about the house, we've been meaning to mention it before but . . .

I imagined some hedge that needed trimming, or the tenants misbehaving, not putting their rubbish out on the appropriate day. But Mrs Lovett nudged her husband's arm.

— No, not now dear, it can wait. Now's not the time to worry Philip with little things like that.

I pictured their garden for a fleeting moment; the bright yellow forsythia and the ground elder creeping around the scorched soil of their bonfire plot. The history of flames. It felt like there was even a mystery in that, another thing I should have asked my mother, or someone, and then I wouldn't have come to feel like this: as if the whole world, everyone, even my own children, they were all comfortable with things, they knew what was going on, but I . . . I . . .

Then the Lovetts and Rachel and Simon were ushered away.

Sarah, with Arthur fast asleep in her arms, shut the door firmly behind them and the hubbub of voices was instantly muffled to a drone.

— What's wrong Philip?

— What do you think?

— I know, your mother . . . it's difficult, having to sort everything out, having to be the grown up in a house where you've never been allowed to be . . .

— No, it isn't anything to do with that.

— I didn't think it was . . . so?

And still I felt the pummelling, inarticulate questions. I wanted to ask Sarah: why it went wrong, why she seemed so happy, why I didn't. What was the secret? What did she know, what did everyone else know that I didn't? I wanted to ask her why Rachel was wearing such a short skirt and looking at me the way she was. Since when did our daughter start wearing lip stick? And I wanted to ask her what I should have asked my mother, all those things that had flashed before me as I looked down on the coffin. But what were they? What did I need to ask? No matter how hard I strained I couldn't quite get to the place and shape of the questions. I didn't know what to say.

As if in need of respite, I pictured K briefly, crying and tearstained in accusation. I even fleetingly recalled her laughing all those months before, enunciating the question. Asking: *Are Simon and Rachel your children?* Inquiring. Prying. I knew exactly what she was really saying: everyone's unfaithful, betrayal seeps into everything. I wondered who K was with now, at that very moment. I couldn't help myself. It had only been a week but I was alert for the signs. I'd phoned a number of times, I'd asked her to send my driving license so I could hire a car, I had left in such a rush. She said she was nearly done and would hop on a plane as soon as she could. I didn't believe it would happen, let alone take time out to consider whether I wanted her to.

Sarah was still waiting.

— So, what is it?

— Sarah . . .

— Yes?

— Are Rachel and Simon my children, am I their father?

I knew of all the possible questions, this was the wrong one, and I didn't mean it in any petty sense. No blood tests or dabbling with my past, with their pasts, with our pasts. I just wanted something more, something that transcended it all, something to say that Sarah and I once met and that there had been a sort of wonder when we touched, when we looked at each other; I wanted confirmation that what I remembered wasn't a dream, wasn't some sort of eidetic memory or confabulation. I knew it was gone. I didn't want the wonder back; I didn't want to touch her now, or for her to touch me. I just wanted the stranger holding the stirring baby boy in front of me to resume as the person in my memory, stashed away like some personal treasure.

But Sarah's smile was unrecognisable, incredulous.

— It doesn't mean they don't love you, the way they are. They're like that with everyone. It's just a phase, they're just kids . . .

We both looked out of the window. The children were in the garden now, Rachel's carrot top glowing like a beacon. She was my daughter all right: no getting away from it; and Simon too, and it was more than just the eczema. The face and the body movements, he was like a splintering off. I was just a face in the mirror. He was three dimensional, more me than I could ever be. That wasn't what I meant though.

— It's just . . . I was blind to a lot of things when we were together. I didn't see any of this coming.

I nodded towards Arthur, who was smiling in his sleep, wind most probably. Sarah and I fell into that child-admiring resignation, the sort of off-wards look that says: this is as far as it goes. And it felt as if that was the closest we would get to articulating the future: looking blankly at children.

— Life's lived forwards and understood backwards, who was it said that?

I didn't know and didn't care. There was nothing else to say. Sarah later told me she and the children were moving out of The Ranch. The two fathers hadn't lived up to expectations, though she didn't say it out right.

— The Ranch is more a place for adults to be kids, not really a place for growing up.

Reading between the lines it appeared the fathers had been a little aggressive with one another; one of them had suggested blood tests. This made me feel better, but Sarah still wanted to live in the sticks. Everyone was talking about the new possibilities: computers and the new software, she was going to try and work from home. She'd rented a cottage on the borders and wanted my consent to put the house in London up for sale so she could buy somewhere.

Why did she need my consent? I was still paying the mortgage, or part of it. Was I really? We'd have to come to some sort of agreement. Did we need to involve the solicitors again? It all costs money. Inexplicably, I felt a pang of nostalgia for the chaise longue, as if that particular seat would never have the same *je ne sais quoi* in any other house. I restrained myself from saying anything. I was sick of the clunk of my own thoughts. I was chasing an answer but what was the question? My father, after a brief flurry, was no longer a possibility in any respect. Neither my mother. My ex-wife, happy on her own with whoever's offspring, was also off the list. And my children: they were banging away at the 'we-don't-know-you, we-don't-want-to-know-you' drum. I couldn't go near them and could see no hope anywhere. Until K phoned.

CHAPTER 12

The line was bad, we had to shout. In trying to find my driving license she'd come across the snapshot again on my desk: Janet Burns' daughter, Holly; the baby who'd been adopted. Later, when the story was up and running in my head, I guessed she'd found the picture right next to the school photos of Rachel and Simon. K asked about Holly's hair.

— Was Janet Burns a red head?

— No.

— Could she have dyed it?

I recalled the teenage photos of her at the Greenaways.

— No

— Was Holly's dad a redhead?

— Not as far as I know.

— Then where did it come from?

She sent the driving license by express and slipped a photocopy of the snapshot in the plastic casing, so the face sat just above my name. There was a mark, like a smudge, on Holly's face, and the hue was heightened by the colour copying: she had hair like a blood orange. And that's all I saw, as if for the first time: the hair. Even allowing for the barmy copying, the detective in me was roused. Janet Burns' hair was almost black. The man in prison, Holly's father, God, or whatever his name was, he had rasta locks: blond, no carrot tips to be seen. I didn't know the gene thing for red-headedness, whether it was recessive, heterozygous or just pot-luck. But I knew my father wasn't the only flame-haired procreator on the planet; I wasn't entirely stupid. Hair alone wouldn't have convinced me. The thing that sealed it was what Mrs Greenaway had said about the Janet's real father being an older man – that and the sight of the hair and face together.

The last time I'd seen Holly, when she was twelve months old, I hadn't seen anything familiar. She was still a baby. But now, in this badly duplicated portrait – a child's face, a bud still forming – it felt like the answer and question bundled into one. Destiny. No other word for it. I cursed myself for not seeing it before; not just in the snapshot but when I'd seen Holly in the flesh. What stopped me from seeing? And what about Janet? Was I blind to her as well? I scrutinised every memory I had: all my dealings, the interviews, the whole case.

Did this explain everything – my fingers in her hair and my compulsion? It was commonly known that blood relatives – fathers, daughters, brothers, sisters, those separated from birth – when they encounter each other accidentally in later life they experience an attraction. Like meets like. K had talked about it once; there was a name for it but I couldn't remember. The one thing I didn't do was reflect, for even a moment, on my unfaithfulness and why I might be so promiscuous with the possibilities. I even thought I'd solved the riddle of the dream – Simon looking back from the doorway with those big black eyes. It was all prophecy, a warning: telling me to keep clear, to stay away from my own blood. But it had nothing to do with Rachel or Simon, nothing at all.

Checking what I still had on file in Richard's office, I had remembered the dates accurately: Janet's mother would have been about the right age; from Wales, a country girl, just how my father liked them. There was nothing in the files to enlighten me further. Luckily Richard didn't ask too many questions. He was harangued by phone calls most of the time I was in the office. Divorce solicitors. He was going through it again; I should have placed money on it.

I rang the mental hospital but received no clear cut answers. They weren't allowed to talk about patients over the phone, no matter that all I wanted to know was whether I could come and visit. I finally got through to Dr Katherine L. Romme. A few days earlier I'd been intent on avoiding her at all costs, while I mopped up my mother's affairs. Now I dropped everything, cancelling the accountant and an appointment with the estate agent in case I overran. I had to see Janet Burns. I needed permission, an excuse, a direction or pass or whatever Dr Romme handed out for people – so-called non-relatives – in order for them to see patients. There was a time when I'd never wanted to find out anything about my supposed half-sister, let alone speak with her. Now I couldn't wait. I didn't stop to think about this revolution in my feelings. I had a thing I thought I'd never have. Certainty. I knew what I was going to do and nobody was going to stop me.

Dr Romme didn't want to meet at the hospital: something about an awkward colleague and the case being officially out of her hands. She had an 11.30 meeting in town. We arranged a rendezvous in the old market square, she said it was on her way, we could grab a coffee. I got a parking space on an adjoining street. With certainty came a change in *modus operandi*. No time for walking now. I rented a nice two litre, five gear Renault, complete with electric windows; feeling a little off kilter, like a tourist in my own home town.

I found her under the old horse chestnut at the edge of the square. A thin woman, almost emaciated, with greasy blonde hair parted in the centre. She sat lightly on the edge of the bench like a troubled bird, clutching a scuffed leather bag to her chest; I briefly imagined all her cases, the lives stashed inside, floating out should she ever open it. We went to a small, thatched cafe with oak settle seats. No time for ceremony, I gobbled my shortcake and drank the coffee straight down. She sipped tentatively at hers, pushing it to one side to cool and nibbling privately behind a hand at her Madeira cake. She got a file out of the leather bag. Inside the file there was a little black notebook and another book covered in grey canvas. She looked in the black book fleetingly then tapped her fingers on the cover.

— I am unable to say anything specific about Janet's condition, you understand. But I think you should know, during her stay in hospital she experienced certain difficulties.

She used the past tense, I didn't understand.

— Is there still a Section Order in place?

— No, the restraint lapsed some while ago, in fact . . .

She hinted at a couple of incidents since Janet's admission, which of course she wasn't permitted to elaborate upon because of patient confidentiality. But these incidents were partly the reason Dr Romme had written to me.

— Can I see her?

Dr Romme looked like she was ignoring me.

— Did you know, Mr Eyre, that Janet entertains fantasies about you? Fantasies of a sexual nature.

She said it with a note of menace in her voice, as if it was a warning. Far from being embarrassed, I thought we were finally getting somewhere. I hadn't yet revealed my hand but I wasn't about to hide it away either. It didn't strike me as at all odd that this doctor could play the confidentiality card and then come up with a sexual fantasy or two, as if these might be less private than whatever else had happened. Could I see her? That's all I needed to know. But something was pushing Dr Romme forward, the bony face pinched to a point in determination, she almost spat as she tried to emphasise the importance of what it was she'd just told me.

— You do not seem that surprised, Mr Eyre? You should be aware that the fantasies are of rather a sadistic variety. Er, dark, shall we say.

I think I may have twitched at that, but I must have smiled as well. Maybe it was because she hesitated about her choice of words, it seemed to slacken her purpose.

— No, Mr Eyre, you misunderstand. Janet's fantasies, they are largely to do with your death, your demise. What I am saying is, you are most definitely not the perpetrator, Mr Eyre, you are not the do-er but the done-to. And in all of the fantasies, without exception, the sadistic intent appears to be an act of revenge. Janet would appear to be aiming to get her own back on you, Mr Eyre.

— Revenge for what?

— That I cannot yet say. Janet seems to hold you in peculiar regard, she appears fixated by you.

This was a little on the edge but it was feasible. Janet was bound to sense something, some affiliation, some connection. Dr Romme paused to look at me, and I looked back, attempting to show where I stood: no culpability on my part, and Janet isn't as mad as you're making out; she's my sister. I didn't say it but nonetheless made it clear; I wasn't scared of any half-baked fantasy.

— Could I just see her?

I nearly got the snapshot out of my wallet and held it up like they do in the movies. Do you recognise this face? Does it ring a bell? Wrong sort of plot and definitely the wrong moment.

— Perhaps that would resolve her problem, if she saw me in the flesh. Can I just see her? Is that possible?

— If you can find her, Mr Eyre. That was the other reason I wrote to you. She left the hospital, against our advice, without provision being taken for her medication. She left in the middle of the night without word, as the result of an incident.

There had been some trauma, the details of which the doctor was unable to divulge, for reasons of patient confidentiality, or so she said.

— She left us some while ago now and we really need to locate her. I think she may be in danger, Mr Eyre. Or, in extreme states of stress, she may even pose a danger to others.

She looked at me gravely, her eyes bulging, appearing like they might finally give something away. But I was too disappointed to take heed.

— Then why wasn't there a Section Order?

The doctor turned briefly to the black note book, flicked its pages as if judging whether to tell me something, then closed it and sipped her coffee.

— Ah, that's a complicated matter, Mr Eyre. What we need to ascertain is . . . has Janet attempted to contact you at all recently?

I answered in the negative, just as the Lovetts came into

the cafe and looked as if they were heading my way. I should have known; it was their sort of place, timbered and twee. They looked like they had some news. I cowered but something stopped them, I don't know what. I eventually looked up and they were in a window seat, waiting to order, as if they hadn't spotted me at all. The doctor got up to get a serviette from the counter and I kept my head turned away, just in case the Lovetts were trying to catch my eye. I spied the doctor's black book and was tempted to pick it up and take a look. When she returned to her seat I decided I might try a different tack.

— Oh, I just remembered. She sends me paintings. I suppose I did get a painting from Janet, must have been about a month ago.

— Did it have an address on it?

— No, it had been sent weeks, if not months, before. She was probably still in hospital.

— Are you sure?

— Yes. It had gone via my old address. The tenants usually send them on but with this last one, rather than sending it on themselves they had handed it to the agents and they, in turn, passed it on to my mother. Then she forgot about it, it didn't get sent on for a while.

— Did it have a date on it then? How do you know all this?

— My mother told me before she . . . she phoned to make sure I received it, she felt bad about keeping it for so long.

It was a disappointment to say the least, getting asked questions when I was supposed to be the one conducting the inquiry.

— So, Mr Eyre, since then there have been no paintings, or letters?

— No . . . and yes, I'll get in touch if she happens to . . . contact me.

It was clear Dr Romme wasn't going to divulge more, and what she had said sounded to me like scaremongering. There was a madwoman on the loose, she might be dangerous and she had her eye on me. Dr Romme, with her pinched nose and popping eyes, was just closing ranks. I'd done enough of it in my time. As five minutes ran to fifteen, she gulped the last of her coffee. It left a rim on her upper lip. She gathered her jacket and papers in a rush, not putting the file back in the bag, or the books back in the file. I offered her a lift and she sat in the passenger seat with this bundle on her lap. I dropped her off and watched her for a moment, shuffling items from hand to arm, scuffling like a wilful accident, full of chaotic purpose. But who was I to mock? Her rushed departure had left me with a gift. There, on the seat beside me was the little black book, the one she'd taken out of her file and referred to fleetingly in the cafe. I checked the inside cover and sure enough, in a spidery scrawl on the first page – *Janet Burns: Supplementary Case Notes*. I could and should have shouted out. Instead I stashed the book in the glove compartment. I was in fourth gear before checking the rear view.

I knew I might not have much time. A few hours, a day or two at most, before the dilemma of handing it back kicked in. Yet I found myself driving out of town, to the hill with the pine trees, the one I'd walked up with my father all those years before. I parked up and all but ran to the top, leaving the notebook in the car, a last pause of conscience or a final prising at the memory. I conjured a picture as I walked: the barrel chest, pushed to the fore by the straps of the rucksack. Was Janet Burns really his daughter? As I reached the top of the hill the breeze riffled through my hair; it brought no clouds but buffeted the marauding crows above the trees. In amongst the fallen cones and broken branches lay a dead, eye-less rabbit, like a sacrifice between the pine boles; it was almost hidden by the erupting, shallow roots. I wondered why the crows hadn't yet devoured it. I scanned the burnt rolls of land, the pitiful river and dried up plain, and recalled that my father had brandished a walking stick, one with a knot for a handle, and that he was wearing a pin-check shirt and green corduroy trousers. His bright hair flapped in the wind much as mine was doing now. I'd never managed to remember this much before. But I saw it now, and I thought again of who he might have been; I reviewed the tapes: the doctor, the eugenicist. And I was flushed with a quick pride. Perhaps my mother had lied after all; perhaps she hadn't known the full story or was too bitter.

All I wanted was some glimmer of commitment and faith; to be able to believe in him. For him to be worthy.

Yet as I snaked back down between the hurdles of gorse and heather I remembered more and worse: I was walking the hill in vain, playing the wrong tapes. I remembered Janet Burns. There were no words, no more words to come from him, would never be. All that was left was a sordid possibility. The past was gone, and would always be silent, blank and blurred. How could I have thought otherwise? His trousers may even have been brown and woollen. I wasn't sure anymore. His shirt may have been plain blue. I couldn't see it now. Within ten minutes I was sitting at my mother's bare desk, her papers all but cleared, with Dr Romme's notebook open in front of me.

PART THREE

Janet Burns (formerly known as Janet Greenaway) – admitted June 1987.

15.6.87

Janet has been sectioned after attempting to take her own life. It is thought this attempt was made on hearing of the crimes allegedly committed by the father of her daughter, Holly. A consideration in this case is the fact that although Janet agreed to Holly's Adoption Order there is often a backlash when a mother realises she will never see her child again. Janet was considered a severe risk even without this, for family reasons (as detailed in the case history).

5.7.87

Janet attends the voice workshops but is often silent. It was three sessions before she spoke at all. Today, by her standards, she was vociferous. Marius was in full voice, with his preacher's rant, talking of 'Him up above' and looking from side to side, as if God might be spying on us all. Janet interrupted him by asking a question: 'But what about the hands?' It was apparent she feared the hands so much that she felt compelled to say something, despite everyone looking at her. I asked her to say a little more. She stared at me as if I was not there, and Marius was soon talking again.

Marius has always been difficult to manage during the sessions. Curiously, at the moment he regularly dons a pair of bright yellow washing-up gloves. Some have started calling him 'Marigold'. This is strange because he has never volunteered to partake in cleaning or portering duties as some patients do. Neither has he ever suffered from OCD, under its more common definition; he is not preoccupied with cleanliness. I am more inclined to see the gloves as another attempt at imitating tangible illness. I thought initially it was his gloves that prompted Janet's remark about hands.

6.7.87

Janet insists that she does not hear voices, yet I suspect she might not be telling the truth. She struggles to string two words together and fails to fit in with the group. Once trust has been established, Marius and the others are rarely reluctant to let the group know what they hear; often they cannot help themselves.

I explained to Janet that the voices should be heard not denied, and that by giving them expression they might be calmed; I claimed, not disingenuously, that they were always better out than in. I reassured her that the medication was important as well, but that it was not a cure-all. It might dull the voices in the short term and I assured her that while some of the voices might be hostile, they might be tamed even without the drugs.

Janet continues to react to the sessions as if being asked to play a game without knowing the rules. Given this vulnerability, I was not the only one to warm to her. In a room full of real and imagined voices, silence can stand out. Dr T commented today that Janet appeared to have become my *cause célèbre*.

Yesterday Janet received one of her regular visits from Guillermo B, a younger male friend. She also receives occasional visits from Alan J, an older male friend, who it appears formed an unreciprocated regard for her at a previous clinic.

10.7.87

Janet's confidence has grown in the group so I decided to address the issue of voices directly. The conversation went roughly as follows:

'What voices do you hear, Janet?'

'I've never heard voices. I see hands.'

'Yes, the hands. But do the hands speak to you?'

'No, they looked after me, they got me out of trouble, they, they . . . but now . . .'

'And what did they say to you when they were helping you?'

'I thought he was . . . I thought he was God.'

'No need to be embarrassed. What did God say?'

'I can't remember.'

'Try.'

'He was real. You don't understand!'

'You wouldn't hear them if they weren't real.'

'No, I didn't hear him . . . he was real. It was just his hands that come back.'

'And what do they say?'

Janet paused here, as if trying to remember. There was a palpable horror in her voice when she eventually responded:

'Hate and love . . . love and hate.'

She has never before talked this much in the sessions. The rest of the group broke into spontaneous applause, and Marius, emulating my own enthusiasm, touched Janet's arm. His hand inevitably strayed before being repelled; Janet evidently knows how to handle him.

15.7.87

I was mistaken – 'hate and love' were not heard by Janet. These words are the tattoos on the hands – they are part of the visual hallucination. It is increasingly clear that Janet hears no aural hallucinations. In today's case conference I reported to Dr T, amongst others, recapping on what progress had been made. The hands first appeared after the birth of Janet's daughter. They related directly to the child's father. As well as emotional factors, a repressed rape perhaps, there were obvious postnatal, hormonal considerations. Dr T's contribution – 'the poor tortured soul, thank goodness for the depixol'. He hinted that he had something else he wanted to try. I suspect this might mean something more radical than an increase in dosage.

17.7.87

Janet seems to barely consider Holly, though she did say this morning that she 'missed something'. She went on to say she could recall Holly's face instantly – 'I don't need to try, it's always there'. I continue to encourage her painting. Last week I also provided her with a journal. The painting goes on regardless. She often enters the therapies room in a somnambulant state and emerges an hour or so later with a spring in her step. The journal seems a less successful outlet. She moaned today about its matt grey cover, saying it restricted her in some way. She said it looked like the fog in her head. She ripped some pages out, saying that she intended to send them to people but, almost as soon as she did so, she became baffled and forlorn, not knowing who she could send them to. The only person she corresponds with is a Mr Philip Eyre, the Guardian ad Litem in her daughter's adoption proceedings. She sends him paintings. I took the opportunity today to inquire why she continued to send Mr Eyre paintings. She did not seem to know herself, yet she did offer a somewhat confused explanation of how she came to give him a picture in the first place.

It was on the occasion of an interview, in connection with Holly's adoption, one in which I suspect Janet had been particularly vulnerable. The interview in question took place at the respite clinic. It appears Mr Eyre saw some of her paintings and asked if there was anyone to whom she would like to send a painting. This is a common tactic for social workers, but more usual in their questioning of children. It establishes levels of bonding with those to whom the child is supposedly close. I assume Mr Eyre was trying to ascertain the level of Janet's bond with Holly. From what I can make out Janet made no mention of her daughter, according to her own account: she was just struck by the fact that she could not think of anyone she wished to present with a painting. The next time Philip Eyre visited she gave *him* a painting, and from that time on Janet has continued to send him the occasional picture. I understand Mr Eyre has never responded.

It is clear that Janet fixed on Philip Eyre as a paternal figure, someone not only to 'father' (or at least make provision for) her own child, in the absence of the real father, but also as someone to father herself.

20.7.87

In the morning we sat together on the patio outside the TV lounge; both of us watched a line of ants carrying crumbs of food. She was engrossed for some considerable time, probably ten minutes or more, and then she asked whether I could hear the brook babbling beneath the ground. She tapped her foot on the lichen-mapped paving slabs to confirm her meaning. I assured her there was no river anywhere near; indeed, no water at all save the hospital's hidden pipes and sewers.

In the afternoon I was told by the ward sister that a stream had been diverted into underground channels and tunnels when the hospital had been constructed, some hundred years before. She assured me though that no one in her time in the hospital had ever heard the running water below.

21.7.87

Janet spent much of the morning observing the small pied birds that wag across the flagstones and the songbirds rustling from bush to bush in the grounds. When her friend Guillermo visits he tells her all about their habits and gives them their proper – sometimes even their Latin – names. One or two of the other patients are prone to laugh at Guillermo. He is only a young boy, barely eighteen, but very bright and most knowledgeable about the natural world.

The hospital is host to a number of cats and I have often seen Janet perched on the small stuccoed wall which runs parallel to the dining room windows, watching the cats creeping or sleeping on the soft green moss of the neglected patio beneath. I have seen her more than once around the back of the hospital, in the pebble-dash court yard where the cats scavenge near the bins. Guillermo, alarmed at the threat the cats posed to the birds, brought in bells, though many of the cats were feral and it was impossible to approach them.

Only Guillermo visits regularly. Alan J. has come once or twice but now seems to have stopped, most probably realising his affections were not being returned. No-one else has visited. A bunch of flowers was once mysteriously left with the receptionist, shortly after Janet was first admitted. On reflection I think this was Alan J., though it was never confirmed. Guillermo is the only person who seems to offer relief for what Janet describes as the 'thudding and fog' inside her head. This is surprising because he could well have proved an aggravation. His compulsion to name everything amounts in its worst extremes to a personal mission. He does this with trees and flowers as well as birds, not to mention architectural features and cars. Janet told me that when he first saw her paintings, he even asked why she liked crimson lake and vermilion so much. She admitted to being astonished: everyone called it red; no one had ever called the colours by their proper names before.

The day before yesterday I came across Dr T peering out into the grounds, watching Janet and Guillermo on one of the benches under the old beech trees near the gate. He shook his head when I suggested Guillermo was a good influence on Janet. This is another matter on which our opinions differ. We also talked about the problems I was having with Marius, and the latter's worrying interest in Janet. Given Marius' history I think we should intervene. He was sectioned after an incident at his previous clinic, the same respite clinic at which Janet had been resident prior to admission here. He assaulted a nurse, grabbing her breasts and not relenting for some while, and only then after being forcibly injected with a sedative. The nurse in question has not worked since. Marius has been in prison several times for sexual offences, but on this particular occasion escaped lightly. As per his notes, I have never decided whether Marius' voices are genuine audio-hallucinations or just role-playing in an attempt to avoid criminal prosecution for his miscreant behaviour. Dr T remains convinced that such behaviour is entirely caused by the voices.

Marius has done the full circuit of possible institutions: respite clinics, therapy wings and worse (as can be seen from his notes). Last week he captivated and horrified us all in the group session, Janet included, by talking about being PP9'd while in gaol. I thought at first this was a prison regulation or another form of sexual deviance. It soon became apparent, however, that it was in fact the name given to a form of prison beating. A PP9 is a large cube battery, used by inmates in the older prisons to power their radios and cassette players. The punishment is meted out by inmate on inmate. A battery is placed in a sock and swung like a cosh, about the head and other vulnerable parts of the body. Sometimes the acid leaks from the battery into the wounds. I subsequently discovered the punishment is almost exclusively meted out on sex offenders.

23.7.87

It is now apparent that Janet is beset by two hallucinations – one recurring, one haunting. The former is the image of the hands; they bear the tattooed words 'love' and 'hate' on the knuckles. These appear regularly, though the medication is having some effect. The main variation, not caused by the medication, is that on occasions she sees the hands as beneficent (they come to her assistance) and on other occasions she sees them as malevolent (they are pursuing her). The latter version has been more common during her time with us.

The episode at the guest house where she was staying with Holly shortly after the birth (as recounted in the case history) is a prime example of the benign hands. A shop fitter doing contract work in town was also staying at the guest house, according to Janet. He initially joked with her, but his attempts to be humorous became increasingly lewd. At the dinner table on the night in question he put his hand on her thigh. She repelled him. Later that night, after he had been to the pub with the other workmen, he tried to get into her room. Janet says she was half asleep in bed at the time. She reported that the hands materialised out of the wallpaper and locked, then shored up the door, while the man pushed at it. In effect they saved her. Eventually they vanished through the door and sent the workman back to his own room, or so she presumed from the subsequent silence.

It is recorded in Janet's case history that the landlady of the bed and breakfast house denied that any of these events could have taken place. The guest house in question, being requisitioned by social services, was not supposed to take in male boarders. It has since been struck off the Social Services' list.

It appears that the hands became malevolent after Janet learned about the crimes of Holly's father. Janet now often fears they may harm her, and when they appear it tends to send her into a severe state of panic.

The haunting hallucination is similarly related to her daughter's conception, and particularly Janet's perception of the so-called 'virgin birth'. This hallucination is not necessarily fearful or benign, though on occasions it can become either. It does not recur but is relived. She recalls it and it has become a riddle that she is unable to solve. Her rational self cannot come to terms with her irrational recall of the event. The memory in itself seems to be psychotic. She continually denies intercourse took place with Holly's father, and yet she fell pregnant. No matter how many times she tries to rationalise different possibilities, different causes and successions of events, she is always left with the impossibility of what she remembers. Similarly she has failed to explain to herself why she calls Holly's father 'God'. A crisis of belief, not least in her own perceptions, has ensued.

25.7.87

The therapeutic programme (the medication coupled to the group sessions) is enjoying a modicum of success. The horror of the hands is at least controlled. The hands now seem to be disempowered. Today Janet told me that she had seen them floating across the room in handcuffs. They made no sound but, according to Janet, looked like they were convulsing and struggling. She even admitted to feeling sorry for them. In my opinion this change was in spite of, and not because of, the increase in the dosage, which Dr T insisted upon.

Dr T expressed concern at today's meeting about the visits from Guillermo. I am of the opinion that they are entirely positive. Janet tells me that Guillermo can calm her when she is agitated. He gets her to imagine a lake and to picture the trees and clouds all around the water, to feel the wind washing over the scene and stirring up the waves. He then tells her to imagine the wind dropping, ebbing slowly, so she can see the trees gradually fall calm, and the clouds slow until she can see a reflection of the leaves and branches in the still water. Janet says that it almost sends her to sleep.

Apparently Guillermo carries a lump of rauwolfia root around in his pocket, something his mother sent him to keep him calm. I warned Janet against using the root if Guillermo ever offered it, yet saw no harm in his meditations. They appeared to help her in a way that our treatment programme could not. It has become apparent that Guillermo talks extensively to Janet, not only about the types of plants they see in the grounds but also about their usage for medicinal purposes. Janet relayed some of these conversations to me: how meadowsweet and willow both contained salicylic acid, used in the production of aspirin; how shepherd's purse could stop heavy bleeding ; how scabius was good for skin disease ; how hawkweed was good for jaundice. Such talk engages Janet's enthusiasm and she was even motivated to obtain a Collins Wild Flower guide from the hospital library.

I perceive this contact with Guillermo, and Janet's consequent innervation, to be a necessary antidote to the effect of the drugs. I see no harm in the talk of natural remedies, providing it remains talk. Dr T is of a different mind. In the meeting he used the fact of the continuing hand hallucinations as vindication. He insisted on a further adjustment to the dosage.

26.7.87
Today Janet described the hands in a most worrying fashion.

They had changed, apparently developing a new potential. It seems that they can now become her own hands. She described seeing them circling the dining room, hovering over all the other patients, over the nurses and auxiliaries, and told me how she suddenly recognised them; the lines on the knuckles, the broken nails, the silver ring on the little finger. The only thing she did not recognise as her own was the 'hate' and 'love' tattooed across the knuckles.

After discussions with the staff nurse and ward sister I have gained a further insight into Dr T's perspective of the case, one that has not been entirely evident in the case notes or meetings. It appears that Dr T views Janet to be promiscuous.

Janet has never had many visitors but those she has received in the past, as I have detailed, have all been male. Dr T interpreted these visits, and Janet's tendency to walk with her friends in the hospital grounds, as sexual liaisons. For various reasons, partly to do with her medication, there is no contraception plan in place. However, in my opinion, Janet has shown no sexual inclination towards either Alan or Guillermo, or anyone else for that matter. Guillermo, according to the ward sister, is gay in any case. This is apparently disputed by Dr T.

29.7.87

Janet's second attempt to take her own life may have come as a direct result of Guillermo's departure. Apparently he has gone travelling for a year before taking up a place at university. This attempt was more serious than it might have been. The nurse checking the wash room first thought Janet was washing red paint from her hands, as she does on most days.

29.8.87

Dr T has used the suicide attempt as a reason to increase the dosage to the upper limit. I suggested more alternatives but Dr T denied there was sufficient evidence to alter the medication programme, inferring the group work might be wasted on a case such as this.

On the full dosage communication has proved almost impossible. Janet looks as if she has fallen into a hole; her voice, when she manages to speak, is just a trickle. I remonstrated with Dr T; I have had these struggles over dosage levels in the past, with different patients, but he has never before been as unwavering. I happened to suggest that there was likely to be some connection between Janet and her mother, that suicide leaves a trace. Dr T enquired whether he had heard me correctly. Evidently he had not checked the case notes thoroughly. He was unaware of the family history and that Janet's mother had committed suicide. He seemed to think this might offer many explanations for Janet's state.

10.9.87
Janet said today that she knows something is missing. She sat staring at the cemetery beyond the hospital grounds and commented on the headstones sitting 'so still and keeping quiet'. She told me how she sometimes sees the men who work there, the groundsmen, digging graves and cutting the grass. She said 'they're alive, they're great, they've escaped'. I made a point of observing the men for myself but found it hard to see what Janet found attractive about them. They wore boots caked in mud and grass cuttings. All wore standard blue overalls, one or two had beards, even those without had burgeoning, unpruned moustaches and stubbled chins. A couple were balding, with unfashionable pudding basin haircuts circumscribing gleaming bear crowns. They appeared insouciant and I could only think that it was this that Janet was remarking upon.

Janet said that she thought she might know someone in the cemetery. As she put it: 'someone out there, under one of the stones, someone might be under a cross or a vase, someone I love'. She talked as if death had lost its meaning, as if she might pop out for a cup of tea with whoever it was. The dosage is a considerable obstacle at the moment.

21.10.87
This morning Janet was transferred to a medical ward for a

surgical procedure without my prior knowledge. Her social worker knew nothing of it either. When presented with the consent forms Dr T claimed that Janet had signed them of her own free will. I reminded him of the dosage he himself had insisted upon and that 'free will' was hardly the appropriate term to use in this instance. He argued that this was exactly the issue: in the absence of her own prerogative, as her carers we were duty bound to act in her best interests. He said it was the only course of action given her obstetric problems. I was unaware of any such problems. He spoke, as he often does, about 'poor tortured souls' and assured me it was the 'medical chaps who made the call', and that there was a considerable history, detailed in her health records.

Whatever might be detailed in the records, Janet, I have no doubt, did not in full conscience give considered consent for the hysterectomy.

1.12.87

This week marked the second full week of sessions since Janet's postponed operation and the subsequent lowering of her dosage. Dr T offered no objections to my suggested programme; I suspect he may have received a reprimand from the anaesthetist at least – besides the problem of her medication Janet was also suffering from a bad cold at the time. The full medical details leading to Janet's obstetric treatment are still not available. The new treatment programme will consist of the eventual abandonment of the medication altogether in favour of hormone trials; there will be no voice workshops but regular and informal one-to-one sessions.

After several weeks muddling through each day without seeming to know whether the sun had risen, Janet now appears to be experiencing a period of sustained improvement, both in mood and levels of rational reflection. She mentioned the hands and the shed today, and I might well be forced to re-examine my earlier assumption – that the denial and repression evident in her accounts of what happened in the shed resulted from a possible rape. Janet today recounted certain descriptive details of her relationship with the character she calls 'God' – Holly's putative father. From these accounts there is still no mention of intercourse but it is apparent that such intimate contact as she recalls was indeed warm and tender. If anything it would seem that *he* was the unwilling, or at least tentative, participant. She is convinced of the reciprocal nature of the relationship, and is convincing in her description of it.

The shed remains crucial to Janet's problems. The source of repression, whatever it is, will surface there, I am sure. It is a highly eroticised site which has gained significant literal and symbolic importance. It is the only venue in which Holly's father ever appears. He is not in prison as far as Janet is concerned, he resides in the shed. As she talked today it seemed as though the shed was merging with other memories. She talked of a river with a stone bridge, and I asked her whether she was talking about the shed or the village in Wales where she spent the first few years of her life. She didn't reply but it appeared that fantasy and reality, biography and confabulation were merging in such a way as to cause her severe confusion.

In yesterday's case meeting I mentioned the erotic significance of the shed to Dr T. He quipped about the 'earth moving' but declined to comment clinically.

3.1.88

Janet has declared summer or late spring to be her favourite time of year (chiefly because of the flowers and migrant birds). This link with nature appears to be a positive force in Janet's life.

This afternoon I adopted new tactics: I related some personal details about myself. I told her that when a young girl I wanted to be a writer, and now consoled myself by reading. I mentioned her painting but did not ask the inevitable question about what she might have wanted to be. That was not my purpose. I chatted generally about how my father was Dutch and how, as a consequence, I liked a pinch of salt in my coffee;

how my mother was Surrey born and bred, to be a Doctor's wife and so a little shocked to end up a 'lady doctor's mother' as well. I attempted to lighten the mood, joking that there was no longer much Surrey left in me. Our conversation continued for some time, with Janet looking at least as if she might be interested, though she remained reticent for the most part. The medication is still having an effect.

25.1.88

Janet has mentioned on a number of occasions that she thought she 'knew someone' in the adjoining cemetery. This suspicion culminated last week with the suggestion that her mother might be interred there. Having made the necessary enquiries, today I was informed by a council officer that the grave of her mother would probably be unmarked but could be located on the cemetery's East Avenue: I have been given a number.

Before the expedition to the grave I consulted with Dr T about my apprehensions. I was aware that the exercise was potentially futile, not to mention dangerous. He tried to dissuade me. He suggested the lack of adequate medication threatened the exercise. My counter argument was already familiar to him: if no initiative was taken Janet would almost certainly regress, another suicide attempt would surely follow.

Janet commented on the plants in the cemetery, some snowdrops and aconites, remarking on how they were flowering early. This was a very good sign, reminiscent of the progress made when Guillermo was a regular visitor and when she used to consult her Flower Guide. I asked her whether it was Guillermo who had first told her the names of the flowers. She explained:

'Guillermo told me the names, he's good at names. But I knew them already, I knew what the flowers were, I just didn't know what to call them.'

I asked her how she could know them without knowing their names? She replied:

'Their smell, I know what they're like, when they come up,

when they flower, where they grow, the type of shade they like, how damp they need to be.'

She spoke with certainty and confidence, as if everyone knew that a plant's name was its least significant feature. I was unconvinced. This all sounded to me like childish wish-fulfilment: finding something out and then saying you knew it all along. It appeared to be working cognitively at the fantasy level and it seemed appropriate not to encourage it. I attempted to change the subject by asking about the first voice she ever heard, when she was a child; whether it was her mother, or indeed whether she could even remember a voice. At the moment I asked her she stopped in front of a Victorian gravestone, and proceeded to narrate aloud the inscription instead of answering my question. It made rather morbid reading:

Joshua Morgan – passed away 1875 aged 31 – To be with Christ.
Infant twins – Mercy and Grace Morgan – Passed away 1876,
aged 2.

At the bottom of the headstone a terse line, all on its own:
Reader what think ye now of Christ?

Janet's voice sounded fearful, but I persisted with my question: was she able to recall any voices from her childhood? She eventually said she could not remember. I reminded her that she had previously told me things that her mother had told her when she was very small. She remained obdurate:

'Did I? I can't remember. Why are you asking if I've already told you? You should tell me, I've forgotten.'

I interpreted this to be more than just the residual effect of the drugs. I pressed the question, asking if she could recall a male voice: whose was the first man's voice that she could remember hearing? She said something about her adoptive father, how he always spoke with a pipe in his mouth:

'I used to think it was his ventriloquist's doll. His words looked like smoke, and I remember thinking they sounded mean. His mouth was always clenched. I remember thinking his words could burn.'

I have previously considered her adoptive father, Mr John

Greenaway, as a figure of overbearing authority and even possible abuse. Nonetheless I have been brought to reconsider this because of his positive influence. It was his allotment and his shed in which Janet used to grow her seedlings. She pursued such activities largely as a result of his encouragement. He himself had grown too arthritic to use the allotment, but even after Janet had left home and given birth to Holly, he maintained its rental, purely for her use.

It was only after considering this conversation for some time that I realised what was perplexing about it. I had asked about words and voices and she had replied, effusively by her standards, but with pictures and images: the pipe, the smoke and the ventriloquist's doll. Janet appears to have no aural memory at all. She is marooned in a landscape which is tangibly silent, yet it appears a landscape rich in colour and texture. This is most apparent in her paintings, which are, as I have variously observed in the past, strangely eloquent.

When we eventually found the grave there was no cross or name, it was completely overgrown with just a piece of weathered wood sticking out of the ground. I might have checked the site beforehand; Janet was shaken by the sight. Last year's brambles were encroaching from an adjoining, older grave which was ornamented with black clay edging. Janet asked why her mother's grave did not have similar ornamentation. She became increasingly angry and started tending the grave, wading into the old, dead grass, her arms soon becoming covered in burs and old leaves. She tugged and tore at the vegetation despite my assurances that we could return with some implements should she wish to do so.

Walking back to the hospital from the grave I asked her if she now remembered her mother's voice from when she was young. Janet reacted as if sleep walking. This again was not just a hangover from the higher dosage; there was something else at work.

27.1.88

Two days after the trip Janet admitted that a part of her thought the wildness of the vegetation on the grave to be beautiful and in some way appropriate. 'It fits her,' she said, 'it's how I imagined her.' She pictured what the grave might be like in the summer. She described this image to me: 'the grasses full of seed, all purple and green, swaying with that little tree, all on its own,' This was the sycamore sapling, which was just a year or two old; it had sprung up by the grave's wooden marker. Janet told me how the sapling would, in the summer, come into leaf, offering a little shade to the smaller plants below. She described it all in great detail in a way that extended far beyond the confines of the grave and the cemetery; it was as though she was describing somewhere out in the country. She talked about getting her own bramble bush for the grave, and giggled at the thought of her mother's grave producing fruit. She asked: 'Is that what they mean when they say the hair carries on growing?' She may or may not have been joking. In Janet's perceptual world she often confuses the literal and the metaphoric.

She also recalled the negative feelings aroused by the visit. She recounted how Guillermo had talked about *his* mother, how she had returned to her homeland and refused to come back to Britain because, and this is what Guillermo had told her, there was no one to tend her mother's grave. She has told me this story before but this time Janet cried as she asked, 'who was there to tend *my* mother's grave?' The tears were borne of anger as much as anything else. The impact of the medication was finally less apparent than a definite emotional response. This was the most promising development arising from the venture.

The visit to the grave provoked a considerable rage, and, noticeably, she expressed anger towards me, not directly for taking her there, but whenever I questioned her about the voices from her past. It appears that such questions are causing a vibrant irritation. This is most encouraging.

Janet later in the session admitted that some part of her had expected to see a face; she had gone to the grave with fantastical expectations, as though her world would change forever after finding it. The fact that she could reflect upon this and call the expectations unrealistic was a gauge of just how far she has progressed. She said 'there might have been a name at least, a vase or something'. She just wanted to see the signature of some care, however small. Sight of the grave gave rise to several speculations about her (birth) father: 'What sort of man could leave her like that? What sort of father was he? Did he love her? Ever? Did he think of me?' She also voiced some concerns about her mother's own family: 'Didn't they care either? Didn't they want to know?' Janet has never had any contact with any of her extended birth families.

28.2.88

Janet has become increasingly disinterested, growing wary of me and all the other members of staff, despite my personal approach and the assistance given to her in tending her mother's grave. Because of this today I tried something new; I started reading to her. I happened upon this strategy by accident. Janet showed me a print in a book of bucolic paintings by various artists; she had borrowed the book from the visiting library. The scene in the print was set in November (this was reflected in the painting's title); most of the leaves had fallen and were gathered in damp looking piles, which were situated on a vast lawn. This area was surrounded by well established oak and beech trees, such as you get in the grounds of large country houses. A young woman was sitting alone on a bench; a gardener was raking the leaves nearby while looking at her. Smoke drizzled upwards from one of the leaf piles. I didn't recognise the name of the artist but was struck by the way in which the picture seemed to tell a story and how it had sparked Janet's enthusiasm.

I asked if she had read a certain book (*The Go-Between*), which seemed to me to connect with the scene, in terms of era and setting, if not season. She had not but showed a degree of interest when I summarised the story. She reminded me that her mother had read to her when she was a child. As detailed elsewhere, she could never remember what was read, only the surname of a girl in one of the stories: 'Burns'. As detailed in the case history, Janet came to adopt this surname. She said she was sure there had been other stories, but she could not remember them. I enquired off the cuff whether she would like *me* to read to her. She laughed at first but then agreed.

1.3.88
Yesterday it was just a few pages, not even a chapter, today it was more. If Janet appears interested, I continue. If she starts to doze, I stop immediately and suggest some other activity. I couldn't get hold of a copy of *The Go-Between*; we have started with an abridged version of *Tess of the D'Urbevilles*.

10.3.88
Janet was unaffected by Tess' fate, though she remained interested until D'Urbeville returned as a lay preacher. Then she seemed to purposefully fall asleep. We have since struck on a popular choice in *Jane Eyre*, notably a book containing a female character called Helen Burns. Janet is not entirely convinced that *Jane Eyre* is the book that her mother read to her all those years ago, though she appears interested in all aspects of it, so much so that she got hold of her own copy (same print as the one we read together) and has read ahead. She still wants to continue with our reading sessions though

She is fascinated by the image on the cover – an oil-cracked vignette of a woman, with impenetrably dark surround. The sleeve notes are missing on her copy and this morning I explained these to her: that it is thought the picture might be a portrait of Charlotte Brontë painted either by her sister, Ann, the one who was not so famous, or her brother, Patrick Branwell who, like many of the Brontës, died when young.

15.3.88
Today Janet started talking in a new way about the characters: about Jane and Rochester, about St John Rivers and Helen Burns. It is as if she has suddenly been dragged out of a dire isolation and been rescued by the words and events of the book. She talked as if the story and characters were real, as

if it was a world to which she belonged without inhibition, and as if these people were her own family. She talked of the places, of the colours and smells, with such clarity that I was confused as to whether she had really experienced such things. I was convinced that there was a horse chestnut tree in the grounds of the hospital with a bench ringing its bole, after hearing Janet talk of sitting on such a bench. I happened to remark on how important it seemed to her and suggested it might be an idea to take a walk there together. Her expression gave nothing away, there was no purposeful joke I am sure. Later I checked with the groundsman as to the tree's whereabouts. He informed me there was not a single horse chestnut to be found within the hospital's perimeter fence. After a little research I realised the tree in question was almost certainly one depicted by Charlotte Brontë, and the bench was part of the fiction.

Janet is prone to take the metaphors and similes from what we read and revive them, so they suddenly assume a literal dimension. The other day I noted how a 'ridge of burning heath', which in the novel is used to represent Jane's inner state, became a real ridge, with real flames in one of Janet's paintings. Also, as if to contradict my assumptions about her voice memory, Janet has started quoting lines from the book at odd hours in the afternoon and evening, outside of the sessions. Initially I interpreted this as childlike enthralment, remembering my own credulity on first reading certain books; treating the story as real life, the fantasy time as actual, historical time. Janet, however, is not that young or naïve, and I am beginning to think it is something more. The grey journal has re-emerged, even if she appears to be keeping it well out of the reach of those, doctors or patients, who might want to read it. I have not pressed her on this. If she wishes to show me or discuss the contents she will do so in her own time.

20.3.88

Janet likes to hear me talk of the Brontës' lives. Today she asked me to read from the biographical introduction. It has

179

not gone unnoticed that they were motherless, raised for the most part by their Aunt Branwell. Janet demanded a lengthy explanation of 'Wesleyan' and how and why their aunt was thought to have 'encouraged Anne's tendency to religious melancholy'.

Of all the characters she is obviously most intrigued by Helen Burns, and understandably so. It appears that she is meditating on the character, in an attempt to revive memories of her mother. This has so far appeared unsuccessful. She still cannot say for sure whether this is one of the books her mother read to her. When considering the story, Janet cannot quite understand Helen Burns' illness or why she gets laid up in bed. As she told me: 'Helen Burns wants to die, she wants to give all of herself away'. Janet finds this odd only in that, as she said: 'she knows exactly what she's giving away. She thinks it's worth something, but she still wants to give it away.'

27.3.88

Janet today remarked on the other name connection: Eyre. She joked about if she were to marry Mr Eyre they could name their daughter Jane, or alternatively take her surname and call their child Helen, and so forth. This appeared harmless enough until it started taking on some of the manifestations of her confusion between the literal and metaphoric. She seemed suddenly to take the possibility of a union between herself and Mr Eyre seriously. She recalled an occasion on which Mr Eyre held her in his arms and was stroking her hair. Evidently the fantastical, still prone to take over, was prominent in this recollection. It seems that while discussions are centred on a fictional story (*Jane Eyre*) Janet's problems seem to be in abeyance. When the conversation reverts to elements of her own life the difficulty appears never to have gone away.

I asked her whether she had sent any paintings to Mr Eyre recently. She told me that she had enclosed a photo of Holly with the last painting she had sent. I calculated this would have been around Christmas, when she received photographs from Holly's adoptive parents. Since then, however, she has resumed painting but not sent any. We talked for a while about the fact that Jane herself was something of an artist, and about the Brontës' own bent. Janet was reluctant to talk about her own paintings. She is now much more private about the output; I rarely see the pictures. As with her notebook, she hides them away.

29.3.88

This morning I saw Janet in the therapies room and caught a glimpse of one of her paintings. I asked her why she painted rivers. She replied that she still heard the babbling brook under the hospital. This time she went on and described it as more than a brook, saying that one day she would have to travel up-stream to the place by the river where she had lived with her mother when she was a child. As she gave details of this prospective journey her description grew confused. She said she had recently dreamt of faces reflected in the river – the faces of Helen Burns, Charlotte Brontë, Anne and Emily Brontë, and many other women. Her mother was present in the dream as well. She said she had to follow all these reflections, follow the river up to its source. She described how she would have to trace a route up through the valleys, up to where there were 'more stones and no reeds', up to where the 'hills crowded round' and where she said 'the stone bridge crossed the river'. As she described this journey, in increasingly breathless fashion, it struck me that she was speaking as if she were lost in those hills on a misty night, lost but with a defiant hope.

30.3.88

This morning I took Janet to a garden centre and we bought some items for her mother's grave – some bedding plants and a blackberry bush, so the grave can now really bear its own fruit. Janet has made a wooden cross herself. Hopefully these will act as incentives for her to continue with her treatment now the Section Order has lapsed. Dr T has not changed his mind and still will not support me in asking for the Section to be extended – or, at least, I will not agree to his conditions for supporting me, namely an increase in her dosage.

3.4.88
I feel the more I get Janet to think about the hands, the more likely it is she will see a glimmer of forearm, a torso or a face. Remembering is, after all, the main route to forgetting. I am still convinced that Janet's experience in the shed resulted in her peculiar amnesia. Whatever Janet's conjectures, about how Holly was conceived and about the father's divinity, I have come to very much doubt whether this man, the man in prison accused of killing his wife and child, is in actual fact Holly's father. I suspect he is less God and more of a Joseph.

5.4.88
Janet today became agitated: first she challenged my questioning about the hands, saying that I 'never stopped'. She said: 'You want the hands yourself, you're jealous.'

Then she started moaning about the medication (she remains for the moment on a very low dosage). I explained how her improvement, the fact that she was feeling so much better, and the fact that she could even complain, was due in part to the drugs. She accused me of being 'Dr T's little helper'.

I attempted to explain that medication was helpful, though not the solution in itself. It was sometimes necessary to control behaviour before it could be understood. She accused me of sleeping with Dr T. I did not bother responding. She said she had made me blush. Given Janet's previous energy levels this banter could be seen as encouraging. However, there is also an alarming aspect to it. She went on to catalogue a number of obscene sexual fantasies, all of which featured Philip Eyre. She said she dreamt them the previous night but talked in a way which suggested they were quite familiar to her. In the scenarios Mr Eyre was submitted to a variety of acts involving knives, ropes, poles and chains. In each of these situations Mr Eyre was at the mercy of hands bearing the inscriptions 'hate' and 'love'. It was unclear from what Janet said whether the hands were her own, and it was as if she were simultaneously remembering, inventing and imagining these scenarios as she described them. Her face became animated and she appeared to enjoy telling me what she was telling me.

10.4.88
Janet has been showing increasing signs of irritability, behaviour which is not all explicable in terms of medication withdrawal. Today she screamed at Marius just for sitting in her proximity in the TV room. Although she has had no recent contact with Dr T, she has mumbled a few things about him that might easily be construed as threats. Her irritation is not confined to Marius and Dr T; she is also aggressive towards nurses and other patients, and indeed on occasions towards me. Though we are proceeding with the readings and occasional one-to-one sessions she appears increasingly uncooperative. She is angry with her friend Guillermo for not writing to her. Today she brought in one of his old letters and almost tore it up, saying that she could not understand it. She showed the letter to me and rather than reading *Jane Eyre* we spent an hour pawing over it, discussing Guillermo and what he might mean by certain of his phrases.

When writing the letter Guillermo was engaged in casual fruit picking work, while on his travels – the grape harvest somewhere in Greece (it was impossible to decipher the address). In the letter he described work in the terraced fields, how lunch was taken under the shade of the olive trees, sometimes a pan of soup, sometimes a bowl of salad soaked in oil, and always bread and olives, water and retsina. He wrote about the evenings, of the scent of jasmine, of fig trees in verandas, of cicadas and oleander, of drinking raki and ouzo in the cafes, and how the bark of the trees on the street had been painted white. Janet was puzzled by it all. As well as the exotic descriptions, the letter went into some detail about the work, describing how the sultana grapes were dipped in a siccative and then laid out in the sun to dry. This baffled Janet, as did the detail of how he and his friends had been offered work by a farmer known as Michali Pelicano, on account of the size of his nose. Janet said none of this made any sense to her. She kept on saying, 'why is he telling me all this?' To her, it was as if the letter was written in a foreign language, one she would never be able to understand.

She was angry at the fact that Guillermo had now not written for some time (this letter dated back to the end of last summer, though I believe she has received one or two since then). She appeared anxious and worried, and expressed concern that he had originally said he would be returning in the new year. I reminded her of what she had told me about one of the more recent letters: of his plans to travel to India with his friends. She shouted at me: 'He's going to university. He's got to come back. It's all arranged.' At the same time she complained that by choosing to do a Business Studies course Guillermo was just going along with his father's wishes and that he should really study botany or ecology. She spoke almost as if she herself were Guillermo's parent, admonishing him but also wanting to guide him. She had never previously expressed any anxiety about Guillermo and it was not clear why she should start now. From the passing comments she has made since Guillermo's departure I have always assumed that the letters offered up a ray of hope. She has previously reacted to them as if these stories of foreign climes were to be cherished.

15.4.88
Janet's mood swings continue and have coincided with her occasional disappearances. The nursing staff has expressed concern on a number of occasions. The situation will have to be monitored. Her behaviour and mannerisms are unpredictable, she appears increasingly anxious. In the conversations we do have it has become clear that for Janet the shed has become a confusing paradox; equally so, the hands. She has no way of comprehending such perceptions and accepting them fully, unquestioningly, as her own. As she has appeared to get better, her world, her past, has increasingly come to resemble a disturbingly vivid dream.

The positive side of this is that through her activities – and specifically her painting and reading *Jane Eyre* – Janet seems to be learning to cope. She appears to be making connections that are her own and is starting to ask pragmatic questions about how to lead her life. Today she interrupted the reading, impatient with Jane for always being 'so stiff and right'. Whatever emotional turbulence she may be presently experiencing (she did reiterate the sexual fantasies about Mr Eyre this morning and also shouted violent threats towards Dr T's office door), she is, I am certain, taking considerable forward strides.

20.4.88

I had become increasingly aware that Janet was hiding things from me. Now she is no longer in residence it is difficult to envisage any possible circumstance in which she would return: the Section Order has expired, there is no reason for her to come back and several substantive reasons for her to stay away. Though the exact details of her departure remain unclear, the circumstances suggest several things, as follows:

Janet finds for herself a private space, this time not a shed but a room. This is a sanctuary within the hospital, not contaminated by the ramblings of others; this room is hers and hers alone. She spends increasing amounts of time there, taking her notebook, her paintings, her private letters and a copy of her favourite book, and concealing them all there. The same items were discovered in the room after the fire was extinguished, underneath the fallen body and shelves. Subsequently they were handed over to me.

They also found her tin containing hand-rolling tobacco and cigarette papers, which, in this institution, are the most precious and personal of items. The presence of these alone is odd: why would she leave the tin? But it also reveals her trust in the room's sanctity. It was a place in which she could be free, a haven where no one could get to her – patient, nurse or indeed doctor. This conclusion is unavoidable; from her notebook it appears clear that more than any other 'oppressive' factor, she wished to escape the attentions of myself most of all. The notebook reveals how from an early stage Janet came to resent and distrust me. Judging from what she wrote in the book she often wandered the dimly lit corridors of the hospital, trying to find peace. From her descriptions it would appear as if she moved around unseen, like a ghost. What is revealing, if her accounts are to be believed, is the extent to which she revelled in being untended, as if it were a game of dare.

It is not at all clear how she achieved this freedom of movement given the regulatory regime in force within the buildings and grounds of the hospital. (Monitoring procedures are consequently being reviewed.) It was apparently during one of these adventures that Janet discovered her secret room. According to her notebook she named the room 'the pigeon loft' almost immediately, although it was not quite a loft and, according to her accounts, only ever appeared to have had one visit from a pigeon. It was on the top floor of the hospital, overlooking the back courtyard of the hospital buildings where all the bins are kept, together with old bread trays and food trolleys. Today I visited the room and sat in the broken wheelchair, as Janet often must have done. Through the narrow window it is possible to spy the cats down below, scavenging around the bins.

Barely larger than a cupboard, the so-called pigeon loft was once used by the maintenance men as a storeroom. The smell of turps still lingers, the broken wheelchair and a rack of bent shelving are the room's only furnishings. There are old paint foot prints on the linoleum floor, oily fingerprints on the window ledge, and a pile of old decorating sheets splattered in various hospital shades. Janet used one of the sheets to wrap and hide her belongings.

It appears from her notebook that on the day when she first discovered the room she heard a cooing and flapping as the faulty door stuck ajar. Her descriptions were far more detailed than I would have thought possible. She wrote of the grey feathers littering the floor (some are still there), describing them as being 'like oil on water, with their purple rings and green edges'. She thought at first one of the cats was feasting, but there wasn't a cat. The pigeon, tired and panicking up on the top shelf, was just chasing itself trying to get out.

She guessed that the bird had fallen from the roof cavity, through the broken ceiling tiles, and become stranded. She managed eventually to open the room's small window, no doubt breaking the numerous spiders' webs which have since been re-cast. From her account it is apparent the bird was stupidly reluctant to exit. Yet as she gradually coaxed it out, she heard another cooing above the false ceiling. She climbed on the wheelchair and, looking up through the gap in the PVC tiles, saw only chinks of light in the blackness: 'midday stars' she called them. This proves that her first visit to the room was during daylight hours. Today I too climbed on the chair and saw the little lights, which are caused by small gaps between the roofing slates. The pigeons appear to get in regularly through the eaves, and the one that fell was most probably just a little more stupid, or less fortunate, than the others. Although she did not write about doing so in her notebook, I think it safe to assume, after talking to all the other parties and seeing the site, that she stashed her parcel of books, letters and tobacco, all bound and tied in one of the paint-stained decorating sheets, up above the false ceiling in this roof cavity.

21.4.88

After now studying her notebook I am struck by the clarity of descriptions, but most shocking is the fact that she wrote about several childhood memories. One in particular struck me. She was sitting on a seat by a horse chestnut tree, her feet dangling and not reaching the floor. She remembered being there with her mother. The tree overhung the river and the conkers fell into a still shallow. On sunny days their crowns shone up 'like pennies' through the water so it looked like a wishing place. Some people even threw coins in as well. Janet wrote: 'The water shone back up at you like gold. Everyone called it the wishing tree.' She evidently had many more memories of her birth mother than she had ever admitted to me.

What is more, she had memories of her mother speaking to her.

In one memory her mother showed her the old meadow-sweet gone to seed down by the river: 'its burnt old stems kept upright by the bindweed twisting round' she wrote, 'the weed's just a parasite but that's the darkest green at the back-end of summer.' Her mother had told her how the longer the meadowsweet stood upright the better the chances for its seed to disperse, so it was hard to tell which was 'the clinger', which the 'clung-to'.

The notebook gives no specific insight into her regard for Philip Eyre, except to suggest that the sexual fantasies have, as I suspected, been with her for some while. It appears that *Jane Eyre* has become a book of strange, corrupted providence in Janet's eyes, just because of the coincidence of surnames. She revels in the violence, injury and physical impairment suffered by both Bertha and Rochester, more so than ever revealed in our reading sessions. Yet it is clear from all of this that both the room and the notebook empowered Janet with a form of reflection and expression which was quite unimaginable only a few months ago. The sanctuary, however, soon turned into a trap.

23.4.88

After a little research, reflection and gathering of information I have managed to construct a sequence of events as I imagine occurred immediately prior to Janet's departure. They are as follows:

Someone eventually notices Janet's frequent absences, someone who is also accustomed to seeking out the invisible gaps in the day; this particular someone has spent a lifetime in and out of homes and hospitals. He is accustomed to the workings of institutions. This someone is on a final warning and is aware that if he steps astray he will be charged, as he has been charged before. He will go to prison and not for the first time. This particular person knows what it is like to be PP9'd. At all costs our voyeur does not want this to happen again and so ensures that he keeps a reasonable distance. Yet he is compelled. He waits and watches and he follows. He tracks Janet up to the top floor, creeping along the corridors, tiptoeing closer day by day. He peeps through the door's square, wired-glass window. He watches the private parcel being wrapped and stashed away in the false ceiling. Again and again he spies on her in this fashion. He spies and he waits. This at least is how I imagine it.

On a day when he has checked and seen Janet two floors below in the therapies room – no doubt painting over by the window – he believes himself to be safe and ventures up to the top floor. He pushes open the stiff door, which sticks ajar. He climbs on the broken wheelchair and gropes in the ceiling cavity until he finds the bundle of her secret belongings wrapped in the decorating sheet. With increasing excitement he unties the knot that binds it. This is how I imagine her secret was finally unravelled.

Spreading the paint-flecked sheet and Janet's belongings out before him he helps himself to the tobacco. He smokes, and his trousers fall quite naturally round his ankles. He holds and caresses himself. This, being a familiar sight on the wards, is imagined all too readily, together with the cloud of yellow-blue smoke around his head. He has no idea that he will soon be spotted, that Janet, having tired of her painting perhaps, having sensed something amiss, would soon take the lift up to the top floor.

She no doubt hears the racing wheeze as soon as the lift doors open. She proceeds silently through the fire doors, and then smells the cigarette smoke. Her heart vaults as she gains confirmation of where the noise is coming from. She knows it's her tobacco. She resists the impulse to run, instead clinging to the magnolia walls, as the sighs increase in volume and frequency and become syncopated with the occasional grunt. She pictures a pig greedily at its slops and becomes impatient herself. Suddenly she is standing in the doorway, no longer attempting to hide. She watches the ginger mop swishing backwards and forwards, the smoke billowing up from his head as he puffs without retracting the cigarette (as is his habit). She sees her own precious notebook, the pages wide open and floundering, the words pitifully exposed, with Guillermo's letters trapped in the folds. She might have looked down and seen the cracked-oil vignette on the cover of her favourite book, the hair greying, the youthful face suddenly aging beyond time. All of her recovered hope, the sanctity, the concealment and privacy, all of it would at this moment be slipping away.

By this time she would be burning inside. She would reach through the door, no doubt crying, she would have no option now, no choice but to nudge the broken shelves as they tilt; help them on their way. The hands would play a part here. Love and hate, her friendly ghouls would direct her anger. It is difficult to imagine the race of her thoughts as the shelves creak and fall, and as Marius screams. She might look down at the notebook and her *Jane Eyre*. She could not possibly take these precious items with her, not now. She would realise: they are a part of her past, they are ruined beyond recognition and gone forever.

The clatter of the falling shelves no doubt alarms her; it will alarm others as well. There is no option but to run, yet she has no idea where she should go. She looks back at Marius, hoping him dead, if not believing him to be so. She sees the smouldering cigarette in the decorating sheet. She leaves it. This is how I imagine it. She even has the presence of mind to run down the stairs to her bed, to gather some clothes and a blanket. This much has been noted in the hospital inventory – a blanket missing. Nothing else was reported, the management achieved an admirable cover-up, made all the easier by Janet's absence. The old storeroom is now kept permanently locked; I had to request a key from security. Marius suffered a few minor burns and a bump on the head, nothing compared to being PP9'd. Inevitably, 'Him Up Above' has returned with a vengeance in the voice sessions.

Dr T was glib about the matter, muttering something about 'those poor tortured souls'; his inference was most apparent:

my methods would always be abused. Dr T and I have never agreed about Janet, therapeutically or even diagnostically. Now I can only fear for Janet's welfare. In her present state she is no match for the hands or their owner, whoever that might happen to be; there is no longer any doubt about the mutability of their identity. The hands can belong to anyone, at any time, and in their capacity to love and hate they can be most dangerous. As this incident proves.

PART FOUR

CHAPTER 1

The sheathed wire from the angle-poise lamp trailed off like a frayed touch-fuse. The light shimmered over my mother's silent desk, with its bare, tear-grained book-ends. I trembled. I shuddered at its emptiness; just Dr Romme's notebook in front of me, the natural light long since dimmed. The world had suddenly come to look and feel like a cave; a small and frightening place. I shut the window and drew the curtains. While I'd been reading a strange dampness had seeped into my thoughts and bones; a nearby drip, drip, drip that made me ache deep down, as did a voice, booming out of the dark. The shadows merged, the sniff of naphthalene and old smoke dragged any goodness out of the air. The drip – was it the tap in the kitchen? No question about the voice – it was mine and it was speaking to me. Get out of there, it said; get out of there right now.

I thought of what my mother had said of her husband, my dearest papa: 'Never one for the difficult situation'. And I couldn't help but feel an affinity; like father like son; the apple never falls far from the tree; peas from the same pod . . .. I found myself smiling; I felt like crying. I thought of how probability wraps us up, then feasts on our ignorance, I thought of the stupid faith we hold in our will, thinking it'll always be there to get us out of a fix. I thought of the futility of it, how we're really all fated, pre-determined, blueprinted and planned. We're already stewed and can't ever uncook ourselves. We'll die, and we'll suffer misfortunes, endure happiness, cry a little, laugh a little. All of it will come to pass as if it were meant to be. But are we ever any the wiser?

If this was going to be any sort of sister of mine I was going to have to work at it. Did I want to? After reading Dr Romme's notebook I made inquiries about flights. Sister or no sister, I wanted get out of there fast. Home town it might be, but I felt like I'd just beached up in some hostile, foreign land. I was flagging; even before K hopped on a plane my conviction was on the wane. I looked at the snapshot of Holly again and again, the familiarity, the recognition, all gradually dripping away: the eyes, the nose, even the hair, all losing their precocious resonance. Okay, I saw something, but now the connection wasn't necessarily to me. Increasingly the face seemed odd, worrying; I felt off-kilter just from looking at it. Janet Burns could only ever be a half-sister in any case, and God only knew what genes had been shipped in. I thought the sexual fantasies might be a sick joke: Dr Romme might have deliberately left the book on my passenger seat, she might be feeding me these grim thoughts, though I couldn't for the life of me work out why.

And then there were my fingers in Janet's hair: eggs in the nest. That was no joke. On reflection, that was the part that scared me most of all. When I first picked up Dr Romme's black notebook and began reading I knew where I was going, I was confident in my intent. I just felt as if I needed a few directions along the way. But I came out of it knowing nothing – possibles, probables, likelihoods, certainties – they all dissolved with the first clouds of dawn. Confusion was too small a word for it. I peeped through a gap in the curtains at the puffs and wisps swirling and stalling in the crepuscular sky, threatening to gather but never quite pausing long enough to form cumuli. Still no rain. The world had dried to a bone. There was a clump of Scots pines on a rise at the west edge of town, just beyond the avenues of detached houses, just before the open fields. I could see them whenever I went to my mother's desk and picked up Dr Romme's book to read over some episode or other. And whenever I looked at the trees I thought of my father and our walk. Those were the days, just a boy and his dad. The trees' flaked-red bark glowed in the sunset every night, as I imagined an oracle might. The summer was just past its infancy but it was getting a definite feel. It was never going to end. It felt as if the only way I might catch a glimpse of the future, a snatch of what it might be like outside of all the crackling heat and dryness, was to stare at the trees. If I looked long enough I might get an idea of what was going on, of which way the world, my world, might be turning.

Eventually I slipped Dr Romme's book in an envelope with a scribbled note, apologising for not returning it sooner. I left it with the receptionist at the hospital. Later that day the Lovetts finally came round to tell me what they'd almost told me at the funeral. They dropped by in the afternoon but declined the offer of tea. They stood either side of me, smelt of cold tar soap and spoke with a cold, clean intensity, as if expecting a certain response. Shock perhaps.

— Someone has been standing outside your house.

— They've been watching it, dear.

— Watching what?

— Your house.

— My house?

— Your old house. Next door to us.

Just like at the funeral, they operated like twins. I pictured the forsythia and the trellis fence, and Mr Lovett's precious roses.

— Watching my old house? What would anyone want to do that for?

I pictured the place where the Lovetts burned their leaves, the ground elder creeping around the edges of the blackened ground, the young leaves leaning towards and yet away at the same time, like mourners at a grave. I knew what they were going to say, I knew and yet simultaneously I didn't know. They looked at each other, nodding in agreement before turning and speaking in unison.

— It's a woman!

Apparently she hadn't been seen for a week or two, not since just before the funeral. The Lovetts didn't like to say anything then. The tenants currently living in the house had been so alarmed as to call the police. They'd subsequently told the Lovetts that, partly because of this, they were going to move at the end of the year, when their lease expired. I thought for a moment about the lost revenue, whether the letting agents yet knew, whether they'd advertised for new tenants. Then it hit me.

— Did you see her? Did you see who it was, this woman?

I rang the tenants but they'd never spoken with the woman; they had only ever seen her loitering in the shadows by the street wall. By the time they went out to approach her she had always already gone. The police couldn't do anything. There was no definite ID, but with what I'd been given – dark, shoulder length hair with a slight curl – I was sure.

She'd always had my old address. That was where she'd sent the paintings. That was a mistake in the first place. Who'd given it to her? Guillermo? How did he get hold of it? She'd been sending paintings to that address for quite some time, and all along I'd never questioned how she got hold of it. Given the nature of my work, I was never listed in the phone book. I supposed she or Guillermo could always have checked the electoral register – the town wasn't big. And then I realised, there was my mother's house as well, under the name of 'Eyre'; where I was presently staying; that would be listed too. What was to stop her? I tried to work out why she might be after me. For all Dr Romme's studious note taking I still felt as if I'd missed a vital part of the plot. Perhaps she really was my sister after all and this was just a sister-brother thing; that syndrome, what had K called it? GSA, that was it – but I couldn't remember what it stood for. And all the time she was seeming less and less like a sister to me.

CHAPTER 2

The possibilities soon started to proliferate; I had too much time to think, waiting for the house to sell, sorting out the probate. The paperwork seemed to be taking forever. And, as Richard kept reminding me, I had the small matter of a lecture to prepare, for the conference at the end of the summer. At the rate things were going I would still be sitting at my mother's dingy old desk when that came around. The estate agents kept telling me I should hold out for the top price because the market was buoyant and rising by the day. But no one wanted even to take a look. I was left to view it on my own: the remnants of my mother's life, tinged with fumes that had long since been inhaled and exhaled, the cracked and mossed path leading to the fishless pond with its sad bewildered reeds and crying rocks; the pine trees off in the distance and all those never-to-be-regained strands of memory. Of course, there were more pressing, more addictive speculations to ponder. If I'd once had a couple of tapes running about my father – three whittling down to one (the cad could be included in any compilation) – I had a few possible novels rolling in my head about Janet Burns.

It crossed my mind, a little more than fleetingly, that her mother might be my Jane: yes, my first venture into the world. K's prying about 'not taking precautions' had set the fire smouldering. I spent a crazy afternoon trying to tidy the garden, cutting the tindery grass, working through that particular scenario: the disused bus shelter and the rhododendron bush – both most certainly situated in Wales, near to where Janet was brought up; the same vicinity, and the timescale matched. I pictured the stone bus shelter, overhung with the bush's blood-green leaves. I pictured the shimmering lane, remembered the palpable pulse of the sun, made that much more intense by the grey days that surrounded its appearance. I pictured Jane, the girl from all those years ago, untying the cotton belt of her dress. A white backing with a red rose print. I remembered it unravelling in the dappled light, falling miraculously around her feet, I remembered her glass-white thighs and the brief mound of her young stomach. I remembered that much, the darkness of her hair, the light and shadow of the hour and place, but not her face, not clearly. Was I really the same person? It made my heart shudder. The possibility. Janet Burns, my daughter! It was possible, but hardly probable. I couldn't recall Janet's mother's name from the reports, but I was almost certain it wasn't Jane. I knew it wasn't true. The fact that I pondered and pursued any of this just signalled an acceleration; impatience was coming to the fore, the power of suggestion taking over.

K later said I had a madman's take on the Oedipus complex: 'Something to do with your old job, being the big old Daddy to the world. Even had the Latin tag to go with it; what did they call you, *Pater Noster*? Think you're everyone's old man, and you suspect all your kids want to sleep with you.' That's why I was always pushing Rachel and Simon away, according to K; why I pushed everyone away. I acted as if I'd received a prophecy and was scared witless. The first sign of madness, she said: 'this tendency to assimilate the world and his dog into your own life story'.

It turned out that I wasn't alone. K had been doing the very same thing herself.

She whirled into town like she owned it, proving to be a far more effective Sherlock than I ever was. She put me straight on a few matters, not least the sibling thing. Janet Burns was no sister – full, half, quarter or even eighth – except in that all of us, the whole world, we're all related to one another. In the end.

K had explored all the possibles and probables, some I'd

come up with, some I hadn't even dreamt of. Slipping only momentarily in her 'I-know-where-it's-at' poise, she explained how she herself had been seduced by the potentials on offer. Sitting in my mother's old chair, she looked like she needed a cigarette.

— Go ahead smoke, I really don't mind. It suits the house.

— No, I've stopped.

Saying it made it seem like she needed one even more. We were sipping tea, the taste of nicotine still on the china. K got a piece of red cloth from her bag, somewhere between a handkerchief and a scarf in size and closer to a rag in appearance. She furled it between her fingers and passed it to the other hand for a few moments before reaching back into the bag for the snapshot of Holly – the one I had received from Janet in Canada; the same one K had sent on to me in photocopied form. The red hair in the original was only marginally less bright than the copy. There was a long, creaking silence as we both stared at it. Finally she looked up at me.

— Did you work it out then?

— What?

— The likeness.

— Of course, you'd have to be blind not to.

She unravelled her red scarf and passed it back to her left hand.

— Was it really that obvious?

— Yes.

I affected a laugh as she worked the red rag between her fingers. I surmised it was like a comfort blanket, to help her stop smoking; it gave her something to do with her hands, especially while she talked.

— I guess it was a bit of a give away. Moles like that aren't too common.

I stopped laughing.

— Moles?

And just then K touched the mark on her own face, not quite middling her cheek. I looked back at the photo and felt suddenly nauseous. The redness of the hair faded instantly, it may as well have been blonde or brown. I didn't see it any more, it was gone. All I saw was a little dot on Holly's left cheek . I'd previously thought it to be a smudge resulting from the photocopying or developing even, some mark from the process of reproduction. So did K. Not the same place as K's, not the same shade, or shape, or size. But given time . . . and a little imagination.

K a grandmother, Janet Burns *her* daughter. It took a while to comprehend the possibility. Wales again (how small could a country possibly be?). She had a thing about red heads. I then recalled her strange inquiry over the phone, a week earlier: 'Does Janet Burns have any distinctive facial marks?' K explained how she too had pursued the recessive, heterozygous trail. Such features – kinks in appearance, hair colour, shape of nose – these sometimes get lost for a generation or two and then resurface. If K hadn't laughed I'd have believed it. Again the timescale made sense, give or take a year, even if there was the slight problem of Janet having a mother or two already. And was it possible to inherit a mole? Later K excused her own madness: she'd been raddled and seduced by the eternal possibility. A child, her child, was out there somewhere, always and forever, and it could be, it could always be . . .

— You can't give a child away and not have strange thought processes.

But she smiled as she said it, in a big secret way, sipping her tea, fondling her scarf, as if I would never understand, but also as if those weird thoughts were, for some reason, less of a burden nowadays. She went on to explain how she'd already, weeks before, worked through my plots: Janet being my sister, Janet being my daughter. The snapshot didn't look anything like me, according to K, but she knew how my mind worked. She'd put the photocopy of Holly's flaming features in the driving licence as a joke. Ha! Ha! But what about the *Jane Eyre* thing?

— What about it?

— Well, it must mean something mustn't it? She chose the name 'Burns'.

— What are you trying to say?

— She chose the name because she saw that we . . .

— Ah, come on! You both have surnames that come from the same book. So what? A book somebody wrote a hundred years ago? If you look long enough you could find our names together in a book already. Choose any two names and you'll find them together in a book somewhere.

— But she chose Burns, don't you see?

— But she didn't call herself Helen Burns.

— So?

— The girl in *Jane Eyre* is called Helen Burns, not Janet. Helen Burns, and she was just a little bit of a character. And as I recall I don't think the main character was called Philip. Wasn't it Jane?

She smiled wryly, sipping her tea, as if there was more to it, much more, but I just wouldn't understand. And it was true: to me none of the novels were making much sense. Holly – that odd, familiar, old-young face in the snapshot – matched none of the strands. Not anymore. Not K, not me, nor my father. Recognising someone didn't necessarily mean that person was kin. I might have felt relieved at the realisation, a kind of liberation, if I hadn't known the hands were still out there somewhere, the ghoulish inscriptions, hate and love, love and hate, jostling with one another. Thinking of them served to remind me: there was a question still to be answered, still a mighty hole to be filled.

K said she had managed to get a new job but she wasn't going to tell me the whole story until it had been confirmed. First she had to tell me about her old, walrus-moustached boss.

— You just won't believe what I found on that guy.

— What? Professor Slater?

— The very same. He's in it up to his abbreviated neck.

And she proceeded to tell me what she'd been doing in the library all this time. It turned out the Professor had an impressive lineage, his great grandfather being one James. W. Slaughter, a colleague of Galton's in the early days of the grand 'breeding hygiene' project. Slaughter had retired from it all, foreseeing the less than egalitarian possibilities. He became a circuit judge in Pennsylvania. A later generation of the family completed the disassociation.

— One of them, set on getting his son to run for Congress, thought it wise to change 'Slaughter' to 'Slater'.

— Didn't want his son to sound like a murderer, eh?

— Yeah, I guess, an aesthetic consideration, but they wanted to ditch some family history as well, given all the bad press coming over from Germany and some of the stories filtering up from the southern states.

— Carrie Buck and the sterilisation programmes you mean?

— Hey, I forgot, you're something of an expert.

— Yeah, yeah.

— Well, the Slaughters or Slaters or whatever you want to call them, they didn't want to be tainted with all that. It was a statement of fashion, don't you know. Being socially concerned was one thing, wanting to stop people from reproducing was a whole other ball game.

She paused, coming to the juicy part.

— Now when we come to the good old Professor's place in the bloodline, turned out there had been a retro-fashion. Slater sees this old Judge James W. Slaughter as some sort of misguided hero. He thinks his great grand pappy should have stuck it out with Galton, gone on and snipped a few tubes.

According to K, her old duckbutt boss might as well have reverted to the old family name, so keen was he on bloodletting.

— He wants to wipe out half the population, under the banner of public interest: those prone to violence, those prone to obesity, those prone to thinking he might be wrong. Waving the flag of this new evolutionary genetics, leastways his brand of it.

— He's a fascist?

— Yeah, only they don't call them that nowadays.

I wanted to ask her what they did call them but she was anxious to tell me all. She'd discovered Slater belonged to more than half a dozen clandestine organisations, he'd written in journals under a pseudonym and made donations. She'd traced it all and sent her evidence to the student body of the university at which he held an honorary chair. She hoped they'd do the rest.

K stared at me as I filled my mother's grease-stained kettle for more tea.

— Why are you looking at me like that?

— I thought you might feel a little uneasy.

— Why? Should I?

I recalled the articles by my bedside and K uncovering them, and I caught the full meaning of the stare. Slater was a recruiting sergeant; he'd had his eye on me. And, okay, I'd found the articles mildly interesting, yes, I thought they had a point, but . . .

— I always said they were nothing . . . nothing other than naive.

— Did you?

— Yes, I did!

— Just naive, eh?

What I couldn't understand was why K had put so much effort into proving Slater to be some sort of bad guy, when all hell was breaking loose elsewhere. During her time locked up in the library looking up family trees, my mother had become compost for an ash sapling and some mad woman was threatening to act out her homicidal sexual fantasies on me. I was being stalked, for God's sake! But K could just laugh it off.

— Janet Burns is obviously saying something to you.

— Is she?

— And you probably, the way you're behaving, are trying to say something to her as well.

— What do you mean, 'the way I'm behaving'?

— Only you aren't able to talk the same language, on the same frequency. You can't understand each other.

— You don't say!

— Not now, at any rate . . .

— What do you mean, 'behaving'?

I didn't want to talk to anybody, Janet Burns least of all. I was a mess and was the first to admit it. But the last thing I needed was a calming, transcendental hand on my inner core. I wanted to rise above things, sure, but I wanted to do the telling, not be told. The investigation had stalled. The person I was chasing turned out to be chasing me. Dr Romme, in the continuing search for Janet, phoned to ask where the shed was. I gave directions but declined the invitation to accompany her. She thanked me for returning her case notes and, in the embarrassment, I forgot to mention Janet's loitering. I doubted whether it mattered. Dr Romme didn't look like she could help me. And neither did K.

The next day we went for a walk, up among the pine trees. K had spotted them from my mother's bay window and suggested we break the monotony of packing boxes and meetings with solicitors. Since her arrival the red scarf hadn't left her side, and now as she walked it dangled inevitably, like a soaked bandage from her knuckles. K said it was strange I was taking such an interest in Janet Burns, a person who, just a few months ago, was being cursed just for including me on her mailing list. The sun hit the tops of the trees and a gust of wind blew up spoils of dust from the path, parching the air and our mouths. K had a furtive look, even as she coughed. I reminded her about what Dr Romme had written about Janet's fantasies; I played down the sexual part, pointing up the malevolence. This was something to be scared of, not to get jealous about. But the twinkle didn't shift. I'd already told her most of what was in the doctor's notes, though thought it best not to mention Dr T and the postponed operation. That would just encourage her, I could picture the 'I-told-you-so' smile: evil was still abroad, and now it was plain to see; she'd been right all along, these things were still going on.

I offered her one of the apples we'd brought along and we sat on the edge of the knoll, K speaking with her mouth full.

— Where do you think she is?

— Janet?

— Yeah.

— I don't know.

But as I said it I remembered Dr Romme's notes, and Janet's fractured memories of her mother: the talk of a river and the bindweed on the bank; for some reason that had stayed with me. When she'd finished K threw her apple core into the gorse bushes down by the path.

— Her life's a nightmare. Can you imagine? Each breath she takes eating away at her.

I grunted some agreement, thinking about the river and the bindweed round the meadowsweet.

— Perhaps she's gone back to the shed.

I said it in a blank, formulaic sort of way. A kind of joke: that's the way all good plots go; back to the scene of the crime. K got up awkwardly, rubbing her back, then walked off down the hill. I felt suddenly left out again. I was still the one with the problem. I was the one searching for some ineffable, some unqualified, unquantifiable, impalpable something. But Janet Burns was the one getting all the attention; she'd become the big victim. And K was doing most of the questioning; she'd become the detective.

Janet Burns was now a grotesque, Bosch-like image; a horror, a shame. The arm around her shoulder; eggs in a nest; my sister; my daughter: all these appeared like ever-darkening shadows. I could barely tolerate the memory of thinking such things. The places we go to try and make sense of the world! They were all mistaken; errors of judgement, things I was desperately trying to forget and forgive myself for thinking. But they were still things that beckoned me.

Far from the brave knight a breath away from the object of his quest, I found myself cowering, quivering, and I didn't know why. What prevents us from stepping forward at such times? What stops us from knowing? I was nearly there. All the answers I'd ever need, all the questions, all the probable possibilities and possible probabilities; resolution was before me. The end and a new beginning were staring me in the face. But I was blinded, my eyes filling.

To compound matters I found that I was shocked and alarmed by K. Not because she looked at me the way she sometimes did, as if I were a little boy and she were my mother, not because of the smile in her eye. There was something else about her – a new smell, like the gorse in flower on the hill; a sweet, subtle perfume. She stroked my arm on the walk back along the road from the pine trees. Just briefly, a few seconds, but it felt like I'd never been touched before. This on its own might once have set me thinking. I'd have pictured her stroking the forearms of the world. But something had shifted. Something about K was different. Her eyes glistened with a secret and strange determination. She was even different with Richard, who sped round on hearing of her arrival. We found him on the doorstep on our return from the walk. K and Richard went through the French windows into the garden, while I went to the kitchen to get some lemonade and beer. I looked back, compelled, to see K accidentally drop her red scarf. They crouched together to pick it up, Richard getting there first and hastily placing it on her bent thigh.

Maybe there were words exchanged, maybe it was the touch of his hand on her summer-bare leg, I don't know. I could only hear the fierceness of her response, not its content. Richard stood instantly, within that moment, and with bent shoulders and lowered head. I'd been trying all my life to strike such a blow. K rose and took her place on the bench, in the shade of the laburnum. And there it was – this new, or renewed, confidence. Not certainty, no, she accepted her own fallibility: just look at how she had wanted to believe Janet was her own daughter; how she had readily admitted it. And there was a glow, a redness in those olive cheeks; she looked like my mother after one of her sojourns. She was basking in a new knowledge but it appeared to be the sort of knowing she would never have been able to articulate. It was for others to see. No secrets, no problems, no short-legged bosses. All was possibility. She was revived, strong and intent. It scared me almost as much as the thought of Janet Burns turning up on my doorstep. K appeared to know something that I perfectly did not.

CHAPTER 3

What did possibility mean for me? I woke every day in a sweat. I dreamt of suffocating in clouds of cigarette smoke. I continually heard the shuffle of shoes, the clip clop of severe heals, on the pavement outside. Possibility meant: today might be the day. Possibility had also come to mean escape: not only from Janet Burns and this perverse chase; not just from the stacked boxes and the sniff of Peter Stuyvesants in a now empty, light-soaked house. The truth was I wanted sidewalks again instead of pavements, bagels not buns, I wanted snow – yes, I even wanted winter. A mantra built up in my head: 'Today, I'm leaving', it chanted, full of gravity and intent, 'I'm breaking free now'. But I never got any nearer to doing anything about it. The more I said it the louder the other things clamoured. My father and his few lines of poetry; my mother's blue smoke rinsing the air as if she was right there in front of me; my arm around Janet's shoulder, my fingers running through her hair. I still had a problem believing that particular picture. The more I thought about it the less I knew where I might be escaping to or from. The watery eyes became a regular feature in the mirror. I put it down to hay fever, an allergy to dust. The drought dragged on. And on. There seemed always to be a song starting up in my head, every morning, every afternoon and evening, I heard it vaguely at the edge of my memory, right on the tip of my musical consciousness – wherever it might be that tunes come from and return to. But I couldn't ever quite get the melody, I couldn't sing the words. And I couldn't sleep, too many things stirred. I sensed the next move in the plot, the outcome. But it was only ever an inkling; I never really knew.

The temperature rose even higher, as if summer's peak had returned. But no one season held sway over the sleep-fled half light of those early mornings. I saw so many crisp, bird-loud dawns I lost count, shivering at every one of them as if thrown into the depths of a dreary, autumn brume. And each time the world felt as if it was about to change and never be the same, as if the sun would soon be rising on the end.

Sleep when it did come was like treacle, thick and cloying; it left me feeling nauseous, my head aching. I dreamt nastily but not anymore of Rachel and Simon. Now it was Janet; she was my child, the helpless victim of some mysterious prophecy, the cause of each and every bad feeling I'd ever endured. In some of the dreams Janet became Jane Eyre, dressed to the neck and ankle in dark linen governess's gowns, all wilful and prim and morally correct. At other times Richard was Rochester, predatory and licentious. Janet was also sometimes Bertha in the dreams, in others she appeared to be Helen Burns on her death bed, coughing up vermilion-threaded phlegm. Even K appeared on occasions: once as St John Rivers, once as his sister. I sensed a meaning in the exchange of parts, some elusive portent just beyond my comprehension. Some nights I woke up convinced the dreams were all Janet's doing; that she was playing a trick on me.

There had been three offers on the house, but nothing was certain. The market was buoyant perhaps, but the vendor-chains were unendingly long; buyers lives were umbilically linked to those of sellers. If you believed the estate agents everyone was on the move; in reality everyone was stuck. Yet despite all my desperation and frailty, I was determined to hold out for the best price. Sarah said that was just typical. She dropped Rachel and Simon off once a week in her inimitable fashion; I returned them in the Renault. It was as if I'd never been away. Sarah and K met and seemed to reach a workable peace almost instantly, though K watched whenever I went out to greet the kids from the car. Seeing the twitch of the green linen curtains in the bay, the only ones left hanging downstairs, I couldn't stop myself feeling a little satisfaction.

On one occasion, the verge poppies dancing lightly with the movement of the passing traffic, Sarah asked.

— When are you going back then?

— Canada, you mean?

— Yes.

— As soon as this place is off my hands.

— But you can't go straight away.

— Why not? There's nothing to keep me.

It was crass; I knew it as soon as I said it. Luckily Rachel and Simon had already raced in. They were getting on fine with K, thanks to a selection of conjuring tricks (for Simon) and a small, well-travelled pile of American Vogues (for Rachel). I saw the curtain give a big twist before falling still, as the children found their target. Sarah broke the silence.

— Surely, there's no point you leaving and having to come all the way back again.

— What do you mean?

I immediately suspected some plot to keep me here for ever.

— Your lecture, the Social Services thing.

The matter of Richard's invitation loomed ever closer: the child care conference and my 'little talk', as Richard called it. Sarah had threatened to come along. I was sure she just said this to compete with K, who had not only arrived in good time to help in my preparations but was a little too keen in offering suggestions as to what I should say. It was advice, and both Sarah and K were prospective spectators, I could do without. The lecture had become part of the burgeoning black shadows that lurked at the edge of my mind. I knew I would have to get something down on paper soon. But as the days passed, I felt less and less able. Whatever I might or might not know about anything, it would be of no interest to anyone, I was sure. This was more than stage fright or passing self-doubt. I put it off by saying: 'I'll do it later, I'll do it when the time arises, I won't have any problem then'. But the time was arising fast, and I kept getting visions, day-mares: a lectern, a sea of eyes and a wash of red-faced silence, loud and stomach churning. I didn't tell K, pretending instead to sit at my mother's old desk, telling her I was working. But I just sat there, staring out at the pine trees. One day she came over and sat on the edge of the desk.

— You kinda like it here don't you?

— I wouldn't go so far as to say that.

I gestured with my eyes around the stacked boxes. K shook her head.

— No, I mean, looking out of the window, that window ... it must bring a lot back for you. Your childhood and all.

— Not really.

— Well, you give it a lot of time.

I was scared she would find me out; scared she would ask to see a draft of what I was preparing for the lecture, a product from all of this supposed endeavour. Scared I'd find myself out.

— Do I?

— Yeah, I mean those trees, where we walked that day. Are they special or something?

She pointed with her eyes.

— No ... no, why.

— It's just I've been watching you, and ... and you seem to be scrutinising them.

— Scrutinising?

— Well, just looking at them hard as if you're trying to find something.

— And what might that be?

— You tell me.

Both of us stared out toward the trees. The windows were all open and the breeze, which we could see in the distance testing but not bending the upper limbs of the pines, whispered round the room, rustling the papers on my desk. For a moment I swore I could see a shape, a woman all in white, dancing between the trunks of the trees; she seemed to be hiding and calling, both at the same time. I said nothing, looking to K and seeing from her face that she could see no one. I looked again and now the woman was all in black, a shift in position perhaps so the sunlight silhouetted her. Still no recognition on K's face, I looked back at the trees. The woman, if that's what I'd seen, was gone. I smelt a sweet rush of jasmine from the garden, enigmatically whisked off by a breeze before it could be savoured. K perked up, rising from the desk and humming in agreement with the scent. She came round behind me folding her arms around my shoulders and chest in uncharacteristically wholesale, 'I'm-yours-do-with-me-what-you-will' fashion.

— Given the choice, would you live here then, with your precious little old trees?

— What do you mean? I've chosen not to...

I looked again but neither the woman in black nor the woman in white were anywhere to be seen.

— No, I mean ... I mean if you had kids to raise.

— You seem to forget ... I do have ...

— Yeah, but ...

At which point I thought I saw her glancing at the doodles on my notepad, so turned quickly round to kiss her.

❧

It transpired that Sarah couldn't make it to the conference after all; Arthur had a tummy bug and had been up half the night. But, as if to make up the discomfort quotient, Dr Romme phoned on the day, just as I was knotting my tie.

— I need to see you urgently, Mr Eyre.

— Has she turned up then?

— Who? Oh, Janet. No, no, it is not about Janet, well, it is, but ... it is Marius Pritty.

— Who?

— A fellow patient of Janet's. Marius Pritty, you may have come across him when you conducted your initial investigation.

I remembered only too well: outside room A213, turning and seeing the sprung red coils, watching them bounce, seeing the zealous self-absorption in his sunken eyes. I knew him alright. Marius, who Janet had caught with her belongings. Yet, I wasn't supposed to know this: a detail confided only in Dr Romme's little book. And, of course, I hadn't even taken a peep.

— Who is he?

— Well, Marius was a rather worrisome fellow patient, with quite severe and disparate problems. He tended to . . . well . . .

— Tended to what?

I was suddenly amused, and distracted from the rush of my preparations for the lecture, by the thought of getting the doctor to spell it out – 'well, in matter of fact, Mr Eyre, he tends to like himself rather too much'.

— Actually, his problems, his condition . . . of course, I cannot confide . . .

It didn't look like the doctor was going to oblige, and I didn't care to hold on any longer just to learn the technical term for Marius' proclivities. Time was at a premium.

— This is all very interesting, doctor, but I'm at this very moment preparing to leave, I'm about to give a lecture.

I looked down for my watch amongst the scrawled notes which thankfully I'd managed to gather together in a last minute panic the night before.

— I won't keep you, Mr Eyre. But I think it imperative that you know.

— Know what?

I found the watch and fastened it too tightly, so the hairs on my wrist were pinched and pulled.

— You see, Marius Pritty has been arrested on suspicion of drugging and attempting to rape a fellow patient.

Just as I loosened the strap of the watch, the clasp broke and I dropped the phone. And as I swore I heard a tiny little voice on the floor, squealing like a mouse.

— What? What was that, Mr Eyre? Can you still hear me? Mr Eyre? Mr Eyre?

I picked up the phone and rammed it to my ear.

— Look, Dr Romme, I really just haven't got time right now, if you'd just like to ring back at another . . .

— But I need to meet with you, Mr Eyre, there's something else you should know.

— What?

By this time I was shouting, and couldn't tolerate the pause after my enquiry. I bawled again.

— What?

— He has been caught in possession of something that belongs to you, Mr Eyre. Well, not caught in possession exactly, he left it in his locker at the hospital, amongst his own private and personal belongings.

— Dr Romme, please! What item of mine, personal or otherwise, could this Marius Pritty possibly possess?

— A pen, Mr Eyre.

— A pen?

— A pen, yes. It has your name inscribed on the clip, Mr Eyre. An expensive pen I believe, a Mont Blanc.

— A pen?

— What I am saying, Mr Eyre, is that the pen has not been confiscated by the police It was discovered amongst his belongings, it is not forming part of their body of evidence, so to speak. I am in possession of it myself now in fact, and am in a position to return it to its rightful owner.

— Well, that's very kind of you, Dr Romme, but . . .

— And I urgently need to speak with you.

There was no time. I told her to meet me, in the foyer before the lecture, thinking I could answer all her questions quickly, without fuss. Get it over and done, that's what I wanted. Get the pen back; if it hadn't been a Mont Blanc I wouldn't have bothered. Just get the pen back, that's all. Was this doctor playing tricks on me? Was it a trap? What did she want, what could I possibly tell her she didn't already know? The picture I had of Janet had grown steadily grimmer and grimier: from needy patient and possible sister, or even daughter, to malevolent stalker and finally to general, malingering parasite. She'd sunk her teeth in, that was what her type did; desperate for a

212

host organism. Call it father figure if you like; she just wouldn't let go, didn't know how.

K, of course, disagreed, vehemently. But what was new in that.

— I don't know what you've got against her. One minute you want to be her long lost brother, next thing you think she's just some bum.

But K had never had to work the coal face. She didn't know what it was like.

We were in the Renault by this time, the traffic thick and slow. It felt like we were never going to get anywhere, let alone to the conference. I pictured Dr Romme on the other end of the phone, the battered briefcase, all those battered lives. I wondered whether she slept with it under her pillow, the voices whispering into her dreams. I recalled the doc telling me about Janet's fantasies. How long ago was that, a week, a month, a lifetime? Asking in her perfunctory way, as if nothing pended on it: 'This attraction, Mr Eyre, Janet's apparent attraction, the way she regards you. Would you ever say it was reciprocated?' Had she believed my denial, my indignant, deep throated chuckle? Did I believe it? That's what shrinks do. They read minds, read the future into the past; they make it up. I could see that much from her little black book. They were parasites, just like their patients.

Before Dr Romme called I'd rehearsed my talk in the bathroom mirror, and experienced one of those horrible moments. I saw the Dickensian wave in the hair first, then the sideburns. It wasn't as if I was unfamiliar with my own features: the beard got trimmed regularly enough, I was used to looking at myself. And I'd seen glimmers of him before. But suddenly the visage in the glass was bare of facial hair, transparent; I was naked and could see beyond, into the future, into the past. I glanced at my lecture notes then back at the mirror. My father: the very spitting, salivating, youth-forsaken image; even the rheumy, old-man eyes. Oh, God! That growing-in-the-grave look. What had my mother said? 'One of those people who just aren't very good at what they do.'

Somehow, eventually, I don't know how, I dispelled the ghost, I think by staring it away. And it wasn't banished completely, just turned into some strange ally, as fathers, proper fathers, are supposed to be. I looked and looked and looked again, until my father seemed to be helping me. I discovered that I could narrate the spiel at myself automatically almost without reference to the notes.

— Since the war there have been a number of initiatives aimed at the relationship between parent and child. In the last twenty years alone . . .

As I looked at myself enunciating, a song, music started up in my head. I couldn't think what it might be, but I knew that I knew it. Looking down at my shaving-foam scented notes, the words scrambling on the page, I heard the creak of my father's voice – 'whenever you can' – as if we were at cello practice again and he was marshalling my up-bows and down-bows, my arpeggios and adantes. 'Whenever you can, count.' K had burned the toast and the smell wafted into the bathroom as I looked and saw myself mouthing the words. And something in the acrid scent, in the moment of that muddled reflection and rehearsal, seemed to make perfect sense. I touched the mirror, clearing the mist from the cold glass. *Whenever you can, count.*

The conference was being held in a squat sixties tower block just off the ring road, an ugly, local council edifice of sectional concrete, with a pebble dash facade under the road-facing windows. It looked as if it was about to fall down, redeemed only by its brief grounds: strips of grit and well watered grass circling flower beds that were colour co-ordinated in purple and yellow, to match those on the adjacent roundabout. The smell of pine disinfectant filled the foyer where Dr Romme sat waiting in a bucket seat by the reception desk. K, with a knowing smile, backed off a step or two, standing by the door.

Sure enough Dr Romme held her battered leather bag close to her chest, opening it only briefly, to retrieve the pen. It was indeed mine. How could Marius have come by it? How should I know, I only lost it.

— Where did you lose it, Mr Eyre?

— In the shed.

— *The* shed, Mr Eyre?

Yes, of course *the* bloody shed, what other shed was there? I explained how I'd gone there, how the little bird had been trapped by my entrance, how, in the commotion I'd dropped the pen and not been able to find it in the gloom.

— But why were you there, Mr Eyre?

— I was trying to find the father.

— But it was getting dark you say.

This was turning into an interrogation, I was feeling guilty.

— It must have occurred to you, Mr Eyre, it was hardly likely that he would still be there after so long a time. When in your investigation did you visit the shed?

My birthday, I knew well enough, but I didn't tell her that. I told her it was when Janet was in the respite clinic, when I was conducting my initial inquiries: spring of last year. She appeared to lighten up at this, as if it was something she wanted to hear. She asked if I ever went back to the shed.

— Yes, of course, these pens are worth a lot of money you know.

— And yet you didn't report its loss to the police? Did you ever encounter Janet on your visits to the shed? Or anyone else?

She made it sound like I went there for Sunday outings and took a picnic.

— I only ever went back once.

But as I said it I got a sudden flash: holding the pen out in front of me, ready to stab, ready to kill.

It crossed my mind that Dr Romme was really a police detective, but I didn't know exactly what crime I might have committed. I was bemused and angry.

— So, how did Marius get hold of the pen? Tell me that.

— He...

— He must have stolen it from Janet. She must have found it at the shed.

— No, I'm afraid not, Mr Eyre. I fear Marius did not steal it from Janet. He found it in the shed himself.

How did she know all of this?

— Marius was aware of the shed, Mr Eyre. Its location, and the fact that Janet frequented it.

— But how?

— He followed Janet there.

I didn't understand. She went on to explain: she'd met with Janet's adoptive parents and now gained all the notes from her previous treatments. Janet had suffered on-going problems from the age of fourteen. She had been admitted to the respite clinic a couple of times before Holly was born, before she was conceived even. There was no doubt she had encountered Marius on those occasions. It felt like Dr Romme was making it all up, just so it would fit. Possible, but hardly probable. She assured me, patients often came across one another again and again. The patient Marius had most recently attacked was well acquainted with him; in effect, they had lived together in the same buildings, the same institutions, on and off, for a number of years. She made it sound like they were spouses.

— Yes, but what does ... what does any of this have to do with me?

— The woman in question, Marius' latest victim, suffered from, amongst other things, involuntary movements, Mr Eyre, you may have heard of such symptoms. Anarchic arm syndrome?

I nodded.

— Well, her condition, this tendency she had of violently swiping out against her will and beyond her conscious control, had, in the event, saved her.

— How?

I was getting more confused by the second.

— She had most certainly been drugged by Marius, but whatever the effect of the drug it had failed to counter her

216

symptoms. In short, it did not stop her random arm movements. She knocked him unconscious in the middle of the attack.

My impatience snapped into a brittle, incontinent chortle. Pictures of Dr Strangelove flashed before me. Dr Romme was not similarly amused.

— It is hardly a laughing matter, Mr Eyre. The fact that he failed in this instance and with this particular victim, does not mean that he has not succeeded in the past and with other victims. Do you not see the seriousness of this, Mr Eyre?

Yes, but I was about to give a lecture, for God's sake, and here I was *being* lectured. I'd got my pen back, what more did she want? Dr Romme looked at me and casually, but without dropping her stare, pointed out that there was a certain similarity of appearance between myself and Marius.

— What?

— Mainly the hair colour. In fact, only the hair colour. There is no other link as as far as I can see.

— Well, that's reassuring.

Bizarrely Dr Romme continued to observe me as if waiting for some obscure detail to reveal itself. I turned away, dumbfounded, only to see K eyeing both of us, waiting for an introduction. I turned back to the doctor and silently demanded an explanation.

— Janet suffers an unconscious confusion between the two of you, Mr Eyre.

— What? Marius . . . Marius and . . .?

— Yes, I am now all but certain this is the case. It may indeed explain the sexual fantasies and the need to seek revenge.

— Revenge?

I didn't understand. This sounded like a last ditch warning, as if my life was in imminent danger. Didn't Janet have the fantasies about me before Marius Pritty desecrated her things up in the pigeon loft? But I wasn't supposed to know about that was I? In any case, it looked like Dr Romme was on the trail of other desecrations. She hadn't got anywhere near her conclusions.

At that moment Richard came down on the lift to get me.

— Come on, old chap. No time for chit chat, we're on the third floor and this contraption takes an age. If you don't beam up now you'll miss your cue.

He pointed at the lift, looking around timidly, yet still furtively, at K. She ignored him, her eyes keen on Dr Romme. Grudgingly I offered.

— Look, there's no time, not now at any rate . . . you could wait down here or . . . or, if you could bear it, I'll get Richard to get you a pass. You could sit in, but you've probably got a busy schedule. . .

— No, I would be most interested. What did you say your lecture was about?

I wanted her to go away but she insisted, said she was sure she'd be most stimulated. I looked for any sign of a smile, any hint of dryness, but there was none. K, who'd been straining at the leash, took Dr Romme by the arm, looking for all the world like it was Christmas. She'd always wanted a head doctor for a friend.

CHAPTER 4

Looking at the audience, all those hungry eyes, I consoled myself: for the audience the words wouldn't matter, whatever I offered up; it was the vol aux vents they were really after. I looked out to see if I could recognise faces and, though I saw nobody I knew, was struck by something familiar: a slight but unmistakable waft of burning. It took me a while to place it: after shaving, my father always singed his sideburns with a burning straw. This was that same smell. Sometimes he asked me to singe the hairs round the back of his neck, the areas he couldn't see or reach himself. I was always terrified in case I set him alight. And now I was filled with the same sort of terror.

There was a cough or two as they settled in their seats. For a moment I thought the acrid under-scent was growing and that there might be a real fire. Soon I realised it was probably someone in the audience with similar grooming habits to my father. I tried to spot who it might be. A woman in the third row fidgeted, her red hat wobbling on her head; next to her there was a badger-bearded man in herringbone jacket. The beard was thick but tightly cropped; the sideburns too. It could quite feasibly have been him. As I gazed out I realised I could see him and the woman with the red hat clearly enough, but I couldn't quite focus on the lectern even though it was right there between my hands. My notes were indecipherable. There was something in my eye.

Being on the third floor there was quite a vantage. Out of the window at the rear of the hall I could just see the Scots pines on the edge of town, the sun catching their bark in that inimitable way. I could see this vista clear enough; still no sign of clouds rumbling in over the hills from the west, or from any other direction for that matter. The swallows had been flocking for a week, but at this rate they wouldn't need to go anywhere. It was so dry the pine bark looked like burnt, flaking skin, the vegetation like threadbare cloth. Summer had lost its lustre and the red tree trunks, far from being glorious oracles, suddenly looked brash, like lurid icons in the darkest, most sacred corner of a church.

Richard finished his introduction, just as I noticed Dr Romme, over by the green 'fire exit' sign to the right, the distinctive leather bag on her lap. Next to her, K: chatting away and, I thought for a moment, smiling up at me on the rostrum like a proud parent. I almost smiled back. Though I could see K and the doctor well enough, I still couldn't quite comprehend the words in front of me, or get a firm grip on the lectern. A hush set in; all those eyes, expectant and settling as one on me. And the song started up, the music and the orders, my father's words: whenever you can, count. The smell of the singed sideburns seemed to have revived his voice, made it deeper and more commanding. I looked to the left; Richard, his eyes urging me to get on with it: 'begin, go on; get it over and done with, so we can all go home'. I could see him all right. I felt a tear roll into my beard, still not regular or consecutive enough to be called 'crying'. I looked to my notes on the lectern but could see nothing. I was going to have to make it up.

And so, eventually, obeying the command -: 'Whenever you can' – I did my father's bidding and counted, to ten, opening my mouth in hope rather than expectation, praying that my rictus wasn't gaping too wide, too inanely. A gurgle rose up from my churning stomach.

— Rrr . . . rr . . . recently my father died.

I heard the murmur. Too many people knew me, something was wrong, they could tell. I looked to the left. Even Richard, in his disinterest, looked bemused.

— Well, my mother died most recently, but with the death of one parent I came to reconsider both of my parents. It was as if my father still lived while my mother was alive. Up until then I had not fully recognised his departure from this world.

Having strung a few words together, I felt a gush of relief. Then I remembered some of the spiel and found myself talking fluently: what the research was meant to achieve, its scope, its sponsors, its relevance. And while I was talking, bizarrely, I recalled a conversation about Freud: K telling me how the word 'spiel' translated as 'play', and how dear old Sigmund had thought of it as spinning a fantasy. And as I thought this I realised I was saying things I hadn't ever thought before. I was improvising.

— ... history induces in us an appropriate caution, but our more recent history has bred a rampant relativism, a relativism which we have permitted some to use against us. Fingers have been wagged for far too long. Reasonable, if unpalatable, solutions to our problems have been dismissed out of hand. We are fearful of anything resembling a bio-deterministic explanation of the world. Such explanations have provoked the most finger wagging. And yet now, now we are discovering the cost of ignoring such explanations, we are discovering that such explanations could have benefited our approach in many areas of everyday ...

Whatever my earlier problems, and whatever K or Freud or my father or anyone had said in the past, it felt like nothing was going to stop me now. And it was going down well. I spotted the lady in the red hat nodding off. The lectern was wet with my sweat and I wondered momentarily if wood could melt. Even some of my notes were now making sense. I could read again. I spotted the Mont Blanc, rested on the lectern, and searched out beyond the red-hatted woman and her herring-boned companion, over to the right, past K and Dr Romme.

— ... any discussion of the state's relationship to the child necessarily involves us all, not just those present here today, not just the professionals, but everyone. We all have parents, dead or alive, many of us have children...

I picked up the pen, and as if empowered, searched on past the green luminescent lettering above the fire exit, out through the window to the Scots pines, now silhouetted on the horizon. Was I blinking? Could they see the tears welling? Could they see this fear or fever or frenzy or whatever it was that had overcome me? The trees, like crying bones, I could see them weeping, I could hear them. I searched beyond their black silhouettes, like grief skeletons, off towards the hills in the west, off into the void of the sky. And I felt another, isolated trickle down my cheek.

— Our . . . our relationship with our children is reflected in the State's relationship to us, and vice versa. It is a reciprocal set of relationships. As parents we must be tolerant, yes, but sometimes we must be firm. And in this respect I think we have lapsed.

I looked to the fire exit and saw the door starting to open; I looked away, fearing what was to come. I focused on K and Dr Romme, addressing them and the man in the herringbone tweed. I let go of the lectern, no longer shaking; not wavering, not giving an inch.

— When I looked down into my mother's grave I got to thinking about her life and that of my father; both lifelong Fabians, she a woman of moral certitude, he a liberal, a humanist, yes, but also a man of authority. He was a doctor, as some of you may recall, and it was his duty to be decisive, to be authoritative. I believe he never shirked that duty. He could not allow himself to be anything other than firm. And if our present era mourns for anything it mourns, and longs for, just that: that firmness of mind, that authority.

To hell with which father tape I was playing; I knew, as I grabbed at the odd, barely discernible phrase from my notes, that this was a best seller. The words were flowing, those written and those found on the hoof; the syllables pronounced before I'd even thought them, as if I was merely some ventriloquist's dummy. Was this what Freud meant by spiel?

— During the early part of this century there was much speculation and talk about the State's responsibility and role in controlling the population, how much it should influence reproductive patterns, and regulate family size and complexion. It was then seen as incumbent upon the State to be firm, to care for its populace and to stand up and be counted. All were of the same opinion, yes even the apparent dissenters, the liberals and philanthropists . . .

I mumbled something about John Maynard Keynes as I looked over my notes and then back to the fire exit. I couldn't help myself. The door was open but I saw no sign of the metal escape staircase, instead just a vignette, a face in the blackness, filling the frame. In a different mood, a different time, I might have been able to laugh; I would have seen the cascade of ironies. But not now; all I saw was a face bursting into flames. All I saw was horror. Janet Burns. She was there, in all her literal, eponymous glory. In that moment I was sure it was her, and I was sure also of the conflagration. There was no joke, no mistake. Later, when I told K, she failed to stifle a giggle: 'Sounds like one of those horrible parodies. You know, a Catherine-Heathcliff moment, but with a dash of Bertha thrown in for good measure. Ha, ha!'

But what did K know? At that moment it was Janet. I was sure of it. Who could I possibly tell? Who could I tell and be believed? The face I had been waiting all my life to see, the eyes shining grey and bright, the darkness framing those finely cut cheeks; my fingers running through her hair, eggs in the nest; the hair that curled ever so gently into the shadow of a shoulder. I knew now: desire, love, these words were too small for what I saw: the smile, the shadow of a star on my blood; the delicate turn of the lips, like the bright edge of a cloud's dark centre; her face staring, then suddenly flaring up with the flames; raging, alive, glancing, devouring. Yes, just like the ridge of burning heath. Yes, but more, much, much more. Feeling as if I was flying, I shut my eyes and carried on talking as best I could.

— Since the war, and since my father's generation handed over the reins, that firmness of vision has lapsed. We look at the State now and are cynical, filled with derision; all we see is hesitancy. Our collective self-esteem is low; we don't know what to do or what we are supposed to do. As a State we are, in short, depressed. So how are we capable of caring for others? We all know that depression affords only an exaggerated self-regard, often at the expense of a regard for others. The ways in which the modern State tries to care are, more often than not, a damning indictment of its inability, for whatever bureaucratic or economic reasons, *to* care. What I am suggesting is that these bureaucratic and economic reasons are merely excuses, symptoms of the depression if you like. What I am suggesting is that somehow we have to start to care again, but somehow we also have to find it in ourselves to be firm. It is the only way we will, collectively, rise out of the depression. Whatever our better impulses and intentions, caring has to be hard-faced and sometimes, in order to care, we may have to make difficult choices.

I saw the red hat almost topple as the woman woke with a jerk. The first ripples of applause. Richard rose, in his capacity as MC, to thank me. The man in the herringbone tweed thought this to be the lead for a standing ovation and was soon joined; the whole audience stood, eventually as one, all clapping. I turned to see Richard's puzzled face as he approached, then turned back to the audience, wiping another tear from my cheek.

Dr Romme was half up, half down, undecided, as she clung to her bag. K was all but alone, still in her seat. The fire exit was obscured. Richard winked as he gained the rostrum, and spoke *sotto voce*.

— How much have you had to drink, you old evangelist?

Then he turned to the audience to calm the applause.

The lectern wobbled as he passed me and my notes scattered and flew like feathers from a shot bird. In stooping to gather them, my groping arms merely wafted the plumes further, so they floated weightlessly down to the parquet floor at the feet of the first row. I was still on my knees when Richard started to speak.

— I'm sure we would all like to thank Philip for that stirring insight. Perhaps we can now turn to the hall, I'm sure you are all full of questions.

I looked up with crumpled paper falling from my hands. The re-inhabited seats creaking, there was a cough or two, a stifled sneeze, but no hands raised, not yet. Could they see: another tear, the tenth or hundredth, trickling down into my beard? Whenever you can, count! Still not concerted enough to be called crying, but whatever it was it was beyond the facts; there was no cause. Were they going to let me off, were they going to set me free? I shuffled the papers. They crackled in the silence and I heard the music growing louder. What was that tune? What were the words?

— I have a question.

It was the herringbone tweed, his beard swirling like a half-mown lawn as he spoke. I imagined him singeing it in front of his mirror. A smart arse.

— I can only compliment Mr Eyre on the apparent dedication and enthusiasm with which he . . .

No problem with that, yes, I could field those all day. Praise me, yes, I can take it. Praise me, praise me! A woman from the front row handed me some sheets that she'd gathered from the floor. Silence again, sweet and scented. I was almost there, one or two more. Praise me, praise me. But then Richard, trying to wrap it up, trying to get to the drinks, was unable to resist. A little playful irony, a gest.

— Just one last question . . . yes, the woman next to the lady with the briefcase. All the way from Canada I do believe.

Richard's smile was so large his bottom lip nearly cut a canal to his ear. K stood for the occasion. What was she doing? She smoothed down the lapels of her black jacket and even Dr Romme looked a little perplexed beside her.

— I was just wondering if Mr Eyre could furnish us with some specifics, about what constitutes this firmness of vision. He seems to be advocating some quite radical programme. How *do* we care, as you put it? What is this hard-faced approach? Or is it too early in your research to elaborate?

Predictable; this was about pinning and masts and colours again. All quiet. Still. All those starving eyes. A man from the front row handed me the last of the fallen sheets from the floor of the hall. I snatched at them, and looked blankly at the crumpled pile of papers on the lectern; again, there would be no answers there, nothing to see. And I had nothing to say. Except the murmur at the back of my mind: 'whenever you can, whenever you can . . .' Yes. That would solve it. That would show K and her wilful ways. Listen to this, just listen. Are you sitting comfortably? Then we'll begin.

— Yes, it is fairly early on in the research programme. . .

K sat. I searched behind her. The fire door was open: no Janet Burns now, but I saw a wood outside, a forest, and I could see someone, a woman, I couldn't look. Another tear, I wiped my eyes. In the wood, there was blood. Flames. I couldn't look, only hear: whenever you can, whenever you can . . . I couldn't . . . I looked. The fire door was open, and Janet Burns stood there again.

Oh yes, the final possibility was still around, it echoed like a charm in my otherwise empty head. I knew how to answer K's dastardly question, I'd tell her what she wanted to hear, I'd tell them all. The final possibility would always be around, haunting and taunting us. And why not let them have it, right between their right-on, beneficent, liberal old eyes? Whenever you can, count. That's what I wanted to tell them; that old time syntax, that way of looking at things. His Master's Voice being wound up on the turntable, the bronze horn speaker, yes, and the man with the herringbone tweed would nod in agreement, the woman in the red hat would turn bemused.

I couldn't work out why the man in the front row who'd returned the last of my notes was looking so hurt and aggrieved. Richard checked his watch, wanting me to get on with it. And what would I have said, at that very moment, if I'd told them? The technology was now advanced. We should utilise it. That's what I'd say. At this point in time my rather general conclusions are inclined toward a State incentive scheme, similar in structure to child benefit as it now stands. But instead of an ongoing cost, the curse of universal allowances, the State would offer a one-off payment; a benefit that would make it more than worthwhile for those of a certain predisposition to undergo genetic scrutiny. And, sure enough, the whispering would start, like a pan coming to the boil. The red hat would rise, as if of its own volition. She'd be one of the first to walk out, guaranteed. Richard would stumble on the rostrum steps, rushing towards the lectern, trying to shut me up. There'd be shouts from the hall: 'Surely you're not suggesting? This is a democracy you know!' They'd boo and they'd hiss but it would all be so English, so terribly, terribly civilised. I wouldn't want it to end there, I wouldn't let it. They wouldn't understand, they wouldn't want to understand; I could see it all clearly: the future, the past. There was no barbarism involved now. People would agree willingly, a free and informed choice in the matter, they'd be happy; it was the only way to care. They'd reap material rewards, substantial benefits. I would tell them to think of the benefits to all of us; the reduced tax burden, health costs slashed. As I pictured it all the music grew louder, together with my father's voice: whenever you can, count. And I would tell them: if you can reduce the beauty and mystery of music to just a matter of counting and calculation, surely you can do the same with people.

I would laugh, imploringly. Wasn't it clear? And then, seeing them all leaving the hall I would shout at them: they were the only people who'd lose out on the deal. I'd tell them. The herringbone tweed would pause, as if this was my last chance. He would stroke his beard in pensive hope. And I'd tell them: we aren't ants or bees. As a species altruism doesn't come naturally to us. Oh yes, we have these impulses but we don't know how to do it properly. We have to be paid to care. And that was the real problem wasn't it? I'd tell them: within two generations most of us in this room would be redundant. And Richard would finally get to the lectern, unceremoniously pushing me to one side. I would tell him: that's why they're walking out on me, you know, they can't stand the implications. Job security: now, where's the firmness of vision in that? I imagined it all, what I would say, their reaction, their indignation. The final possibility: a slow motion future-play.

In real time the pause in my answer had taken on cough-

and-splutter proportions. They were still looking at me, still pressing for an answer to K's question. How do we care? How should I know? How could I know? How do we reach out our hands to those who might be in need, how do we touch each other? Caring: was that ever at all possible? I thought of Grey Owl and Bjorn Borg, I thought of Marius Pritty and a million others. And as I searched the hall I caught sight of the fire exit again; the green of the sign I was sure had turned a shade of red. Janet reappeared as my eyes rested on the door, this time with her sights set. No longer a vignette, no more in flames; this time her hands were freed from the darkness that surrounded her. They spiralled for a moment, rubbing together gleefully, anticipating the blood, the death-rattle, the corpse. Having now separated completely from their owner they sailed across the room towards me. Vermilion and crimson lake, in unison, intent, over and above all the heads; hate and love, love and hate, tattooed clear as day on the knuckles. All possibility dissolving; hate and love arrowed at me, dripping red, coming towards my neck, heading straight for it. I heard myself starting finally to say something, about universal paternity leave I think, but the words, my words, suddenly cracked into a yodelling scream. Was that really me yelping? Was that nail-scraping voice mine? I remember someone called out my name as I grabbed the pen and took aim.

— Philip! Don't! Philip!

But their shouts rang hollow, a gun chamber echo. The shot had already been fired. Nothing made any sense. I thought I might know him, possibly, but who was this Philip? Who was he really?

K told me that I shouted for my mother a couple of times, as I was being restrained. I screamed more too, but only a little, she said. I think she was being kind. She told me that I shouted something about hate and hands. I stood, as if trying to ward off an attack, with my shoulders up like a boxer. And she told me I took aim with great care, quickly but with unerring precision, as if I was throwing a dart or spear, as if I knew exactly

228

what I was doing. I looked scared but angry, K said. The pen scored a direct hit. The red hat. The woman became all arms and handbags, all fluster and bluster, outraged 'squeaky squawks', according to K. She laughed when she told me, how the woman had garbled something about solicitors and how it wasn't like this last year. But no-one really took any notice of her, everyone was looking at me. And K said I was crying, really crying.

All I remember clearly, uncontrovertibly, is opening my eyes and looking out over the once full seats, the drained, charcoal plush; the last door swinging shut. At the back, the fire door was closed; even the light of its sign was extinguished. There were only three figures left, three people who moved with a mysterious alacrity. Hadn't they seen what had happened? I overheard Richard in the wings confess to thinking I was drunk, while K and Dr Romme hovered over me, both smiling anxiously. This was another picture for my K album, to go with the tear-stained visages, to go with her all-knowing, flirty ways. But it cracked the theme; there was no betrayal here, just care and concern. Wiping the tears from my face, my one-time persecutor looked to me now very much like a nurse. Or an angel.

CHAPTER 5

K once said that we give up a part of our selves when we care, when we love, when we follow a possibility even a little way. I didn't think much of it at the time, but during those days and weeks and months after the lecture I couldn't get these odd lines out of my head. And I couldn't help but wonder about all those lips meeting, or even just eyes, the way those in love touch the air between one another. Some part of us is left behind, that's what K said. We leave belongings, photographs, pictures of ourselves, letters and notes, our words, sometimes not even these, just our thoughts. We leave them, that's what she said. Some part of us is lost and chipped away.

Whether or not I would be able to forget whatever it was that had happened to me I just couldn't say. And I knew – the only thing I did know – I wouldn't be able to say for quite some time. In this new, torn landscape I was met by salvos of sadness and grief at every turn. The various characters I'd once recognised as myself seemed to be smouldering amongst the surrounding trees and roads and gardens. They billowed up at me from time to time like puffs of bonfire smoke then dispersed just as quickly. Every time I caught a glimpse of myself I felt defeated and riddled with gloom; like a balloon bursting, suddenly my world would plummet, spiralling into sucked-out nothingness. I would fall down and down, as if I was falling deep into the soil, only worse, darker; it was so lightless I couldn't move my arms or legs, so black I couldn't pass, or even tell, the time of day.

Sitting paralysed, I sometimes watched old people going about their business from my mother's window, the familiar smells and echoes rife inside the empty house. But it was more than just being reminded of my origins, more than being surrounded by forecasts of my own demise. I watched the old people from the window and I wanted to reach out, to carry their bags for them, to clean their houses and cut their lawns, change their light bulbs and wash their clothes, I wanted to help them onto their buses. I watched them and cried at their lives. I cried at my own; I watched them but couldn't move, not one little finger.

One night, long before the dawn, I woke and heard a bird singing, briefly, on its own. It had the shrillest, most hysterical pitch, jagging like a splinter through the still air. And as I looked about me I realised it was the darkest, the blackest possible moment. Though I couldn't see a watch or clock I could tell it was absurdly early, way ahead of the usual twittering chorus. Over breakfast I asked K:

— Why do some birds sing out in the middle of the night?

— What do you mean?

— Long before the others begin, in the middle of the night, one bird, it sounds louder, as if . . . as if . . . I heard one last night. You were fast asleep, I got up but I couldn't see it.

— A bird?

— Yes, you slept through it, probably a blackbird or a thrush.

— Beats me. Maybe it had a nightmare or something.

A couple of weeks later, just before we received the news, it happened again. the middle of the night, the lonely voice-song, like an un-oiled cog beginning to turn, then, just as shockingly, stopping: a moan of day, and then the silent, screaming night again; only a few seconds, a few cranks. This time, I don't know why but I didn't need to ask K or anyone; this time I knew what it meant.

It was a numbers game: counting, just like my father had said. I had to do some research but the information wasn't that hard to come by. Wales has always had a lot of water, more than its fair share: cwm lakes, tarns, streams and rivers, millions and millions of gallons of it. In the fifties and sixties the conurbations of Birmingham and Merseyside looked to Wales to help them out. Dams and reservoirs were already fairly common, if not without their objectors. Lynn Alwen and Lake Vyrnwy, and the other nineteenth-century lakes, had served their purpose well. But now, with the post-war boom, flush toilets and garden ponds, the demand had surpassed all Victorian imaginings. There was a need to flood more valleys.

It was just a numbers game. In one such valley they decided to control the flow of the river downstream, where domestic water was then abstracted and treated nearer to the population centres in England. An extra 50,000,000 cubic metres of water was needed every year, for an area covering 120 square miles with a population of 1.3 million. They would build a dam and it would act as a tap. Work was delayed for political reasons. Two holiday cottages were burnt down in protest. But the dam was eventually completed in 1975. The need of the few sacrificed in favour of the need of the many.

The inhabitants of the only village in the valley, 35 of them in all, were all tenants of a local JP, Geraint Griffith. Most had lived there for generations. He paid each household a few hundred pounds (£369 was the average hand-out) and offered them caravans on a patch of lowland scrub for which he had no other use. It was a pasture which, after the building of the dam, often flooded in the spring, and which soon proved only of use for summer grazing. Geraint Griffith made a pretty bundle in compensation: tens, probably hundreds of thousands. The exact amount was never made public. So accommodating the need of the few.

When it came to the lake itself, I soon found out it was a question of numbers again. 5 miles long and half a mile across at its widest point; covering 1,100 acres, with a maximum depth of 123 feet, and a maximum capacity of 12,131 million gallons; the dam was constructed with 510,000 tons of masonry and took 4 years to build. We were told by a pub landlord from down the valley that most years the reservoir hid its past. I could see this from the publicity shot: it looked as smooth as a mirror, reflecting the sky's innocent azure and the rather pompous looking hill tops; a negligible passing cloud completing the partial lie. Even on this photograph you could see the water rippling opaquely, and the imported boulders at the dammed, eastern shore, camouflaged by thick moss and lichen, looking for all the world as if they'd always laid there. You could also just make out the route of an old railway line, a real give away: at one point, to the west of the valley, elevated and viaducted, it then dipped tragically down below the water line, towards the lost village.

During the drought-ridden summer just gone, the water level at an all time low, the railway line rediscovered its platform and station. A chapel could also be seen for a number of months. And a stone bridge. A village was re-found as the people of Merseyside used more hose pipes to water their lawns and fill their paddling pools than maybe they were supposed to.

It was after all only a numbers game, that's what my investigations kept telling me. The underlying rocks were laid down under the seas between 400 and 500 million years ago, during the Ordovician and Silurian periods. At the end of the latter all of Wales was uplifted and folded by intense earth movements. The more recent shape of the valley was caused by the glaciers of the last million years. One such glacier scooped a hollow between the hills. For thousands of years there'd been water at the valley's centre. Long before the dam there was a small cwm lake, 300 yards across, no more, some 25 feet deep. On fair days in years gone by farmhands raced to the top of the adjacent hill with cartwheels on their backs, then threw the wheels off the cliff into the valley's watery stomach. When the dam was constructed they excavated the lake and found hundreds of cartwheel skeletons preserved in the silt of the lake bed. The race winner was lauded, gaining the hand of whomsoever he should care to dance with that evening. One unfortunate racer fell with his wheel; it was 2 days before they recovered the body from the lake. Numbers again. The coroner in the nearest town, some 10 miles away, has only ever reported one body found in the water since the dam was built.

Janet Burns must have looked down into the sinewy black, into the opaque mass of water. She must have been convinced it hid everything she was looking for and must have asked. 'What do I do now?' Faced with the impossibility, her amnesia running alongside the flooding and drowning of her past, she would see no irony, only the fact that something of herself, some essential hope, had been wiped out, yet a reminder of it, a trace, had been tantalisingly preserved. It would always be just out of reach. I never checked with her case notes to see if the flooded valley was indeed the place where she was born. There was no need. The half-submerged village was where she was headed from the start, whether or not it was her real home, whether or not it was the actual place she had once lived with her mother. It was the end, the only certainty; checking names wouldn't alter that. She believed it to be her point of origin and that was all that mattered. How did I know this? How does anyone know anything? I believed too. Janet looked down into the water and saw it passing under the half-submerged bridge, the same stone bridge where she once sat while her mother shelled peas, the same bridge over the same river, the source, the hope she'd followed so desperately all her life. She believed it to be so. And I believed this to be the way it was.

I had no idea whether Janet actually came to the conference and saw me giving my lecture. They told me she couldn't have; K said it was impossible. But what did she know. All I could say was that I saw her, a vision if you like. But my life turned as a consequence. It was a miracle. A seeing. When we got the news, and as soon as I was well enough to travel, I got K to drive me up to the lake in the Renault. I had to see it for myself. I had to know. The end, and how she'd got there.

The mist at first concealed the lake's surface, revealing only the pine tops on the far shore. We parked the car and grabbed our coats, K with that gurgling enthusiasm.

— Look at it, just you look at it!

I was suddenly less sure.

— Maybe we shouldn't have come.

— But just look out there, it's like we're on top of a cloud, like you could just walk over to the other side.

I stifled a vague, boyhood urge to skim a stone, an urge that felt as if it was being recalled from someone else's life not my own. We stood on the shore and gazed in silence across the grey fleece for what seemed like an age, the moisture threading our hair and coats with glistening, silver beads, the stillness drugging us into a dreamy lull. We searched across the cloud and way up into and over the pine trees and hills, scanning for clues to this moment of our lives.

K eventually broke the spell.

— Look, it's shifting.

And sure enough, the mist gradually rose before our eyes, unveiling the black waters beneath. As it climbed a swirling rain rushed into the vacuum – even in these parts the first for a long, long time. And as the drenching swathes slashed dismissively through the remains of the fog, the air suddenly and incongruously lightened and I saw what had happened. I saw it all, as clear as if it were being presented to me on a screen. Like a movie, like another vision.

Janet walked at first; that is how she must have set out: following the banks of the river, sleeping in barns, in cow sheds, in half-built houses, half-unbuilt cottages and in the derelict outbuildings of dogless farms. Then she must have hitched rides and had salesmen putting their hands on her knee, lorry drivers smiling at the bunk behind the driver's seat, inquiring, oh, so sympathetically how tired she must be. But nothing could touch her now. She followed the river, up out of the plains, up through the old oaks and beech woods, winding up into the hills, way beyond anything she could be expected to know or remember. Following the river home; so she believed.

And by this time the river had started to babble, to rush over rocks, polishing and honing, sharpening her will; there would have been no resting place now, only a kind of happiness, the hum of being nearly there. No more reeds or sleepy, civilised, weeping willows. Only sallow and alder and hazel – and a pining in her, so strong she'd have all but burst when reaching the dam and seeing the pine trees on the far shore, the head of the valley where the river had been stemmed.

By now there would have been hardly any cars. She would have walked along the road and passed as a rambler, with her bag strung over her shoulder, the bag they found by the giant, lichened stones. The dam could halt the water, it could stem the river and mountain streams but it couldn't stop her believing. This would have been, I was sure, her dying spiel. *I believe. I believe. I believe.* She would have recognised something in the way the hills met the sky, in the burnt bracken slopes, something in the imploring, God beseeching curve of the land, something in the random yet heart-sung swerve of the contours. More permanent than anything man could invent or make, it was etched into her so she could never possibly forget, though she might never have known it from a solitary day or minute or moment from her own past. Not *déjà* but rather *toujours vu*, a recognition that hardened her faith and told her that no matter the doubts she suffered, no matter her fears, she was, after all, on the right path.

And she might have looked at the thick black, oily ripples and yearned for more. The wishing tree, was that down there in the depths? Where she had sat with her mother beside the old gnarled trunk; the chestnut crowns sitting like swallowed penny's in the valley's bowel. And the meadowsweet, just like her mother had told her; was that there too, its dried stalks wrapped in the bindweed's deep, deep green? More than a season was ending now, more than a month or year or day. The black would have called her, offering all these irresistible glimpses, hope flickering like a jinx on the water. And she might have seen, as the sun dipped and the sporadic holiday traffic, the walkers and towed caravans, as they were pausing for the evening; she might have caught sight of herself in the water. Silent and lapping and snaggle-toothed, the hint of a wave in her hair, so dark it seemed to hang down, right into the depths; and the light shining in her eyes, too bright to look at for any time at all. As I pictured her, standing there on the shore, I realised I knew: she had never really been dreaming just of home. It wasn't as simple as remembering her mother; it was more, much more than that. She dreamt of more than the village and stone bridge, more than the hills and dry stone walls, more than the moss-fluffed crags, more than the gorsed slopes curling ever over and upwards. She dreamt of possibility; somewhere you could never see, somewhere just over, just beyond, somewhere . . .

It was all numbers in the end. An open verdict, the coroner said it was a female – 5ft 7in, weight unavailable, aged about 23 or 24. She had been in the water for between 7 and 14 days. And at first they called her Janet Doe: some American who worked in the mortuary. Anonymous. Did anyone know her? Was there a name? Without a name she didn't exist, ever. Any family? Did anyone care?

Yes, I did. I knew her, for what it was worth. I cared. I couldn't explain it, but I cared more than I could say.

CHAPTER 6

As if they had known each other forever, Dr Romme and K were united by Janet's case. As soon as I was well enough K told me the doc's conclusions. I took it with a pinch of salt. What had my mother said? 'Some things just aren't for knowing.' There were always grey areas, always would be.

For what it was worth, Dr Romme's version sounded probable. Even K admitted it made sense, and though I thought I'd heard some of it before, as ever, I was slow to understand. K tried to explain, taking me as part of my recuperation programme to a cafe which looked out over the river. It was the wettest of days and all views, even of the river's far bank, were obscured by the rain bleeding in like a wound from the west. A chill air crept in under the door of the cafe and round the old, dilapidated, blue window frames. We lunched on soup and garlic bread, still wrapped tight and snug in our scarves and coats. And I asked.

— So, Marius went to the shed?

I had a vague recollection of Dr Romme telling me something similar. But I couldn't remember precisely when or what else the doctor had said. I didn't understand.

— I don't . . . I mean, how did he know about the shed? Only Janet knew about it.

— You seem to forget, quite a few people were attracted to that little old shed.

As K said it she slid a crouton between my lips, obviously thinking I was now well enough to have a little fun poked at me. Maybe I was well enough or better even, I didn't know. I could smell her again at least, that sweet gorsey scent, even above the steam of the carrot and coriander potage. A piano played off in the kitchens, Debussy perhaps, but it was too far off to tell for sure. I felt like asking them to turn it up. I could feel the mood of the world seeming, achingly, finally, to change. Well or not, now I wanted to be in on the secrets, I wanted to know what everyone else seemed to know.

— No, but . . . but when? That's what I can't understand.

— Round about the time Janet met God. That's what Kathryn said.

— Kathryn? Who's this Kathryn you keep talking about?

— What do you mean, who is she? Kathryn, Kathryn Romme, of course.

I knew they'd spent some time together but I didn't expect this. I recalled clearly enough that Janet had once upon a time been admitted to a respite clinic. I told K. I knew she spent a lot of time painting and that Marius liked watching her. I pictured too readily the ginger hair bobbing up and down, the hand like a restraining collar with its bulging blue veins. I felt my cheeks redden at this fuller, hard-to-banish memory. K was oblivious, just intent on the tale.

— Marius Pritty, the incubus.

— What do you mean?

— It was a voluntary clinic, right?

— Right.

— She was there of her own free will? She could come and go as she pleased?

This conversation, these questions, these answers, I'd heard them all before. Now I was impatient just to reach an end.

— Will you just tell me what. . ..

— Janet most probably ventured out during the day to her shed, sometimes to see her God, sometimes just to water her plants.

Again the deep, dark déja vu.

— So? Tell me something I might not already. . .

— Kathryn reckons that Marius followed her there and on the day when her spiritual guide and protector went missing. . .

— What?

— The hollyman, when he quit the shed, Marius made his

move, presenting himself as a ready-made, if invisible, alternative.

— Invisible?

K's playfulness was making me queasy. Dr Romme suspected Marius used the same method he'd most recently been accused of using. And that was how Holly came to be conceived. When K explained this I took the old crumpled photocopy snapshot out of my wallet. I'd kept it, I didn't know why. I'd once seen such light in it, such possibility. The face was familiar all right, reliably so, but my memory and powers of recognition much less accurate. There were more questions pummelling away at me.

— So, Marius spiked the apple juice, the food she'd brought for the guy who was staying in the shed. Marius drugged her, then he raped her? In the shed?

— That's what Kathryn reckons.

— How did he get access to the drugs? You can't just buy that sort of dope off the shelf?

— Beats me, but I guess he had ways and means.

— Did the drug cause her illness, her amnesia, or make it worse? And the hands, what about the . . .

— Look, I'm not the doctor in all this, you better talk to Kathryn.

A horrible question rose up before me. I knew it was horrible because it made the gripes grow into waves of nausea. And I knew also, straightaway, I shouldn't on any account voice it. I knew and yet I couldn't do anything to stop myself.

— You sure about this? Are you sure she was . . .

— Hey, mister . . . if you're saying what I think you're saying.

But I wasn't. I was just thinking in an old, old way. The way I once had of thinking, and the way K had once thought too – thinking around. If Janet herself didn't know it happened, if the drugs had worked and she really couldn't remember anything about Marius Pritty and the shed, then surely it didn't happen. We know things because we remember them. If we don't recall things then those things don't exist. I caught a glimpse of the red, corkscrew-headed child in the snapshot, the most vivid mnemonic. I didn't even start trying to explain myself.

— No, I'd just be interested to hear how your doctor friend knows this, that's all.

Even as I said it I suffered sharp pangs of doubt, echoed by the screams of nausea now rising ineluctably from my stomach: it was as if I'd missed something vital, some part of the answer or a question, some part of myself and my own life. I rushed to the toilet, the combination of the coriander, the garlic, and K's scent finally taking its toll. And as I held my spinning, vomiting head over the fathomless, ocean blue of the lavatory, the piped piano playing strangely louder than in the eating area of the cafe, I saw all the possibilities swirling. I heaved and heaved. There would always be more; possibility was like that, a slippery fish. If it was something you could get hold of it would go by a different name. I heaved until my throat was on fire.

When Janet saw Marius untrousered in the hospital, there in her very own pigeon loft, crashing in on her precious room and pawing over her belongings, it might well have washed up the truth in her consciousness. Then again it might not. It might have made her accept her own past and future, her own fate. Maybe it didn't. What right did I or anyone have to presume?

Returning from the toilet I was now grateful for the cafe's cool draughts. I decided to put on a brave face and say nothing about being sick. I declined to finish my soup, getting the waitress to take it away. They must have turned the volume up, I'd brought the piano's loud trills back out with me. Now it was Satie, perhaps. I hummed briefly along; K looked at me, frustrated. She wanted to get on with it and tell me the whole story. Marius had probably returned to the shed repeatedly in the hope of encountering Janet there again. That was how he'd come to find my pen. The important thing, according to K, was that God had been kicked out of the equation. She came up with some highly unconvincing tale, concocted with her precious shrink, about how Janet probably sublimated Marius' religious rantings about 'Him Up Above', turning them into a story of Holly's conception, an hallucination in which Holly's father was the Almighty. All the time Janet was secretly revealing in this story, to us and to herself, who the father really was. This was the gospel according to K and Dr Romme. It sounded all beautifully rational, and far too neat for my mind; a nice try, but I wanted to hang on to God for a little while longer.

Knowing Janet Burns, seeing those hands, and going up, as we did, to the lake, I was turned and I could never go back. Okay, I collapsed for a while, but when I came to it was as if I'd seen or sniffed or sensed something: a re-cognition or a thinking-again, a re-finding of something, something I'd always had but never realised. No, it was nothing to do with my father, or my mother; nothing to do with finding an answer to the world's ills; nothing to do with Slater, or those articles and that old syntax, not that sort of recognition, not that grammar or thinking old, worn-out, unthinking thoughts. And no shining lights either; no old men with beards, no saints or angels or green men. No strange tramps wearing sprigs of holly, only the tune running through my head. In the cafe it was the piano, soaring and racing, dipping and diving, tickling the air. In the end I was so enthralled I couldn't help but talk about it.

— Isn't it beautiful? Makes you feel like dancing, like you're floating on air.

I stood up momentarily and swayed along to it. K was taken aback.

— What does? What's beautiful?

— The music, the piano.

— What music?

And then I realised. On another day it might be a full orchestra, or just a guitar or violin, or a slow, drawl-sweet voice. Cadences and cadenzas, wonderful sweeps, sweet silent pauses, not like those old childhood attempts on the cello. This was the real thing. This realisation was the real thing. I didn't have to recall the words, I didn't have to count or remember to count, to give it a name, know who it was by, who wrote it, who played it, sang it or composed it, I didn't have to know it at all in that way. It was just there in my head and I felt grateful. I felt blessed.

CHAPTER 7

Guillermo returned from his travels with Zinnie, his French friend, just in time for the funeral. He'd come back for the beginning of term, but wasn't starting any Business Studies course (as his father wanted) or ecology course (as he'd once wanted). Born taxonomist he might be, but he opted instead for a course in herbal medicine. As I was fully 'out' as ill by then, he kindly offered me a decoction of St John's Wort for my problems.

— Hypericum perforatum, fills thc holes faster.

He seemed to be making some sort of joke but it was beyond me. He suggested a few other plant leaves and roots, the names of which I didn't write down and subsequently couldn't recall.

The service was held at a small chapel within the cemetery grounds. Guillermo offered to care for Janet's grave. He also said a few words at the ceremony, the only person who felt able. Yet even he stood like a prisoner in the pulpit, mangling a piece of paper between his hands.

— It's strange standing here, knowing how Janet died, knowing that everyone knows how she died but knowing that no-one, me included, wants to talk about it. No, I don't want to talk about it either, but ... but ... well, I've ...

Alan was standing beside me, his one arm wrapped around his torso as if in some sort of comforting salute. He had travelled down from Manchester for the funeral. I whispered a naive introduction, knowing only too well who he was. But I was curious as to how he had managed to keep in touch, how he had found out. He forgot to lower his voice.

— She was living with me.

I almost shouted out.

— Living with you?

— My house was her last address.

— In Manchester?

— Yeah. The police must have found the address on her, in her bag. They came round.

Somebody from the front turned and shushed us, and I felt a burning sensation rise in my head, realising things weren't all as I'd imagined. There was no heating in the chapel and we were all wearing thick dark coats. Yet I felt like flinging mine on the pew, I was beginning to sweat. I thought about it.

— When did she first arrive?

He told me: they'd kept in touch, when she escaped the hospital she'd gone straight up to Manchester. She'd arrived when needed. Alan had been at a low ebb, she'd looked after him, cooked his meals.

— Don't know what I'd have done without her, to be honest.

— She stay with you a long time?

— Right up until . . .

Someone shushed us again and though I couldn't quite see him I heard Guillermo's Black Country voice rumbling on like a very slow train on an old rusted track.

— I reckon we all feel guilty. This sort of thing . . . that's the only way you can feel. But . . . but my guilt feels strange. Maybe everybody feels it in their own way, I don't know, I can't say. I just know I don't feel guilty because she's dead, not dead *now* anyway, I feel guilty because I stopped her from dying once before. Some of you might know, I pulled her out of the river one time.

Yet no matter what Guillermo said, no matter how painfully nervous or moving or sincere, all I could think of was that Janet had stayed with Alan, right until the end, right until the trip up to the lake. I wondered whether I'd even got that part right: had she really followed the river, had she really sought out the village and valley? There was no way of knowing. But it meant that Janet had never dallied outside my old house, never peered into my windows, never stalked me or hunted me or followed me or pursued me in any way. All those glimpses, all those shadows, they had nothing to do with her preying on me or prowling in my vicinity. Nothing whatsoever. I pictured the hands briefly, the smudged ink tattoos, love and hate, bleeding eternally into the grain of the skin. And I shuddered, wondering if the hands had still been with her up in Manchester, whether they were still with her now. I turned to Alan but he was listening intently to Guillermo:

— And when I pulled her out of that river, they say I saved her life, but all I could think of then, and all I think now, is that ... that ... that I prolonged something that she didn't want.

I turned away from Guillermo, away from Alan and the host of crow-coated shadows; I looked down into the darkest corner of the chapel's sandstone nave, into the deep brown, crumbling recesses; I sniffed the mildew, the fetid fungal rot, the dank stonework. Who was the woman then – the woman looking in through my windows? The one the Lovetts and the tenants saw. The one the police could never catch. Who was she? Back on the pulpit Guillermo had come into his element, rubbing his hands up and down the edges of the lectern. Now it was excitement rather than nerves. I looked up into and through his eyes, but still I couldn't see. All I could do was hear:

— She did thank me, before I went away, said she was grateful, that she would always remember; I saved her life. But I didn't believe her, it wasn't that she was lying, it was just that ... just that it was always something that went against her wishes, and I'd always know that, I saved her, yeah, but I'd stopped her doing something of her own free will. That seemed like a crime, and it might sound funny, but it was as if I was killing her by saving her life. Maybe I'm wrong, I don't know. But I couldn't forget that struggle; I couldn't forget how much she wanted to die.

I looked back out through the door, back out through the rows of graves, out to the bushes and shrubs, the vases and headstones. And I thought of my mother and her ash tree, and I thought of Janet's mother and the bramble and how Janet had tended the grave, and I thought of Guillermo's mother all those thousands of miles away, tending the grave of her own mother. Then, finally, I got to my father and I pictured all that growing-in-the-grave hair. 'A bastard,' I heard my mother's voice, 'a bastard. It was a girl. Your father had a baby girl. I'm pretty sure it was a daughter. A bastard.'

As I looked out, every thought of him seemed trite and false, every face, every version, no matter how hard I tried to picture the walk up the hill. I heard a string quartet start to play but still his objectionable, still his brutal, booming voice; deaf to it all. 'Whenever you can, whenever you can', trampling down the hope. And then a saxophone pierced the air, climbing and dipping and pulling at me, churning my stomach until the voice, his voice again, cut through the moment, breaking forever the chain of notes. 'Whenever you can, count. Whenever you can.' I tried to feel pity for him, to excuse him and say all those things you might say to help your father out of being who they are. But none of it could ever work, because I couldn't see him. I looked out and thought for a moment that I should tend his grave, something I'd never done. I could at least do that and then I might feel better. But the more I pondered it the more I knew it was impossible. I knew he was gone, lost forever in the grey skies, never to be forgiven. Never to be known.

And as I stared out through the chapel's doors, through the dreary leaves and barbs of a long, long year's growth, I realised. The woman standing at my gate and peering in my old, once-were windows: she was my father's bastard, my would-be sister. Could it be? Yes and no. Taking a peep and wisely, all too wisely, acting upon what she saw. Leaving well alone. I wondered whether she might still be out there somewhere peering in, and whether or not it really was or could be her. But, of course, I couldn't and never would be able to say for sure.

I looked to my side. Alan was quietly sobbing, not like I might, not like a cry baby. His tears appeared heavy, like jewels, to be worth something. My arm reached out, before I could stop it, and he turned and whispered in response.

— She cared, she cared so much. She helped me so much. I reckon that's what killed her. Because if you care . . . if you look after someone, what happens to you, eh? What happens to *you*?

It was an occasion when I really should have been crying too; it might even have been expected of me given my recent history of tears. Yet I was dry and barren, cold and aloof. Both Alan and I looked back up to Guillermo who had released the lectern and was standing clear of it, straining against the perimeter of the pulpit.

— And now, I'll just miss her, and I know I've been away and haven't seen her for a while. Still, I'll miss her, I will, but I do feel relieved. No, not because the guilt's gone, because it hasn't, not because of that. I don't know whether that'll ever go. No, I feel relieved because now at least, after all her struggles, after all her grief, now at least she's found a way of saying who she was and who she is. Now at least she's expressed her wishes.

This was one way of looking at it, I supposed. But the longer he had gone on the more Guillermo's stuttering drone had gained an edge, a gravelly eloquence. His final hope, that she might be at peace.

— Because she always had a way with her, a way that gave me pictures in my head, pictures that were calm and peaceful. Even if she wasn't able to get much calm herself. She brought me to the peace of being able to know something without having to talk about it.

This provoked a few nods and caused Zinnie, his companion who was standing just below the pulpit, to let out an audible sob. I felt suddenly indignant and mean: what did this Zinnie know of Janet? I thought of Janet's pictures, the paintings she'd given me, but the other pictures too. And I saw them there briefly, as if summonsed: just a glimpse, circling overhead, the knuckles white and clenched, hate and love emblazoned as always. I trembled but in a moment they were gone. At the wake, which was funded by a combination of donations and Social Services, Dr Romme admitted that she'd always thought Janet and her paintings to be prophetic. I nodded but felt like a hypocrite. Farewells again, just words, and all after the event.

The hands didn't stay around or come back to haunt me. Yet they did lend me a new way of seeing. I now looked people not straight in the eye but hard on the knuckles. At first this was a wariness, a horror, as if any hand might, at any moment, separate from its owner and attack me. Any hand might bear the inscription. Soon I picked up on the personal signatures, scanning the finger tips and nails, the creases and crevices, not out of fear, not looking for fortunes but fault lines, those very same lines of love and hate.

It made me look more closely at my own hands too: gauging my nerve, the shake and steadiness, the will and control; looking all the time for random movements. Sometimes when I write, especially with the Mont Blanc, I feel as if the pen has hold of me and is writing the words of its own accord. I look down at the wonderful swerve and curve of the letters, and I marvel. But this isn't the only wonder.

CHAPTER 8

K was my miracle. My saviour. My Lord.

K knew about caring. She nursed me back from the brink, took me for walks, took over the Renault, dealt with estate agents, the solicitors and all. And, yes, she read to me. Not like my father reciting his stiff old poems, not a cold experiment, as I imagined Dr Romme with Janet. No it was more like the mummy I'd always wanted and maybe once had. Memory always plays those tricks of ungratefulness. Not now. A new regime was in place, a new cognisance. The only certainty: I wouldn't have survived without her.

One day she picked *Jane Eyre* out from one of my mother's boxes of books, the boxes and books that were all now officially mine. We sat by the bay window and she dipped into it, not reading from the start, just giving me tasters, teasing me on purpose, or so I thought. I couldn't follow what was going on. I became lost in the rush of characters and words. Jane and Rochester talking under the chestnut tree ran into a dark and terrible scene with Bertha in the attic, then all of a sudden we were on the moor, with St John Rivers proselytising and preaching, so sure of himself, and I . . . I . . . I was so unsure, so . . . so fragile. I didn't know where we were. K obviously thought me stronger than I actually was. Within a few minutes of this dashing around I was sobbing like a little child, the view of the pine trees inconsolably lost in tears. I bleated, blurted, leaking my soreness into the room, filling it and flooding the world. So it seemed: it felt as if my aching face would soon explode but I would die if the burst was in any way stemmed. I wanted my mummy and I wanted my daddy too, I wanted them now, there in the room, their room, our room, with me. I wanted them and knew only too well that I couldn't have them. By this time K had stopped reading, wrapping her arms around me, sitting on my lap and hooking my shaking, dripping head into the warm hollow of her neck. The gorse scent swaddled me.

— Sh . . . sh, sh.

— But I still don't understand, I don't . . . I don't. . .

— Sh . . . What don't you understand? Eh? Sh . . . Here, use this, go on.

She offered me her red scarf and I felt both guilty and honoured. Yet still I couldn't stop blabbering.

— Come here. What don't you understand? Come.

— Our names.

— Whose names? Yours and mine?

— No, Janet's and . . . It was . . . it was . . . weren't we written into the same story, bound together whether we liked it or not. It's like a memory that won't quite come back, won't come to the surface. But you know it's there. It means something, but what?

I reverted briefly, a last refrain, to the desperate rocking and sobbing, but this time just for a few seconds. K waited until I was still, then she paused some more. A minute, ten minutes, looking at me, holding me, waiting and waiting.

— Every book you read is going to be like that. It's the beauty of books, they rouse the memory, they get you going.

She looked at me straight on, at half arm's length, and I chuckled in that conclusive, final, end-of-crying way while she told me.

— No, I mean it. You read a book like this and it brings it all back, what it was like way back then in those days, when was it?

She picked up the book and browsed the first pages.

— Wow! 1847. This is some memory.

I laughed again and wiped my cheeks completely dry,

smoothing the moisture not absorbed by the red cloth down into my beard as she talked.

— And then you've got all those memories of when you first picked it up, how old you were, who gave it you, who else might have read it, all that sort of remembering. Books are like that, they bring it all back, and sometimes there's just too much to deal with.

— Yeah. And sometimes there are things that come up that you recognise, you sort of know them, but you don't recall them from your own life.

She looked into my eyes and I could see that she was floundering. And why wouldn't she be? I was the only one in the end, the only one who could possibly understand what I might be saying. And if I couldn't understand it fully, wholeheartedly, how could I possibly expect anyone else to. I recalled Dr Romme's notebook and the accounts of *Jane Eyre* being read to Janet. And as I pictured it I felt suddenly cheated because that seemed to be part of my past too, a part of me from somewhere I no longer knew. There was probably an irony in the connection of our names to this stupid book, probably another joke that I just wasn't getting. But the joke didn't seem to have an author; nobody, as far as I could see, was getting it. I was supposed to fall in love with her; she was supposed to kill me; we were fated to cross paths in one of those big ways. I knew this. I remembered this. But that's all I could say.

— Do you still reckon she did it intentionally? Renamed herself so she could fit into your famous old tale. Played the trick of literary providence to get you hooked. Is that what you think?

— No, no. I don't know. No, I don't think she called herself anything because of me.

— And like I said she was Janet, she wasn't Helen Burns was she? She wasn't Jane or Bertha.

— I suppose not.

— She was just some mixed up kind of lady who had a name that was vaguely connected to you via this little old book here.

She picked up *Jane Eyre* again and paused at the inside

cover. There was an inscription; no names but I could see
from the handwriting it was from my father, addressed to my
mother: 'love always' and a solitary cross that looked more like
a cancellation than a kiss.

— Look, I'm sorry I read you this, I didn't realise.

— No, it's okay, it's alright, it's just . . . it's just I don't know
what it means, that's all.

— It was a coincidence, all it was, a coincidence. If this was
some cheesy nineteenth century plot, you and Janet would
have ended up marrying each other already, or finding out
you were brother and sister or cousins or something. That's
how coincidence worked back then. Now it's different, now it's
more like you say: 'oh, that's interesting, that's a coincidence'.
You might think it's strange or mysterious or cool or whatever
you think it is. But it doesn't necessarily mean anything, not
in the end.

— You really think so?

— Yeah, sure, I really think so.

And she grabbed the red scarf back from me and wrapped it
round her fingers. It looked like a streak of still wet blood. She
pushed herself a little away and looked back quickly, sharply,
as if she'd just come across the possibility.

— Is that what this is all about?

— What?

— Reader I married him. That part of the deal, the ending
you missed out on?

But before I had even taken in what she said, her jagged look
was wiped away by a widening, glistening smile. She pulled
her deep, dark curls back behind her ears and touched my arm
with her finger tips, tracing the veins, bones and creases down
to their convergence at my wrist. Then she glided lightly over
onto my palm, drawing my lifeline out, and all that crossed it.
And I knew right there and then as she touched me: she was
right, she had succeeded, she had saved me.

Even Sarah acknowledged the fact, on one of her last visits.
She paused over tea and biscuits while leaving the kids, Arthur
awake in her arms but quiet and still, a perturbed and concen-

trated look on his face. She told me how good it was to see me getting back to my old self.

— And you seem very happy together.

There was a wistful stir, a passing moan in her eye, as I'm sure there was in mine. More than passing, I could feel it aching to run out as tears, to blurt out as the forlorn, too-long-delayed declaration: 'but what about us, what about happiness and our lot together!' At that moment, just looking at Sarah, I wanted to reach out, to touch her cheek. Just touch. I was struck by the immediacy and the impossibility of the memory, of what it was to touch her, to be able, to be in each other's arms, without worry, without anxious reference to some irreversible timetable of separation. At that moment I couldn't take my eyes off her for fear that she might vanish, just as Janet had gone, into thin air or into the dark, impenetrable depths. I was sure I mustn't stop looking even for a moment. If my eyes veered she would no longer exist and if that were to happen I would crash completely. My arm moved briefly of its own accord, helplessly, towards her. But on its way something happened. Perhaps the sight of Arthur in her arms, perhaps the fear of meeting with indifference. But no, I was sure that look, it was shared.

In any case Rachel and Simon rushed into the room, both in turn giving me a cursory, defiant glance. Their old man was ill but they still needed and were going to assert: 'I come first, okay, so long as you remember that when you get better.' Rachel, suddenly, impulsively, acting no doubt upon what she saw with her glance, ran to me, wrapping me in a huge, mittened, scarfed and hooded hug. So big it even made Simon scowl and chuckle all at the same time. And suddenly in that moment, just then, I knew why I was scared of my own children. I knew but I couldn't get near to putting it into the sort of ordered words that would make sense to anyone else. It was because they were me, but not in any simple way. It was worse than that. They were more than close reflections in the mirror, more than kin. They were bits and pieces of me, fragments broken off and put back together. Some of it bad, some of it good. The unlikeliest bits, the unnoticed bits, and those parts no-one cares to see. They were my brash desires and defeated will, they were me as master, me as slave; me as nasty, malevolent perpetrator, and me as brow beaten, tear-streaked victim. And as I looked and felt my eyes filling I remembered them as if I was remembering something from my own life. I could say 'I' and 'he' and 'she' and 'we', but really it was, and should always be: 'I' and 'I' and 'I'. Nothing sweet about it, just inescapable. And in that moment I felt like hugging them, and shoving them, pulling them and pushing them. And I would have done if Simon hadn't been standing off, just like he always did, and if Rachel's hug hadn't been so octopus-like. I tried to hide my tears.

— Now, what was that for?

But, before anyone could even guess or see the truth, Arthur let out a long, raspy fart, followed by a contented gurgle. When the laughter had died down Rachel and Simon ran out again, and a familiar stillness fell on the room. I continued to hide my tears.

— How come they've started tying their shoe laces again?

— The benefits of moving from home-education.

— Ah, so the place for untied boots was the commune?

— Community. There is a difference.

An old insistence of Sarah's, and one that brought us back down instantly to where we actually were. My tears were forgotten.

— Is there? Is there really a difference?

— Yes. Yes, there is.

— And?

— A community is where people care for one another, a place where you see your neighbour or your friend in trouble so you help them out.

— And a commune?

— A commune . . . well, the way you say it, it's . . . it's . . . the way you talk it sounds like just a place to have sex.

The stillness felt sticky. This too was terribly, horribly familiar. I reached to open a window.

— Isn't their new school a community? It's got a good reputation.

— You know what schools are like. They notice the superficial things, like shoe laces. They'll put you right on those.

— But they're surviving, aren't they.

— Rachel and Simon?

— Yeah, they look well. They look as if they're enjoying it, and their reports, that speaks volumes.

— Does it?

— I just wanted to say that's all.

— What?

— Just, they're doing well, you're doing . . . I mean not many people could . . .

— No.

Arthur started crying as she told me that she was finally getting more clients too; working from home might prove a good step after all. Arthur continued to blabber, swinging and smashing his arms about in want and need of food, and I pictured her with him in one hand, tapping away on her computer keyboard with the other. Some part of me felt like screaming, bawling out as loud as I could. I looked at her to see if there was anything left of the look between us, anything at all of that exchange of selves. But she didn't see me, busy as she was, fussing over Arthur.

CHAPTER 9

It turned out K got two new jobs, not just one. The first, I discovered, would begin in the spring officially, it had been confirmed, but there was a certain amount of preparation involved. I found out about it one day when I went into the kitchen, a place to which I rarely ventured during those gloomy, grit-in-the-eye days, when even the smallest activity might send me spiralling. K was chopping onions, her red cloth already saturated, her eyes streaming so severely that she had to run to the bathroom just as I entered. And as she left I decided I would try to make amends for my stupor, make at least a little effort. I started to clear away the onion skins. The open pages that lay by the chopping board I presumed to contain recipes. They were splashed with water or oil or some other liquid, and I attempted to wipe them with a cloth. And as I did so I read a little: 'Jasmine; Jenny; Jonathan; Jonny; Joshua'. No menus in this book, just Js in this particular section, very modern: both boys and girls on the same page; first names, whole lists of them. When K returned, still snivelling, she saw me holding the book.

— They say it's good luck to cry a little. Onions or no onions, it's normal.

— Normal?

She was laughing, despite or because of the tears, despite or because of the fact I had hold of the book and was gawping up at her.

— Good luck, that's what they say. Probably an old wives' tale, don't you know.

— Is it definite? Are you sure?

And yes, she was. The doctors had set the date. I was slower than I might have been: it was the one and only possibility that hadn't before that very moment crossed my mind. She hoped for a girl. So, eventually, did I. And yes, there were no other possibles involved. She or he was mine, or at least, I was the one and only daddy.

The second job fitted in nicely, she could more or less work from home. When she told me about it later that afternoon my eyes were tardily, mysteriously, beginning to smart from the onions, even though they'd long been cooked and eaten.

— Do you really think the world is that interested in your Professor Slater?

— Seems like it is, I've got two article deals already, and another three interviews lined up.

— Just on what you found out?

— Yeah, and we're talking about a TV documentary and a book deal if we can show them . . .

— We?

— My agent.

— You have an . . .

Yes, she had an agent, and I just couldn't fathom it. This wasn't envy or stupor or illness, or anything other than plain old incomprehension.

— But what's so interesting about him? He's just a small guy with a big moustache, that's what you used to say. Low centre of gravity, high ideas, why would people want to read about that?

— Just think about it.

— I'm trying.

— An expert in his field, he knows what he's talking about, he cares, he cares passionately. The guy is dedicated, he wants to help.

— Are we talking about the same person? The same duck-butt jerk, remember? Slimy walrus, remember? That's what you used to call him.

— Yeah, yeah. But in his desperation to help . . .

— I don't believe this. Do you remember anything? Do you

have any recall of what you said about this man? Now you're saying he wanted to help.

— This is what I learned, from doing all the research, from finding out about who he was. I learned that despite all the things I'd previously thought and said about the guy, despite my expectations, despite all that, he was after all a human being, a guy who cared.

— A guy who cared?

— Yeah, and in this huge effort he was making, trying with all his might to care, he turned the corner. He turned the corner and forgot he was dealing with people.

— So that makes him interesting to the general public, eh?

— Yeah, the good guy shakes hands with the devil, the story everyone wants to read.

A week later I overheard K talking on the phone to Dr Romme. Some 'yes Kathryns' and some 'no Kathryns', I heard a build up, a momentum rising. Just the odd word or phrase: 'that doctor at your hospital'; 'dosage'; 'poor tortured souls'; and the indignant, outraged 'what he did to her!'. I guessed where they were heading for the next 'case'. K had a career, and a team of confederates in the offing.

Meanwhile, I knew that at some point in time I would have to get back to my own research; start all over again, thinking how I could change the world, or at least how I might devise ways in which that world could turn, a notch perhaps, as I had done. How are people supposed to look after their kids, how do you help them? How *do* people care? Most days the wheel seemed just too big, it felt like no matter how hard I might push, how much I might strain, there'd be no budging it. But on some days, the occasional morning, the sun shone on the lonely, yellowed, year-end leaves, those forlorn and crinkled flags still left on the trees; it shone so brightly that it seemed to gild all my thoughts, it warmed me and gave me hope and made me feel a prickle, a new sharpness in the air. Only odd days, but maybe that in the end is all you need. On those days I couldn't wait to get back to work. On those days I was going to fix the world.

As it turned out K offered to negotiate my paternity leave. With an organisation like the International Child Care Foundation she reckoned they were duty bound to give me two years, minimum.

— Being a dad will make a nice change for you.

Of course, the irony in that could have made me laugh or cry. But I saw the flicker of hope in her eye as she said it, and I knew I held out a hope of that sort too.

The day before my mother's house was finally cleared and sold and we set off back for Canada, something nearing normal service was resumed. I went for a walk on my own, down by the river, and on the way back bought a bottle of merlot from the off-license. Something in the air, some damp and smoky scent, or the way the river swirled in spate, carrying off the golden flecks of last year's growth . . . I couldn't put my finger on it or give it a name, knowing only it was to do with spirits and reviving. When I got back to the house K had borrowed a radio from a neighbour. A jazz piano was doing its thing, the first music, real music, in the house since everything had been boxed away. After toasting and tasting the first sip of wine, K took the glass from my hand and placed it gently on the table. She stroked my forearm in that way of hers, making me feel like I'd never before been touched. And I knew then, a flash-memory. No need to ask, no need to check, no need to talk.

She broke the spell like she always did, unexpectedly, speaking into my shoulder, into the stillness, her words curling up to my ear.

— Will you marry me?

I stared down into her dark, impenetrable curls.

— Wh . . . wh . . . what?

I'd heard this line before, a thousand times, a hundred movies; an echo from way back. You could usually see it coming, but not this time, this wasn't what I knew. I was shocked into silence.

— I just can't stand the thought of my father giving me away. I mean, in this day and age, what's all this business about women being possessed and owned by the men in their lives?

She laughed and shuddered at the thought.

— That's the only thing I'll insist on. Best if he doesn't even come along.

But I hadn't answered, yes or no. I had no possible answer. What was it about me – lost, lonely, pitiful fake-orphan as I was – that attracted such big presumptions? She undressed, apparently oblivious to my silence. I wondered whether I'd inadvertently nodded my head. Had I, somehow, given her permission, or spoken when I wasn't looking? I spied her moles and wondered again which was which, the Jewish and Turkish, and whether it was ever that simple. This spot coming from mama, that spot from papa. From where had she got her sense of recovery and survival? Her intuition of me? She was the one who restored me, brought me, like some half-baked Rochester, back into the world of full sight and sense. But where did she get her sense of humour? And I such a lack?

I did get a little better, I have improved. But at that moment irony truly sailed by me. Later, I understood. Both of us lying on my mother's old divan, the bed-linen already packed, we covered ourselves in the finally pulled-down curtains. Draped in green, the bay window bare, and yes, I could see. It was a joke, it was all a joke. She was having a baby, we were going down that road. But this wedding business, it was just a gag. All it ever could be; one of those possibilities that gets your heart racing, your mind whirling, burns a hole in that part of the brain – what did K call it? – the part that does the imagining. But marriage was never ever a runner.

Kismet – my portion, my future, my lot.

Needless to say: reader, we lived together. K and I and the new, much loved and cared for child – whom we called Jane, in reference to no one in particular. No family link. This one was going to be her own woman. We tossed for the surname, K having a strong dislike for the modern, egalitarian habits:

those double-barrelled hyphens. So, the balance of probability running at fifty-fifty, the dime flicked and peaked and seemed mysteriously to pause mid-fall.

But yes, it dropped heads up. I lost. No doubt our daughter will one day thank her lucky stars.

ACKNOWLEDGEMENTS

In the early stages in the writing of this book I received financial help from The British Academy and Arts Council East, for which I am most grateful. I am also deeply indebted to the many people who looked at chapters, whole drafts and part drafts during this story's long journey into the world. Thanks to all. This is a book about family, a book that wouldn't have been possible without my own family's unwavering love and support.